Someone was watchi

Jilly opened her eyes and blinked, startled by the dimness of the room. It was late, the sky outside the broad expanse of windows was settling into an early autumn night, and the man watching her was blocking the door, consumed in shadows.

The hushed activity of Meyer Enterprises had stilled. It was very late, and she was alone with a stranger. If she had any sense at all she'd be scared to death.

"Are you going to hover there?" she asked in a tart voice, forcing herself to take her time in getting off the sofa.

He flicked on the light, and she blinked, momentarily disoriented after the shadowy dimness of the room. "I'm sorry I kept you so long."

"I wasn't waiting to see you. I don't even know who you are. I was waiting to see Jackson."

He stepped into the room, and his smile was deprecating, charming and completely false. "Your father asked me to handle it, Jillian. I'm—"

"Coltrane," she supplied flatly. "I should have guessed."

"Why?"

"My brother told me all about you."

"Nothing flattering, I'm sure," he said lightly.

Watch for the newest novel from
ANNE STUART
and MIRA Books

THE WIDOW
Coming July 2001

SHADOWS AT SUNSET
ANNE STUART

MIRA

ISBN 1-55166-571-9

SHADOWS AT SUNSET

Copyright © 2000 by Anne Kristine Stuart Ohlrogge.

Visit us at www.mirabooks.com

Printed in U.S.A.

First, I have to send huge thanks to my Genie sisters, Teresa Hill, Christie Ridgway and Barbara Samuel. They are goddesses extraordinaire, and really helped me jump-start this.

And thanks to Jackson Norton for letting me use his name. He's the only Jackson I know, and he really is a most excellent young man, nothing at all like the wicked Jackson in this book.

And as always, for Richie and Kate and Timmy, for making me work when I'd rather play with them.

Prologue

From: Hollywood Haunts, *Hartsfield Books, 1974*

One of the most interesting houses in Hollywood is the famous La Casa de Sombras—House of Shadows. Built by the Greene brothers in 1928, La Casa is a perfect example of Spanish Colonial revival mixed with Mediterranean and Muslim influences. The once lavishly landscaped grounds are extensive, though recently the estate has fallen into disrepair and most likely will be razed.

La Casa de Sombras was the site of an infamous murder-suicide pact in the early 1950s. Fading film star Brenda de Lorillard shot her married lover, director Ted Hughes, before turning the gun on herself. Though a trail of blood led through the ornate house, both bodies were found in the lavish master bedroom. In the ensuing decades their ghosts have been spotted, at times arguing, at other times dancing on the terrace by moonlight, and occasionally, to the embarrassment of certain well-known Hollywood Realtors, in flagrante de-

*licto on the large banquet table. Mystery still
shrouds the reason for the murder-suicide.*

*The house was purchased by Meyer Enterprises
and remained empty until the mid 1960s, when its
grand elegance was tarnished after it was turned
into a hippie crash pad for some of Hollywood's
notorious young actors and musicians. In recent
years efforts had been made to restore the Grand
Old Lady by the present owners, but like much of
Hollywood's architectural history, its days are
most likely numbered. One can only wonder where
the ghosts will go, once the baroque mansion is
demolished.*

Brenda de Lorillard, star of stage, screen, tabloids
and nightmares, stretched her lithe body with a little catlike gesture, then made a moue at her beloved. "It's been more than fifteen years since they
published that dreadful book, darling. I think
they've forgotten all about us."

Ted lowered his newspaper and glanced at her
through his wire-rimmed glasses. When he first
started wearing them she'd teased him unmerci-
fully. After all, why in heaven's name should a
ghost need reading glasses? They were dead, for
heaven's sake. How could his eyesight possibly de-
teriorate? And where the hell had he found those
glasses, anyway?

But he'd simply given her his usual, indulgent smile, and as always Brenda was lost, as she had been when she first saw him across the bright lights of a movie set, when he was a lowly director of photography and she was a grand star. She'd loved him ever since, no matter how illogical. She'd spent almost her entire life, thirty-three…er…twenty-eight years focused on her career, and she'd put it all at risk for a mad infatuation that never faded, through career disaster, through time, through death itself.

"I wouldn't worry about it, honeybunch," he said, taking a sip of his coffee. "The place is still standing, though just barely, and the house tours still stop by the gates occasionally."

"It's the scandal tour," Brenda said. "The same people who go visit Valentino's grave and the place where the Black Dahlia was found. Hardly befitting a gorgeous villa like La Casa de Sombras!" she said with a sniff. "And not very flattering to the two of us. I hate thinking our only legacy was our death."

Ted set his glasses down beside the newspaper, turning to look at her out of those wonderful gray eyes of his. The newspaper was the *Los Angeles Times,* dated October 27, 1951, the day before they died. It never changed, and Ted read it every morning with the air of a man who was seeing it for the first time. As Brenda suspected he was.

"Honeybunch, anyone who sees your movies will remember you in all your glory. Especially the ones I directed," he added with a mischievous grin. "Scandals fade, art remains. *Ars longa, vita brevis,* you know."

"Stop quoting movie slogans at me," she snapped. "I never worked for MGM and I'm glad of it."

"It's a little older than that...."

"Don't condescend to me, either, with your Ivy League education," she interrupted him, glaring at her nails. She filed them every day, searching out little imperfections, and each day she found new ones. There was one major glory in that, though. She never aged. She missed seeing her reflection in the mirrors that filled every room of La Casa, but she knew from the look in Ted's eyes that she was still just as beautiful as she'd ever been. It was all she needed.

"They're not going to tear it down," he said patiently. "It survived the sixties and those repulsive creatures who camped out here. It's survived years of neglect, and at least now we have someone who loves it as much as we do. She'll take care of the place. And of us."

"But what if she doesn't?" Brenda cried.

"What if they tear it down to make office buildings? We'll be left wandering the earth, lost...."

"Honeybunch," he said, his voice warm and comforting, and she slid into his arms so naturally, finding the peace that was always there. "We'll make it through. Don't we always, you and me together?"

She looked at him, so dear, so sweet, so maddening, so eternal. "Always," she said in a tremulous voice. She leaned down to press her carmine lips against his firm mouth, and slowly they began their inevitable fade-out.

1

Jilly Meyer never approached her father's office without some sort of absurd fantasy playing through her mind. The last time she'd come she hadn't been able to shake the image of a French aristocrat riding in a tumbrel to her untimely doom. The reality of that unpleasant meeting with her father had been about as grim, and she hadn't exchanged more than a handful of civil words to him in the eighteen months since.

And yet here she was again, only this time she wasn't the proud but noble martyr heading toward her fate. This time she was a warrior at the gates, ready to do battle with the forces of evil. She just had to persuade Charon to let her cross the river Styx so she could confront Satan himself.

Terrible of her to think of her father as the devil, she thought absently. And steely eyed Mrs. Afton didn't deserve to be called Charon, even if she guarded her employer with a diligence that was downright supernatural.

"Your father is a very busy man, Jilly," Mrs.

Afton said in her clipped, icy tones that had terrified Jilly when she was a child. "You should know
better than to simply show up unannounced and
expect he'll be able to drop everything to make
time for you. Let me check his appointment book
and see when I can work you in...."

"I'm not leaving until I see him." Her voice
didn't waver, a small blessing. Mrs. Afton demor-
alized her, and always had, but her father had
ceased to wield any power over her, whatsoever.
Jilly just simply hated confrontations, and she was
anticipating a major one.

Mrs. Afton's thin lips compressed into a tight
line of disapproval, but Jilly didn't move. She was
still three doors away from the inner sanctum, the
holy of holies, and those doors were electronically
locked. If she tried to force her way in she'd only
wind up looking foolish.

"You can wait in the gray reception room,"
Mrs. Afton said finally, in no way a capitulation.
"I'll see if he can spare a moment for you, but I'm
not holding out much hope."

Abandon all hope, ye who enter, Jilly thought
absently. "I don't mind waiting." After all, it was
past three. Ever since her father had married Melba
he'd been less of a workaholic. Jilly didn't know
whether it was jealousy or lust that kept Jackson
Dean Meyer from abandoning his third wife as

he'd done his first two, and she didn't want to think about it. Suffice it to say, Melba might have mellowed the old bastard a bit. Enough to get him to do what Jilly desperately needed him to do.

The gray sitting room had a tasteful array of magazines, most of them about cigar smoking, something that failed to captivate Jilly. The leather furniture was comfortable enough, and the windows looked out over the city of Los Angeles. On a clear day she could see the Hollywood Hills, perhaps even the spires of the house on Sunset. La Casa de Sombras, the House of Shadows. The decaying mausoleum of a mansion that was her unlikely home.

But today the air was thick with smog from the Valley, and the autumn haze enveloped Century City. She was trapped in a glass cocoon, air-conditioned, lifeless.

She'd dressed appropriately for a paternal confrontation, in black linen with beige accents. Her father was a stickler for neatly dressed women, and for once she'd been willing to play his games. Since the prize would be worth the effort.

However, if he was going to keep her waiting she was going to end up wrinkled. So be it. He'd have to listen to her, wrinkles and all.

She kicked off her shoes and curled up in the corner of the gray leather sofa, tugging her short skirt as far down her thighs as she could manage. She rummaged in her bag for a compact, but it was the Coach bag Melba had given her for Christmas last year, not the usual one she used, and she'd transferred only her wallet and identification. No compact, no makeup, only a rat-tail comb which would be useless with her thick hair. She closed the purse again, leaned back against the sofa and sighed, trying to get rid of some of the tension that was swamping her body.

It was ridiculous. She was almost thirty years old, a strong, independent, well-educated woman, and she was still afraid of her father. Over the last two decades she'd tried everything, from meditation to tranquilizers to psychotherapy to assertiveness training. Every time she thought she'd finally conquered her fear, Jackson Dean Meyer returned it to her on a silver platter. And here she was again, ready for another serving.

Codependency was a bitch. It was relatively easy to break free from her father's influence. He had little interest or affection for her—he probably didn't notice when years went by without seeing her. Her father had made his choices and lived life the way he chose. She couldn't save him, even if he wanted to be saved.

But when it came to her sister and brother things were different. Although Rachel-Ann was probably beyond redemption. All Jilly could do was love her.

And Dean. It was for him that she'd come here, walked into the lion's den, ready to fight. For her brother or sister she'd do anything, including facing the tyrant who fathered them, though in Rachel-Ann's case the parenting was adoptive, not biological.

Dean was sitting home sulking, alone in the darkness of his room with his precious computer. Once more Jackson had managed to crush and belittle him; once more Dean had taken it, refusing to fight.

Jackson had removed Dean from his position in charge of legal affairs, replacing him with his new golden boy, a man by the name of Coltrane. Apparently Jackson trusted a stranger more than he trusted his own son. Dean had been given a token raise and no work, a complete humiliation by their ruthless father.

Jilly was ready to do battle in Dean's place. She couldn't sit back and watch her brother crawl into a computer, surrendering everything, in particular Jackson's trust, to an interloper.

To be fair, Dean allowed himself to be victimized by his father. He'd never made any attempt to find other work—the moment he'd passed the bar exam he'd taken a high-paying job with his father's multimillion-dollar development firm, and he'd been ensconced there ever since, taking Jackson's abuse, doing his bidding, a perfect yes-man still looking for a father's approval and love. Jilly had given up on Jackson years ago. Dean had a harder time letting go.

Of course, he hadn't confronted Meyer about it. Instead he'd come home, drunk too much and wept on his little sister's shoulder. So here she was, trying to make things right for her brother's sake, knowing she stood a snowball's chance in L.A. of doing any such thing.

But for Dean's sake she had to try.

She leaned her head back against the sofa and closed her eyes. She should have gotten a manicure. Her grandmother always said no woman could feel insecure if she had a terrific manicure. Jilly doubted that plastic nails were much of a defense against her father's personality, but at this point she could have used all the weapons she could muster. Maybe she could leave, do as that gorgon Mrs. Afton suggested and make a formal appointment to see her father, and come back with a manicure and even a haircut. Meyer hated her long hair. She could return with something short and curly, like Meg Ryan had.

Except that she wasn't cute and pert, she was tall and strong with unfashionably long, straight, dark-brown hair, and nothing was going to turn her into a bundle of adorable femininity. Even a manicure wouldn't help.

Deep breaths, she told herself. Calm down—don't let him get you worked up. Picture yourself going down a flight of stairs, slowly, letting your body relax. Ten, nine, eight…

Someone was watching her. She'd fallen asleep while trying to meditate herself into a calmer state, but suddenly she'd become aware that someone was watching her. Maybe if she kept her eyes closed he'd go away. It couldn't be her father—he wouldn't let a little thing like sleep interfere with his agenda.

It couldn't be Mrs. Afton—she'd have crossed the room and given Jilly a shake.

But hiding behind closed eyes was no way to deal with life.

Jilly opened her eyes and blinked, startled by the dimness of the room. It was late, the sky outside the broad expanse of windows was settling into an early autumn night, and the man watching her was blocking the door, consumed in shadows.

The hushed activity of Meyer Enterprises had stilled. It was very late, and she was alone with a stranger. If she had any sense at all she'd be scared to death.

She was a sensible woman. ''Are you going to

hover there?'' she asked in a tart voice, forcing herself to take her time in getting off the sofa, resisting the impulse to pull her short skirt down over her long thighs. It would only draw his attention to it.

He flicked on the light, and she blinked, momentarily disoriented after the shadowy dimness of the room. "I'm sorry you were kept waiting so long. Mrs. Afton left a note on my desk that you were here to see me, but I didn't see it until I was ready to leave."

"I wasn't waiting to see you. I don't even know who you are. I was waiting to see Jackson."

He stepped into the room, and his half smile was deprecating, charming and completely false. "Your father asked me to handle it, Jillian. I'm—"

"Coltrane," she supplied flatly. "I should have guessed."

"Why?"

"My brother told me all about you."

"Nothing flattering, I'm sure," he said lightly. His voice lacked the California softness—she couldn't quite place his accent, which meant he was probably from the Midwest. It was the only clue that he didn't belong in the sharklike environment where Jackson Meyer thrived.

"Depends how you define *flattering*,'' Jilly said, wishing there was a way she could slip into her shoes without him noticing. He was already too tall as it was—she didn't need the added disadvantage of being barefoot.

What had Dean called him? A pretty boy with the soul of a snake? It seemed accurate. He was pretty, indeed, though he lacked the feminine softness that usually went with such extraordinary good looks. She couldn't tell whether he was gay or not, and she didn't particularly want to know. Either way, he was strictly off-limits. Anyone connected with her father was.

Still, he was astonishingly easy on the eyes. Everything about him was perfect: the slightly shaggy, sun-bleached hair, the Armani suit, the Egyptian cotton shirt unbuttoned at the collar, exposing his tanned neck. He had a long, strong-looking body, like a runner. His eyes were hooded, watching her, so she couldn't see either their color or their expression, but she had little doubt they were bright blue and frankly acquisitive.

She bent down and shoved her feet into her shoes, no longer caring that he was watching her, no longer caring that her silk shell probably showed too much cleavage. He wouldn't be the type to be excited by cleavage. "I appreciate that you finally got around to me," she said, "but it's my father I wanted to see, not one of his minions."

"I haven't been called a minion in years," he said with a drawl.

She straightened to her full height. Still a lot shorter than he was, but her high-heeled shoes made her feel less vulnerable. "Where is he?"

"Gone, I'm afraid."

"Then I'll just have to go over to the Bel Air house...."

"Out of the country. He and Melba left for a short vacation in Mexico. I'm sorry but I have no way of getting in touch with him."

"I can see you're devastated," Jilly muttered, not caring if she sounded rude.

He didn't seem to care, either. His smile was cool, unnerving. "Look, I'm here to help. If you've got some sort of legal problem I'll be happy to look into it. A traffic ticket? Some problem with your ex-husband? The legal department can take care of things...."

"Can the legal department get rid of an interloper who stole my brother's job?"

His eyes opened at that, and she got a shock. They weren't blue at all, they were a dazzling emerald green. So green she figured he was probably wearing tinted contact lenses. And they weren't acquisitive. They were calmly assessing.

"Is that what your brother told you? That I stole

his job?'' The idea seemed to amuse him, and Jilly's anger burned even brighter.

"Not just his job. His father," she said in a voice as cool as his.

"His father? Not yours? Jackson Meyer isn't a sentimental man. I don't think he gives a good goddamn about me or your brother. He just wants the job done well. I do it for him."

"Do you?" she said in a silken voice. "And what else do you do for him?"

"Cold-blooded murder, hiding the bodies, anything he asks," Coltrane responded offhandedly. "What are you doing for dinner?"

"I believe it," Jilly muttered, and then his question sank in. "What did you say?"

"I said, what are you doing for dinner? It's after seven and I'm hungry, and you look like you have at least another hour left in you of berating me for ruining your baby brother's life. Let me take you to dinner and you can rip me apart in comfort."

She was speechless at the sheer gall of the man. "I don't want to go out to dinner with you," she said, flustered.

"We can order something in, then. Your father keeps a caterer on call twenty-four hours a day."

"And he's not my baby brother. He's only two years younger than I am," she added inconsequentially.

"Trust me," Coltrane said, "he's definitely your baby brother." There was no missing the faintly mocking admiration in his voice, but it only made Jilly angrier. She'd failed, her father was out of reach. As usual.

"I'll talk to my father when he gets back," she said coolly, reaching for her purse. "Thanks for your help, Mr. Coltrane."

"Coltrane will do," he said. "And you haven't finished with my help. You can't get out of here without me."

"What do you mean?"

"The place has a top-of-the-line security system. No one can get in or out without the code once it's past seven. It's seven-fifteen, and I don't think you have the code, do you?"

"No."

"And where did you park your car? In the garage in the building, right? There's no other place to park around here. You won't be able to get in there without a different code. If you want to get home tonight you're going to need my help."

She would have said this was all some evil plan on the part of fate, but she didn't tend to think fate had that much interest in one Jilly Meyer. She stared at Coltrane, her eyes narrowed as she considered her alternatives. She could call Dean, but he often ignored the telephone. Besides, he might be too drunk to answer, and she certainly didn't want him driving to pick her up. God knew where Rachel-Ann was. And it had been so long since Jilly had been to the Meyer building that she no longer knew anyone who worked there who might be able to help her, with the exception of the draconian Mrs. Afton, and even Coltrane was preferable to the gorgon.

"I'd like to leave," she said in a steady voice. "Now."

"And you'd like my help? Pretty please?"

"Yes," she said, hoping there was a special place in hell for men like him.

"My pleasure." He flicked off the lights, plunging them into unexpected darkness just as she started toward him, and she almost slammed into him in her hurry to get out of there. Some blessed radar stopped her seconds before she did, but she was close enough to brush against his jacket, to feel his body heat in the enclosed area. It was unnerving.

But she had learned years ago not to let her unease show, and she stopped, following him at a more reasonable pace, determined to keep her distance. Trust Jackson to put her at a disadvantage, she thought sourly. Not only did he ignore his daughter, but he sent The Enemy to deal with her.

If she hadn't been pissed off before she was pissed off now.

The place was completely deserted, an astonishing circumstance. Jackson Meyer encouraged his employees to work long and hard, and he usually matched them in overtime. But there didn't appear to be a soul left in the building as she followed Coltrane past the ghostly forms of neat desks, empty offices, echoing cubicles.

She had no idea what the people who worked at those desks actually did, any more than she knew how her father made his money. Meyer Enterprises had been her grandfather's company. He'd started out in real estate in the 1940s, buying huge tracts of land, derelict factories and ruined mansions. The place where Jilly lived with her two siblings was one of the old man's last acquisitions before he died in the early 1960s, the only building that hadn't been razed and redeveloped to benefit the endless coffers of Meyer Enterprises.

And it never would be if Jilly had anything to say about it. It was one of the few things temporarily beyond her father's greedy reach. Jackson Dean Meyer and his mother had had a falling out, and while Julia Meyer hadn't been able to deed La Casa de Sombras to her three grandchildren outright, she'd still managed to keep Jackson away from it. It belonged to the three of them, Jilly, Dean and Rachel-Ann, for as long as even one of them wanted to live there. The moment the last one moved out it would revert to Jackson, and he'd have it torn down.

He'd been trying to get them out for years. Threats, bribery, anger had made Dean and Rachel-Ann waver. But Jilly was made of sterner stuff than that, and she'd kept the others firm.

Coltrane punched in a row of numbers on the security keypad by the door, too fast for Jilly to read them, then pushed the door open, holding it for her. She walked past him, too close again, and gave him her cool, dismissive smile. "Thanks for your help, but I can take it from here."

"The elevator won't come without the security code," he said. "We're on the thirty-first floor, it's a hell of a long walk down, and when you get to the basement you'll find the door is locked and you'll just have to climb back up again. Besides, there's the little problem of the parking garage."

"I've got my cell phone—I can call a taxi."

"You'll still have to come back here for your car sooner or later. Unless you want to just go buy a new one with Daddy's money."

His easygoing contempt startled her, and she glared at him. "I'm surprised you don't know that I don't live off my daddy's money, as you so sweetly put it. Maybe you're not as involved in his affairs as Dean thought.''

Coltrane simply smiled. ''It's your choice, Jilly. You want to spend the night wandering up and down thirty-one flights of stairs, or do you want my help?''

Being trapped in a stairwell seemed vastly superior to being stuck with Coltrane in one of the bronze, art deco elevators Jackson had brought to the Meyer Building, but she wasn't about to say so.

''Call the elevator,'' she said, resigned. She was back in the tumbrel again, heading toward Madame La Guillotine.

He punched another rapid set of numbers on the keypad, and the doors opened immediately. She had no idea why the elevator would already be on their floor, but she wasn't about to ask. It was going to be hard enough to step into that bronze cage with her brother's nemesis.

She didn't like heights, she didn't like enclosed spaces, and she certainly didn't like men like Coltrane. Tall, gorgeous, self-assured men who knew just how intimidating they could be. It was a subtle, sexual intimidation, the worst sort, and Jilly was usually invulnerable to that sort of thing. But for some reason she still didn't want to get in the enclosed cage with him.

She had no choice. He waited, watching her, and she could no longer see the expression in his eyes. She walked into the elevator, hearing the jeering crowds of the angry peasants. He followed her in, and the doors slid shut with a subtle hiss, as Jilly steeled herself to ride to her doom.

2

Jackson Meyer's daughter was scared shitless of him. It was a fascinating realization, and Coltrane wished he knew a way to slow the rapid descent of the elevator, to stall it completely, anything to keep her with him for just a little bit longer.

He'd watched her while she slept, absolutely astonished at how far off the mark he'd been about her. He'd let his opinion of Dean influence his expectations about Meyer's other children; that, and stories he'd heard about Rachel-Ann's voracious appetite for drugs and sex. He'd assumed Jilly Meyer would be cut from the same self-indulgent, self-destructive cloth. He hadn't met Rachel-Ann yet but Jilly was as different from Dean Meyer as he could have possibly imagined.

In a land of California blondes she was dark, with an unfashionable mane of thick brown hair, a big, strong body and endless legs. She was no delicate flower—she had a physical presence that was both aggressive and arousing, even as she tried to make herself disappear into the corner of the elevator. He wondered if she was scared of heights or of him.

He wouldn't have thought she'd have the sense to be frightened of him. He'd done his absolute best to present himself as a laid-back and easy-going, slightly unscrupulous Southern Californian. No one had the faintest idea how dangerous he really could be.

Except for Jilly Meyer, who looked like she wanted the floor of the elevator to swallow her up. Her linen was rumpled, her hair was tangled, and she looked sleepy, wary and hostile. It really was an irresistible combination.

He allowed himself the brief, graphic fantasy of slamming his hand against the emergency stop button, shoving her against the elevator wall and pulling up that too short skirt of hers. Those long, strong legs would wrap around his hips quite nicely, he could brace her against the wall while he fucked her, and she'd stop looking at him like she wondered whether he was a scorpion who'd wandered in from the desert. By then she'd know that was exactly what he was.

The doors slid open on the basement level with an audible sigh, and Coltrane's fantasy vanished, unfulfilled. He punched in the garage code and the door buzzed. He pushed it open, and she walked through, brushing past him, and he wondered if she was going to take off in a run. He might enjoy stopping her.

But she was too well-bred for that. She held out her slim, strong hand to him. Silver rings, he noticed. Elegant and plain. And he took it, touching her for the first time.

His hand swallowed hers, and he used just enough pressure so that she couldn't keep ignoring him. She glanced up at him through her thick lashes. "I'm not biologically equipped for a pissing contest, Mr. Coltrane," she murmured.

He released her hand. "Where are we going for dinner?"

"I have no idea where you're going. I'm going home."

"Can you cook?"

"Not for you."

He was baiting her deliberately, to annoy her. He still wasn't quite sure why he wanted to—she was easy to get to. Far easier to get on her nerves than to seduce her.

Or maybe not. He intended to find out.

There was only a handful of cars in the deserted garage. He wondered whether she owned the red BMW convertible or the Mercedes. And then he saw the classic Corvette—1966, he guessed, lovingly restored, a piece of art as close to an antique as Los Angeles could boast.

He didn't make the mistake of touching her again, he simply starting walking toward the car, knowing she was going in that direction. "Nice Corvette," he said.

She cast a wary glance up at him. "What makes you think it's mine?"

"It suits you. Are you going to let me drive it?"

He might just as well have suggested they act out his elevator fantasy. "Absolutely not!"

"She'd be safe with me. I know how to drive— I've had a lot of experience. I'm good with a stick shift. I'd take it slow, I wouldn't strip her gears."

Her expression was priceless. "Mr. Coltrane, if you drove her with the same deftness that you're using in coming on to me then she'd stall out before you could even put her into gear," she said. "You're not driving my car or me. Is that clear?"

"Crystal," he drawled. A week, he figured. A week before she'd lie down for him, two weeks for the car. "I don't suppose you'd give me a ride home."

"Where's your car?"

"In the shop. I was supposed to take one of the company cars but I got distracted up there and forgot to get the keys."

"You can go back up and get them."

He shook his head. "The door has a time lock.

Once the last person leaves no one can get in until morning.''

''What the hell does my father keep up there, the Fort Knox gold?'' she said irritably.

''Just private files. Your father's involved in some highly complex, sensitive business arrangements. It wouldn't do for just anyone to walk in and have access to them.''

''Just anyone like his daughter? Who's obviously far too simpleminded to understand the great big complexity of his sensitive business affairs,'' she mocked him.

He ignored that. ''I live near Brentwood. It's not that far out of your way.''

''How do you know where I'm going?''

''You said you were going home. You live in that old mausoleum on Sunset with your brother and sister. I'm right on your way.''

''Call a taxi.''

''My cell phone's dead.''

''Use mine.'' She was rummaging in her purse now, obviously determined to get rid of him. A moment later she pulled out a phone, holding it out to him.

''Why do I make you so uncomfortable?'' he said, making no effort to take it.

''You don't,'' she said. ''I have a date.''

Two lies, he thought, and she wasn't very good

at lying. Unlike the rest of her family. Dean Meyer seemed almost oblivious to the truth, whereas his father used it as he saw fit, mostly to manipulate people.

But Jilly Meyer couldn't lie with a straight face, and that was oddly, stupidly endearing. Coltrane wasn't about to let that weaken his resolve.

"Then you'll probably want to go home and change before your big night out, and my apartment's on your way," he said in his most reasonable voice.

"Get in the damned car." She shoved her phone back into her purse and headed around toward the driver's side. He wondered whether she'd chicken out, try to drive off without unlocking the passenger door to let him in. She wouldn't get far—the garage doors wouldn't open without the right code.

But she slid behind the wheel, leaned over and unlocked the door, pulling back when he climbed in beside her. The Corvette was beautifully restored, perfectly maintained, and he had a sudden moment of sheer acquisitiveness. He wanted this car.

He didn't want a car exactly like this. He could afford to buy what he wanted on the exorbitant salary Jackson Meyer was currently paying him, and in L.A. you could find anything for a price.

He didn't want a 1966 Corvette. He wanted the one that belonged to Jilly Meyer.

She was strapping the metal-buckled seat belt across her lap, and she threw him a pointed look, but he made no effort to find his. "I like to live dangerously," he said. Her short skirt had hiked up even higher in the low-slung cockpit of the car, but he'd decided the time for ogling was past. She'd gotten the initial message, he could back off now. At least for the time being.

He didn't even waste a glance at his Range Rover. Sooner or later she'd see it, but he didn't know whether she'd figure out it was his. Probably not—he was doing far too good a job at rattling her. She wouldn't notice any details.

She drove like a bat out of hell, another surprise, though he expected the squealing tires and tight corners were a protest against his unwanted presence. The moment the garage doors opened she was off like Mario Andretti, racing into the busy streets of L.A. with a complete disregard for life and limb. He gripped the soft leather seat beneath him surreptitiously, keeping a bland expression on his face.

She knew how to drive the 'Vette, he had to grant her that. She wove in and out of traffic, zipping around corners, accelerating when he least expected it, avoiding fender benders and pedestrians

and cops with equal élan. It was all he could do to
keep himself from reaching for the steering wheel,
from voicing a feeble protest. She was out to scare
him with her driving, and she was doing a good
job of it.

She'd grown up in L.A., learned to drive on the
freeways and the boulevards; she knew what she
was doing. She was getting back at him for intimidating her.

She didn't even waste her time glancing at him
during her wild ride through the city streets. She
didn't need to. She was focused, concentrating on
her driving with an almost gleeful energy, and he
simply gripped the seat tighter and said nothing,
wishing to hell he'd put on the seat belt.

She pulled up in front of his apartment building
with a screech of tires, going from fifty to zero in
a matter of seconds, and he had no choice but to
put his hand on the dashboard to stop his certain
journey through the windshield. She turned and
gave him a demure smile, all sweet innocence, the
triumph gleaming in her brown eyes. "You're
home."

He kept his expression bland. "If that was supposed to scare me you've made your first mistake.
I like living dangerously."

"Hardly my first mistake," she muttered.

"You're home," she said again, pointedly. "Goodbye."

"And what about your brother?"

"What about him?" she said warily.

"Don't you want to know what your father has planned for him? Isn't that why you came to see him?"

"What does my father have planned for him?"

"Tomorrow night. Dinner. I'll pick you up at seven."

"I'm busy."

"Cancel it. You know perfectly well your brother comes first. You have that codependent look to you." He was pushing just a little too far, but he sensed she could take it. He needed to keep her angry, interested, willing to fight.

"I'll meet you."

"And miss my chance to see the legendary La Casa de Sombras? I'll pick you up."

"If you're interested in famous Hollywood houses you can always take one of those bus tours. La Casa de Sombras used to be on most of them."

"Including the one that takes you to all the famous scandal sites? I think I'd rather see it with a guided tour from its owner."

"Dean's one of the owners. Treat him well and maybe he'll invite you over."

"I'm not exactly Dean's type," he said.

"You're not mine, either."

"And what is your type? I wouldn't have thought Alan Dunbar would have been the kind of man you'd marry."

She'd obviously forgotten he'd have access to all of Meyer's legal affairs, including her divorce settlement. "I think I've had enough of you for now," she said in a deceptively even tone.

"For now," he agreed, opening the door and sliding his long legs out. "I'll be there at seven."

She gunned the motor, speeding away into the oncoming traffic without looking, the passenger door slamming shut of its own volition. He stood beneath the towering palm tree, watching her go.

Unable to decide whether it was the car or the woman he wanted more. And which one he intended to keep.

He shrugged. Probably neither. After almost a year things were finally moving into high gear, and he was more than ready. Breaking Jilly Meyer's stubborn, defensive attitude would simply be the icing on the cake.

He'd been planning on working through Rachel-Ann, seducing her first while he worked on bringing down the rest of the Meyer family. She was the most notoriously vulnerable, but in the time he'd been in L.A. she'd been noticeably absent, honeymooning with husband number three, going through a quickie divorce, disappearing on retreats and binges and detox outings. He'd never even seen her from a distance. At thirty-three she was still beautiful, they told him, and she'd be easy prey.

But maybe he wanted the challenge of Jilly. The indefinable treat of Jilly Meyer, the family outcast. Or maybe she'd just be a delicious side dish on the banquet table of truth and revenge.

But first he needed to get close to them. To Meyer's three disparate children. He glanced up at the expensive, upscale apartment building where he'd lived for the past year, surrounded by upscale wheelers and dealers as soulless as he was.

Maybe it was time for a touch of arson.

It was all Jilly could do to make it through the five-minute drive to La Casa. She sped up the long, overgrown driveway, gravel spurting beneath her tires, and slammed to a stop inside one of the bays of the seven-car garage. Her hands were shaking when she turned off the motor, and she sat there, seat belt still fastened, her eyes closed as she tried to will the tension from her body.

She'd screwed things up royally. It was all fine and good to arm herself for a confrontation with the old man, but she'd let the gorgon slough her off, then reenacted some damned fairy tale by falling asleep, letting her father escape scot-free. She should have known—she'd been awake half the night before, worrying about Dean and how she'd deal with her father. She never did well without enough sleep.

And she'd let that goddamned man rile her. He was everything Dean said he was—smooth, gorgeous, so damned sure of himself she wanted to smack him. And Coltrane was dead wrong—part of the problem was that he was *exactly* Dean's type. Unfortunately he didn't seem to share Dean's sexual orientation, which would have made things a lot easier. Then he wouldn't have been coming on to her like she was Julia Roberts. He'd already be involved in a bitch-fest with Dean, and she could have just stayed out of the entire mess.

She leaned forward, resting her head on the leather-covered steering wheel. She didn't want to deal with this. She was so tired of taking care of everyone, taking care of this house that was falling down around her. The house that she loved with complete abandon.

It was late. Everything was still and silent around the legendary La Casa de Sombras—even the supposed ghosts were quiet. Dean was either off somewhere or lost in the glow of his computer screen, and God only knew what Rachel-Ann might be doing. She'd been back from treatment for three months, and it was usually around that benchmark she began to slip. She'd been out almost every night, coming back early and sober and silent. If she was home tonight there was a good chance she'd want someone to pick on, and Dean had a talent for making himself unavailable.

Jilly climbed out of the car, suppressing a sigh. She could handle this. She was the one who was mercifully free of addictions and needs and runaway emotions. She was strong, a survivor, and she could hold the others together when they needed holding.

She yanked down the heavy wooden door on the garage bay, wondering why she bothered when the locks were too rusted to work and the keys were long gone. If the house itself hadn't kept demanding so much money she would have invested in an automatic garage door opener. Dean had two cars, neither of which ran terribly well, and Rachel-Ann had her BMW, not to mention the rusting hulk of the Dusenberg that had once belonged to Brenda de Lorillard's doomed lover, and the cost of equipping the entire building with automatic openers was prohibitive, especially considering that the wood framing was in a state of rot.

Jilly started up the gravel pathway to the house, letting the blessed stillness wash over her. There was something to be said for lack of money. The estate was so overgrown that the palm trees provided soundproofing from the city that surrounded them, making it an oasis of peace and safety—a perfect sanctuary. At least, until Rachel-Ann went off the wagon.

There were only a few lights burning in the house as Jilly climbed up the wide, flagstoned terrace, and she breathed a sigh of relief. She'd have the place to herself, at least for a few hours. That was all she needed, a little time to think through what had happened, to devise a new plan to help Dean.

In the meantime she was starving. She headed straight back to the huge old kitchen. She sat down at the twelve-foot-long wooden table and ate two containers of yogurt with a silver serrated grapefruit spoon from Tiffany's, then followed it with a peanut butter sandwich on a cracked Limoges dessert plate. She'd have to go food shopping tomorrow—there wasn't much left. Rachel-Ann seemed to subsist on sweets when she was clean and sober, and Dean was always on some strange diet or other. Which didn't keep the two of them from suddenly emptying the refrigerator and cupboards of anything remotely interesting when the mood struck them.

Jilly set her plate in the old iron sink, then

headed toward the back of the house where her brother kept his separate apartments.

She knocked, but there was no answer. Pushing the door open, she was, as always, assaulted by the room. Dean had claimed the servants' wing because it was relatively unadorned with the Mediterranean kitsch that flowed through the rest of the house. He'd had the walls knocked down, everything painted white and then buffed into a glaring, glossy sheen. The furniture was sparse and modern, and Dean lay facedown on the bed. The only light in the room came from the computer monitors—Dean always had at least two going at a time.

She moved quietly to his side, looking down at him tenderly. Dean had his air-conditioning unit on high, but she didn't make the mistake of turning it down, nor would she be fool enough to touch the computers. She simply covered him with a blanket, wishing things were different, even if she wasn't quite sure what she'd change.

She left him in his sterile, frozen cocoon, moving back into the dark, decaying warmth of La Casa de Sombras. The House of Shadows. Except that it sometimes seemed as if Dean's stark, white room held the most shadows of all.

3

Zachariah Redemption Coltrane was a child of the sixties, born in the middle of that turbulent decade. His name had been an albatross around his neck until he was thirteen, and yet it had been the least of the various crosses he'd had to bear. At age thirteen and a half he'd been almost six feet tall, everyone he cared about was dead, and he'd taken off into the world he'd already learned was cruel and hostile, changing his name to Zack. That is, when he bothered to use his real name at all.

Odd, how some family histories were straightforward and others seemed like the stuff of legends. From his great-aunt Esther's bitter-toned stories to his father's whiskey-soaked reminiscences, he could never tell what was truth and what was fantasy. How his mother had died, or what her real name was. He only knew her as Ananda, and his memories were of light and laughter and the sweet, acrid scent of marijuana floating in the air. They'd lived in a castle, he thought, and there had been dragons and danger and his mother was a lost princess.

But that was before she'd been murdered.

He couldn't really remember a time when he hadn't lived in that dreary little house in Indiana with his drunken, defeated father and his tart-tongued great-aunt. Couldn't really remember the magical place, or the princess who'd been his laughing mother. And no one would ever tell him about her.

Great-Aunt Esther had died first, eaten up by cancer. His father had followed, breaking his neck in a drunken fall. And Coltrane had taken off before Social Services could get their hands on his rebellious, thirteen-year-old hide, bumming his way around the country as he grew into manhood.

He'd ended up with an education despite himself, more a fluke than a plan. Lawyers made money, lawyers manipulated the system, lawyers were the scum of the earth. It seemed a perfect career for him, once he got tired of living life on the edge.

He'd been in New Orleans, working as an assistant district attorney prosecuting the lowest of the low and doing a piss poor job of it, with no knowledge of his real past and no interest. He'd put it behind him, including the vague memories of his long-lost mother. He didn't know what prompted him to pick up the magazine the first place—he had no interest in Southern California or haunted mansions or the excesses of the young and beautiful.

But for some reason he'd picked up *L.A. Life,* thumbing through the pictorial on scandal sites of the century, and he'd stopped at an old, grainy newspaper photo, staring at his mother's face. Back in the 1960s, a ragtag band of Hollywood street people had been arrested for trespassing on the deserted grounds of La Casa de Sombras, and his mother had been one of them. He couldn't tell if his father was in the photo or remember if he'd ever been in L.A.—it was his mother who'd stood out, young and luminous even in black and white.

No one had bothered to prosecute and the interlopers had simply gone back to make their home in the ruined mansion in true sixties communal brotherhood, thereby hastening the decline of the historic property and sending the wealthy neighbors into apoplexy. And the Ivy League dropout, whose family owned La Casa, joined them.

That was how he'd found Jackson Dean Meyer, the first name he'd come across from that turbulent time that had ended in the loss of his mother. He'd learned early on not to ask questions of his family—his father would start to weep and drink even more heavily, and his Great-Aunt Esther would tell him to shut his mouth, accompanying the admonition with a crack across the face. She had mean, hard hands for such an old lady, and she'd died before he got bigger than she was and could stop her. Before he could find the answers to his questions.

But once he had a name, it had been easy enough to track down the black sheep. Jackson Dean Meyer had mended his ways, gone back to Harvard, acquired a graduate degree, three wives in reasonable succession, three grown children from his first marriage, one of whom was adopted, and two young ones from his third.

And control of a billion-dollar investment and development firm. He'd done well by himself, but then, he'd started off with several advantages, including a wealthy family. The house where he'd once dabbled in communal living now belonged to the children from his first marriage, and the old man lived in modern luxury in an estate in Bel Air.

Coltrane knew he was the man who would hold the answers to his past, to what happened to his mother, and Coltrane had every intention of asking politely.

His father used to tell him that his half-Irish mother had "the sight," a curse Coltrane wondered if he'd inherited. He'd looked at his father one day and known he was going to die. Unfortunately he hadn't known how soon it would happen.

That sight had reasserted itself the day he'd bluffed his way into Jackson Dean Meyer's office, no mean feat given the layers of protection that surrounded the old man. He'd taken one look into his clear, calm eyes and known that this man had murdered his mother.

Of course Meyer had no earthly idea who Coltrane was. Nor did he care. But Coltrane was gifted at giving people what they wanted and getting them to trust him. It had been easy enough to work his way into the inner sanctum of Meyer Enterprises, into a position of power. The old man was a ruthless snake, and he detected a soul mate in Coltrane.

What hadn't been easy was learning patience over the long years, the great gift of biding his time. He'd been in place for almost a year now, working his way into Jackson Meyer's confidence to the point where he had total control of the legal department at Meyer Enterprises. Zack Coltrane, with the phony Ivy League degree, the charming smile and the California laid-back ease was poised and ready to take Jackson Dean Meyer down.

But he couldn't make his move until he had all the answers. It wasn't going to be enough to destroy Meyer financially. Killing him would be too easy. Coltrane had never killed anyone in his life, though he'd come close a few times. He suspected in the case of Jackson Meyer it wouldn't require much effort. He hated him that much.

But death ended things. And he wanted an everlasting torment for the man who murdered his mother. Once he had proof. He wanted Meyer to know who destroyed him, and why.

Destroying his business and reputation would be merely a start, and he'd been working on that since he'd come to L.A. Destroying his family would be even better, an eye for an eye. Coltrane had grown up in the grinding, soulless poverty of the icy Midwest, with a father too drunk to even notice him since they'd lost the one thing that mattered to either of them. The least Coltrane could do was return the favor, no matter what that made him.

The problem was, finding someone Jackson Meyer cared about other than his own sleek, artificially tanned, fitness-center-buffed hide was no easy task. He treated his trophy wife like an impatient parent, his two young children like puppies who hadn't been housebroken. As far as Coltrane could tell he didn't even remember their names. And his daughter Jilly might as well not exist for all the mention that had been made of her.

But Rachel-Ann was different. Rachel-Ann was Meyer's one weak spot, and that was who Coltrane intended to work on. He'd already managed to put enough pressure on Dean to get him out of the way—Meyer's only son had conceded the battle without firing a single shot, retiring to his computers and an impressive case of the sulks. As for Jilly, she was simply a casualty of war—if he had time he'd take her, but she was merely a sideline.

From all reports Rachel-Ann had been hovering on the brink of destruction for most of her life. It seemed only fitting that he'd help push her over the edge, and then stand back and watch while Meyer went flailing after her. And he refused to think about what kind of man that made him.

He poured himself a Scotch, straight up, carrying it out onto the patio as he slowly sipped it. It was the best Scotch he could find, a single malt from a tiny distillery in the Hebrides, and it had become part of a ritual—a silent toast to the father who drank his life away. An arrogant daring of fate to try to do the same to him. After a decade he still hadn't learned to like the taste of it, but he drank it, anyway, a small spit in the eye of the vengeful gods.

His plan was simple. He'd use Jilly to get to her fragile older sister, then go from there. He was a patient man, but he'd waited long enough. Time to up the ante. It wasn't that he particularly wanted to harm innocents. But if Dean was anything to go by then Meyer's grown children were far from innocent.

The Los Angeles night was settling down around him, and he stared out over the city, his back to the perfectly decorated apartment that was nothing more than a stage setting. He could feel the cool tingle of anticipation in his veins, a headier drug than the whiskey. By tomorrow night he'd be in the legendary Casa de Sombras, well on his way to the answers he'd spent years of his life looking for. And if he felt even a faint twinge of regret that Jilly Meyer was going to be one of the casualties of war, he dismissed it with a stray grimace.

He answered the phone on the third ring, just before the answering service would get it, knowing who it was.

"Did you get rid of her?" Jackson Dean Meyer barked into the phone.

"For now. You didn't tell me you wanted me to do anything permanent," he said lazily.

There was a pregnant pause on the other end of the line. "Is there something permanent you could do?"

"I suppose I could find a hit man if you think it's necessary...."

"I don't find that amusing, Coltrane," Meyer said icily. "I'm not in the habit of murdering my children."

No, only your lovers, he thought calmly, eyeing his drink. "Then she's going to keep after you until you give her what she wants. You know what women can be like."

"She always was a stubborn bitch. Just like her mother," Meyer snapped. "What is it exactly that she wants?"

"She wasn't particularly clear about that, but I imagine it's something along the lines of you loving your son and me being at the bottom of the ocean."

Meyer's dry chuckle sounded faintly asthmatic. "Made a good impression on her, did you? I warned you she could be difficult. What are you planning to do about her?"

"Take her out to dinner tomorrow night."

"You won't get her into bed. She's the prude in the family."

"Why would I want to get her into bed?" Coltrane took another sip of his Scotch. The ice had melted, watering the drink down slightly, and the sharpness danced against his tongue.

"To keep her occupied. Don't tell me you haven't noticed she's a good-looking woman. Can't hold a candle to Rachel-Ann, of course, but she's still pretty enough even with that hair of hers. And last I heard you weren't involved with anyone."

Coltrane had no doubt that Meyer knew exactly who he'd been sleeping with over the last year and how long each relationship had lasted. His employer's efforts at surveillance were laughably blatant, and Coltrane always fed him just enough to keep him satisfied.

"You want me to marry her, boss?" he drawled. "Or just shack up with her?"

"Don't push me, Coltrane," Meyer said. "I want you to distract her. I've got too much on my plate right now. Getting the Cienaga estate shouldn't be causing these kinds of problems, and I don't need the Justice Department breathing down my neck. You were supposed to give them stuff to distract them. Send them off on another tack."

"I took care of it."

"Goddamned bureaucrats don't seem to have a realistic idea of how things are done out here. And where the campaign contributions come from. Get them off my back, Coltrane."

"It's been done," Coltrane said soothingly. Indeed, it had. The Justice Department investigations of Jackson Dean Meyer's covert business practices had gone from one investigator to an entire team. And Meyer hadn't the faintest idea how little time he had left.

"I don't want to waste my energies distracted by inconsequentials," he said.

Inconsequentials like your children, Coltrane thought, but didn't say it out loud. There was a limit to how much leeway Jackson Meyer would give him. The man was convinced he needed Coltrane for all his little schemes to fall into place, but he needed his sense of omnipotence even more.

Meyer was going to find out that his trust in both Coltrane and in his own invulnerability were sadly misplaced. And while it would be the icing on the cake for him to lose his children at the same time, it hadn't taken Coltrane long to realize Meyer had really lost them years ago.

"All right, boss," he drawled. He was the only person who called Meyer "boss," the only one who could get away with that faintly mocking tone. "I'll sleep with your daughter. Hell, I'll sleep with both your daughters, but I draw the line at your son."

Meyer chuckled humorlessly. "He'd be too easy for you. And you keep away from Rachel-Ann. She's fragile right now, and I don't want you interfering with her. She won't be a problem—she's never been any trouble to me, unlike the other two. My fault for marrying their mother. You just keep Jilly busy until this deal is finished. Then you can dump her. You know it'll be worth your while."

It was a good thing Meyer couldn't see the slow smile that curved Coltrane's mouth. "That's what I like about you, boss. Your sentimental streak."

"Fuck you, Coltrane."

"Yes, sir." But Meyer had already slammed down the phone, certain that he was going to get his own way. Coltrane would sleep with his daughter to keep her occupied while Meyer did his best to deal with the unexpected financial calamity that was bringing his empire down around his ears.

Little did he know he was asking the fox to guard the henhouse.

Jilly never entered her bedroom without making a great deal of noise. It was the master bedroom, the largest, most elegant of the massive rooms in the old mansion, but no one had argued with her when she'd chosen it for her own. Dean preferred his sterile haven, and Rachel-Ann was too superstitious to care.

Not that Jilly believed in ghosts. La Casa had been in the family since before she was born, and she'd spent enough time there to have run across a ghost or two if they'd actually existed. Dean had tried to scare her when they were younger, telling her elaborate stories of the murder-suicide pact and the ghosts who roamed the halls, but for some reason he'd never succeeded. If there were any ghosts in La Casa de Sombras then they were benevolent ones, no matter how harshly they died.

But even so, she didn't fancy walking in on one, unannounced. Clearing her throat, she rattled the doorknob before pushing it open and flicking on the light switch. No shifting shadows, no dissolving forms. Just the same bizarre room it had always been.

It looked like a cross between a bordello and a Turkish harem, with a totally peculiar touch of chinoiserie. It was whimsical Gothic horror, from the elephant-footed stools to the ornate, gilded, swan-shaped bed, and Jilly loved every tacky inch of it.

She filled the huge marble tub, stripping off her clothes and sliding into the scented water, letting it engulf her as she closed her eyes. It had been a long, miserable day, one for the books, and not only had she not accomplished a damned thing, she might have made things worse. She'd certainly added to her own discomfort. She didn't want to go out to dinner with Coltrane—she'd done her best to keep her distance from all the sharklike young men her father employed. He was everything she despised—ambitious, aggressive and too damned good-looking. He knew it, too, which was probably why Dean found him irresistible. Dean always had a weakness for smug, clever, pretty boys, especially those who were unattainable.

Rachel-Ann would probably find him just as enticing. He wasn't as outwardly dangerous as the usual losers her sister surrounded herself with, but he was gorgeous enough to make up for it. They'd make a stunning couple.

The water had grown cold in an astonishingly short amount of time. Jilly pushed herself out of the deep, marble tub, grimacing at her reflection in the mirror. There were too damned many mirrors in this house—everywhere she turned she got an unwanted glimpse of herself. She had no idea who had installed all of them in the first place, the silent movie star who'd built the house or Brenda de Lorillard, who'd died there. As someone singularly devoid of vanity, Jilly found them unnerving.

Particularly when Rachel-Ann was convinced the place was haunted. Every now and then Jilly would catch her reflection in the mirror, but she wouldn't be looking at herself. She'd be looking for a ghostly image of someone long dead.

It was a cool night, and she pulled on cotton sweats rather than close her windows. She liked the fresh air infusing the house. It swept away the cobwebs and the trace of mildew. Oddly enough it could never rid the house of the smell of fresh tobacco smoke, or the faint note of perfume that lingered, a scent she half recognized from her childhood. It must have been her grandmother's. Probably Julia Meyer had dropped a bottle and the stuff had penetrated into the woodwork. Jilly rather liked the scent. It made her think her grandmother was watching over her, somehow. Even if Grandmère hadn't been much more than an adequate guardian in life.

She heard the slam of the door echoing through the vast house. It was odd how certain sounds carried—she always knew when Rachel-Ann came home. She brought a nervous energy with her that spread throughout the place, like the charged air before a thunderstorm.

Jilly held very still, listening vainly for the sounds of voices. Nothing. Rachel-Ann was alone, thank God. Had been alone for the last three months. It was aiding her uncertain temper, but it was a step toward recovery.

A moment later she heard a crash and the sound of running footsteps. By the time Jilly was out in the hall Rachel-Ann was halfway up the stairs, thin and ghostlike, her flame-red hair trailing behind her as she raced up the remaining steps, an expression of pure terror on her pale face.

She went straight into Jilly's arms with a grateful sob, shivering. She was so slight, so fragile, so small, and Jilly wrapped her strong arms around her, making soothing noises. "What's wrong, sweetie?" she said. "Did you trip over something? I heard a crash."

"I don't know! Something must have broken, but I didn't see what." Her voice was soft, panicky, but entirely sober.

"Don't worry about it," Jilly said in her calmest voice. There wasn't much left of value at La Casa to break. "What frightened you?"

Rachel-Ann pulled away, staring at her sister in momentary confusion. Her green eyes were huge, staring, but she didn't look drugged. Jilly breathed a silent sigh of relief. "I don't know," her sister said finally. "They were watching me. I could feel them. They watch me all the time. I know you don't believe me, but they're there, I can sense them."

"Are they?" Jilly had learned from past experience that Rachel-Ann hated to be patronized. "You want to come in and tell me about it?"

"Not in that room," she said, looking toward the master bedroom with an expression akin to horror. "I don't know how you can sleep in there, knowing what happened."

"I don't believe in ghosts," Jilly said.

"I do. They were watching me a few minutes ago." Rachel-Ann's usually soft voice was high-pitched with strain. She'd lost a lot of weight recently, weight she couldn't afford to lose, and she looked like a frail, red-haired sparrow, lost and frightened.

"Then we'll go into your room, and I'll sit with you until you fall asleep."

Rachel-Ann's mouth twisted into a smile that was both bitter and longing. "Always the good sister, Jilly. Don't you ever get tired of us?"

"Never."

"You don't need to worry about me. I'm fine in my room. They never come in there. I've seen to that."

"Rachel-Ann, there are no ghosts—"

"Humor me for once, Jilly! They're there. The only way I can make them go away is to drink, and I'm not ready to pay that price. Just let me go to bed and I'll be fine in the morning. They don't usually bother me in the daylight." Rachel-Ann grimaced. "Don't look at me that way. I'm not crazy. This house is haunted."

"Did you talk to your therapist about the ghosts?" Jilly asked.

"What, and have him think I'm crazy?" Rachel-Ann's laugh was only slightly hysterical. "The ghosts are in this house, not in my mind. But don't worry about it. They leave you alone for some reason. Be grateful."

"Maybe I just don't have enough imagination."

"Maybe you're just too levelheaded," Rachel-Ann said wearily. She gave Jilly a quick hug, and the tremor in her slender arms was pathetic. "See you in the morning, darling. Not too early."

"I'll be glad to sit with you...."

"No need," she said, suddenly breezy. "I'll be fine."

Jilly watched as her sister skirted the hallway, putting as much distance between herself and Jilly's open bedroom door as possible. A moment later she was in her own suite of rooms, the door shut tightly behind her.

Jilly stayed where she was, wondering whether she should go after her. She hadn't been inside Rachel-Ann's rooms since her sister had come back from her most recent hospitalization—it was a matter of honor that she wouldn't search for empty bottles or pill containers. Rachel-Ann said she had a way of keeping the ghosts out, and Jilly couldn't even begin to guess what that was. Or whether it would work to keep other, more resourceful demons at bay.

She had no idea what time it was—probably after eleven. It had been a piss-poor day. She'd accomplished nothing and only managed to unnerve herself with her abortive visit to her father's office.

And she'd met Coltrane. A treat she could have happily done without. She was going to have to find a way to either get rid of him, or get him to help her. And he didn't look like the kind of man who made an effort to help anyone unless there was something in it for him.

She reached up and pulled the pins out of her thick hair, letting it fall down her back in a heavy mass. She'd figure out what to do about Dean and his problems in the morning. At least for tonight she could rest easy, assured that her sister and brother were safe in their own beds, and that Rachel-Ann's specious ghosts couldn't come into hers.

"You scared her," Brenda said in a cross voice. "Haven't I told you the girl's fragile? She always has been, ever since she was a child. She reminds me in many ways of myself when I was that age."

"Honeybunch, you died before you reached that age," Ted said with a particular lack of tact. "And you were as fragile as an elephant in labor. The girl's too easily spooked if you ask me."

"She can see us."

"So can a lot of people. They don't turn into raving drunkards because of it," Ted said. "Most of them figure it's a trick of the light or something. That girl's the only one who's gone around the bend, and if she wasn't so busy throwing things at

us she'd realize we're just worried about her.
We're perfectly harmless.''

''Perfectly,'' Brenda murmured, leaning over to
kiss him. ''And besides, she shouldn't be drinking.
If we hadn't shown up when we did she would
have taken that drink instead of throwing it at us.''

''Maybe. Maybe not.'' Ted shrugged. ''She's
poured them before and then left them. It doesn't
really matter. We terrify the poor girl, and it's not
as if we can sit down and explain it to her. We'll
just have to be a little more circumspect. We don't
need to feel guilty.''

''Guilty,'' Brenda said in a hollow voice. ''No,
we wouldn't want that. Let's go for a walk, darling.
We can sit on the terrace and watch the stars.''

He tucked her arm in his, smiling down at her
fondly. ''It sounds heavenly, darling.''

''Heavenly,'' Brenda echoed. A place she was
never going to see. ''Any place with you is
heaven,'' she said.

And Ted leaned down and kissed her.

4

By late the next afternoon Jilly was in a thoroughly bad mood. If Wednesday had been bad, Thursday was even worse, and the evening didn't look like it was going to be any improvement. She'd gotten up early, as always. She'd never needed much sleep, and the ornate, swan-shaped bed was more oppressive than comfortable. For years she'd thought about buying a new mattress and box spring, but the swan bed was custom-made and of no standard size, and she couldn't justify spending so much money on a mattress when she spent so little time there. And as Dean had callously pointed out, the mattress had to at least date from after 1951. The previous one would have been soaked with blood.

Jilly shivered, rubbing her arms in the warm evening air as she sat on the deserted terrace at La Casa. Would it have been too much to ask, to have a good day for once, just to make the ordeal of this evening easier? But no, her job wasn't overburdened with good days, and today was one of the worst.

Working as an historic preservationist in Los Angeles was a classic exercise in futility, and she'd known that going into it. Los Angeles was based on money and power, and history and aesthetics were commodities of little value. In the three years Jilly had worked for the Los Angeles Preservation Society she'd watched landmark after landmark be turned into rubble and then transformed into Bauhaus boxes. The best she could preserve were memories.

Today was particularly bad. She'd spent the day scrambling over debris at the Moroccan Theater, snapping pictures with the digital camera, taking notes, taking measurements. In a few more days it would be gone, its last reprieve used up. And at one point Jilly sat in one of the dusty, plush velvet seats and wept, not sure if she was weeping for the building or her own life.

Dean and Rachel-Ann were gone by the time she got home in the middle of the afternoon, and chances were they wouldn't be back until late. Just as well. Handling Coltrane was difficult enough— she didn't want to have to worry about her siblings at the same time.

She'd showered the dust and rubble off her body, made herself a tall glass of iced tea and wan-

dered out on the terrace to watch the sun set over
the huge expanse of overgrown lawn. She loved
the terrace, the old iron furniture, the flagstones,
the stone columns weathered and chipped from the
years, the towering palms surrounding them. But
down in the middle of the lawn, some two hundred
yards away, lay the dank, algae-covered pool, and
Jilly could never look at it without shuddering.

It was past time to get someone in to drain it
again, she thought idly. It hadn't been used in
years. As a child she'd had an unexpected dread
of it, even though she spent all her free time in her
friends' pools. Maybe it was the trees looming
overhead, or the odd patterns in the tiles, or maybe
an excess of teenage imagination. Whatever it was,
Jilly had stayed away from the pool most of her
life.

When they'd inherited the house she'd had it
drained, but each year it would fill again, water
seeping in from a crack in the lining. There was
no way she could afford to hire heavy machinery
to come in and bulldoze it, so it just sat there, dank
and malevolent, with only the wild tangle of rose-
bushes to shield it.

Jilly perched on the wide stone railing, breathing
in the scent of roses mixed with the acrid perfume
of exhaust from the surrounding city. There was
nothing she wanted more than to climb into her

huge marble bathtub and stay there until her skin got wrinkled. She didn't want to see anyone, talk to anyone, save anyone. Not tonight. She most particularly didn't want to have to deal with Z. R. Coltrane.

At least she'd found out that much about him, even if she couldn't fathom what Z. R. stood for. It seemed an apt enough name for a Hollywood cutthroat.

Not that she had any particular reason to consider him a cutthroat, apart from her instinctive dislike of all lawyers. She wasn't particularly trustful of good-looking men, either—years in Los Angeles had taught her to be wary, and Alan had finished the lesson. Of course Coltrane didn't look the slightest bit like her former husband. Alan was dramatically beautiful, with long, flowing dark hair, a poet's face, an artist's hands, a butcher's soul.

Coltrane, on the other hand, was a shaggy-haired, bleached California blond, a lawyer, not an artist, a businessman, not a poet. Unlike Alan, he made no pretensions to being a gentle, noble soul. And yet he was a phony, a liar, just as much as her husband had been. What you saw was definitely not what you'd get, or so her instincts screamed at her.

Coltrane was the sort of man who could easily figure out what appealed to certain people and tailor his approach accordingly. If anything, he'd seemed determined to annoy her rather than seduce her into thinking he was harmless.

Bad word, *seduce*. Particularly in connection with him. They'd have a business meeting tonight, a calm, rational discussion of how Dean's situation could be made more tenable at Meyer Enterprises, and then she'd bow out, gracefully, and never have to see Coltrane again. She never went to her father's lavish holiday parties—for all she knew she hadn't even been invited the last couple of years. There was no reason she should ever have to run into one of her father's employees again.

It was all quite simple once you put it in perspective, she thought, sipping her tea and averting her gaze from the swimming pool. She'd let her imagination get out of hand, which was downright silly of her. She'd learned to change what she could and let go of what she couldn't fix. There was a good chance she could at least help Dean. And if she couldn't, she'd simply have to work on backing off and letting him deal with it on his own.

She heard the sound of tires on the overgrown driveway, and her stomach lurched unpleasantly. She didn't recognize the sound of the car. It was just seven o'clock, and her unwanted date must be arriving.

* * *

Coltrane knew exactly where La Casa de Sombras stood behind its curtain of overgrown trees. He'd developed an odd sort of fascination for it, though in truth it probably wasn't that odd. He knew from the photograph that his mother had spent time there in the sixties, though he had no idea how long or if his father had been there, as well. There'd been no dates on the newspaper photo, and no one to ask. His father had flatly refused to ever discuss his mother. But La Casa de Sombras was part of his family history, a place where some of the answers to his past lay buried, and it had taken a long time to finally get inside. Things were beginning to fall into place.

He'd considered breaking in at some point during his tenure. It would have been a piece of cake—during his hellion youth he'd learned all sorts of skills from the motley group of lowlifes he'd hung around with, and he knew how to break into a house without leaving any mark. He'd chosen not to risk it, relying on his patience. Sooner or later he'd walk in through the front door. He could wait.

But now that the time had come he found he was oddly tense. The last few years of his life, maybe his entire life, were coming down to this night, and all he could think about was Jilly Meyer.

He had to remember that she wasn't the weak

link. If anything, she was the strong one, and he wasn't particularly interested in a challenge. He'd already been working on her brother, but it was her fragile older sister who was going to provide the key. He knew it by instinct, instinct bred in him by his Irish mother. Rachel-Ann Meyer was the way to Jackson's heart, and to his destruction.

The ornate gates at the bottom of the overgrown driveway were stuck open, rusty even in a place where it never seemed to rain. He drove slowly up the winding drive, dodging an overhanging tree limb here, a raised hump of grass there. In Los Angeles, one of the most developed areas on earth, there were sport utility vehicles in almost every garage. This was one place where one might actually be needed. He wondered how Jilly managed to avoid the potholes in her gorgeous, low-slung Corvette.

He first caught sight of the huge garage. The slate roof was cracked and damaged—it was a good thing it seldom rained or the place would have been worthless. There were seven garage doors—three of them were closed, three were empty. The Corvette stood in pristine glory in the remaining bay.

He parked directly behind it, blocking her in. There was no sign of anyone around, so he immediately headed over to the red car, letting his hands brush the shining finish like a tender lover's. He'd always thought his dream car was a Gull Wing Mercedes, or perhaps a classic Jaguar XKE. He'd never realized how deeply American he was, after all.

He reached for the door handle, unable to resist, when he realized he wasn't alone. He didn't even jump when he heard her caustic voice.

"I told you, you're not driving my car."

He kept his hand on the car, letting his fingertips caress it lightly, knowing Jilly was watching. And then he turned and peered at her from beneath his shaggy hair.

"I'm glad you didn't put yourself to any trouble on my account," he said. She was wearing shorts and a T-shirt, and he let his gaze travel up her long legs. She obviously had no idea how very much her long legs turned him on, or she wouldn't keep exposing them like that. It didn't matter that the shorts were baggy cargo shorts—it was the legs beneath them that got him going.

Rachel-Ann, he reminded himself. *She is the key. Meyer wouldn't give a damn what happened to this daughter.*

"Sorry, I've changed my mind. There's no reason to go out—we can discuss the situation here as well as anywhere. Guess you'll have to rethink your plans," she said breezily.

"How about McDonald's? I wouldn't have thought fast food was the best arena for negotiations, but I'm game if you are. Especially if we get to eat in the car. That way no one will notice if I accidentally grope you." He wasn't quite sure why he'd added that—mainly to get a reaction from her, he supposed.

"Yeah, right," she said, foolishly unconvinced. There was nothing he'd like better than to grope her, if the time and place were different. But for right now she was simply the means to an end. "Negotiations?"

"Isn't that what this is about? You convince me to help your baby brother win Daddy's love and approval? I'm going to be fascinated to hear what I have to gain by doing it, but I'm always open-minded."

She didn't bother denying it. "Maybe out of the goodness of your heart?"

"I don't think there's much goodness in me. Much less a heart," he said, giving her his most dulcet smile.

She blinked, a good reaction. He believed in warning people. They seldom believed him—people always tended to downplay his honesty. It was only later when they looked back, battered and bruised, that they realized he'd simply told them the truth.

"You're not going to convince me with that diffidence crap," she said.

"Convince you of what? I'm telling you the truth."

"I'm not sure you'd know the truth if it bit you on the ass."

"I guess you'll just have to find out." He stepped back from the Corvette, hiding his reluctance. "So, are you going to give me a tour of this place? And don't tell me I can take a bus tour. I want an owner's perspective. Or at least the temporary owner. Your father's the one who'll end up with this place when you finally give it up."

"That's not about to happen. You're awfully conversant with the legal ownership of this place," she added suspiciously.

"I'm head of legal services, remember? It's my job to know." Hell, he didn't usually make slips like that one. He had to be careful with Jilly—she was a lot more observant than her brother. "Anyway, I like old Hollywood legends," he said. "I also like old houses. I studied to be an architect before I switched to law."

Her disbelief should have been scathing, but he wasn't easily scathed. "I got my degree in architecture from Princeton," she said, warning him.

"I know." He smiled at her. "Want to cross-examine me about architectural detail? You seem convinced I've got something to hide. What you see is what you get." He held his arms out.

"Not if I can help it," she muttered. "I don't suppose you'll be willing to leave until I show you the place."

"As always, you're very astute. And I'm looking forward to meeting your sister." He liked how casual it sounded.

"Why?"

"I'm curious. As your father's lawyer I've dealt with everything, including your divorce, Dean's traffic accidents, and Rachel-Ann's various... issues."

"You'll have to stay curious. She's not home tonight. Neither is Dean, for that matter."

"So we're here alone? Maybe I don't mind not taking you out, after all."

She looked completely unflustered. "Depends on how you define *alone,* and whether you believe in the ghosts. I never see them, but a lot of other people have. I wouldn't want to irritate them if I were you. Ghosts are notoriously unstable."

"Fortunately I'm not very irritating," he said, deliberately setting himself up for her hoot of disbelief. "Tell me about the place. Give me your best tour guide impersonation, and then we'll talk."

She wanted to get rid of him, she made that

perfectly clear, and he still wasn't quite sure why. He'd been his charming, unsettling best with her, and most women were reluctantly fascinated by him. She was fascinated, as well, but more along the lines of someone caught in the gaze of a snake. Maybe she was more intuitive than she gave herself credit for, despite her inability to see ghosts.

Coltrane didn't believe in ghosts. When he was younger he used to try to see his mother, floating over him like some sort of guardian angel. But his mother was no restless spirit—he would have known by now if she were. His mother was at peace, no matter how she'd died. He was the one with the restless spirit, seeking answers, seeking resolution.

"All right," she said finally. "Follow me."

It took an effort to keep his eyes off her sexy butt and on the overgrown path leading up to the main house. She was rattling off details in a monotone, and he let them filter into the back of his efficient memory, to dredge up later if and when he needed them. Built by the Greene brothers, site of Hollywood parties, witness to the infamous Hughes-de Lorillard suicide pact, home to a roaming band of dopers in the sixties and seventies. Nothing he hadn't heard before, though she didn't seem to realize her father had been part of that pack. He listened with half an ear for any inconsistencies as they turned the corner and reached the edge of the extensive terrace, the house looming over them in the shadows.

He stopped dead, her words no more than a meaningless hum in the back of his head, like an annoying insect.

The stone railing was crumbling. Weeds grew up beneath the flagstones, the stucco on the house was cracked and streaked with water marks. The slate roof was missing several tiles, and the furniture on the terrace was rusting, broken, derelict. The house looked like a grand duchess turned hooker, out on the streets, her finery faded and torn. A magic castle for a lost princess. But suddenly he knew with a certainty his mother wasn't the only Coltrane who'd lived there, decades ago.

He realized Jilly had stopped talking, and he tore his gaze away from the house to find her staring at him, a curious expression on her face.

"Not what you were expecting?" she said. "There's been barely enough money to keep it from falling to pieces entirely. I don't know how much longer I can keep it together."

"You don't strike me as someone who admits defeat." He was amazed at how calm his voice sounded.

"I'm a realist, Mr. Coltrane. Not a fool."

"Just Coltrane." And if she was a realist then

he was an altar boy. She was as idealistic and starry-eyed as anyone he'd ever met, at least when it came to what she loved. Which was old houses in general, and this old house in particular. "Let's go inside."

He was half expecting her to refuse, but after a moment she nodded, leading the way in. It was just as well—he wasn't about to leave without finally going through the place. Not since that cold wave of shock had washed over him when he first looked up at the house.

He'd lived here. No one had ever told him—as far as he'd known he'd spent the first thirteen years of his life in Indiana. He'd simply assumed that picture had been taken before he was born, before she'd met his father.

Wrong. He'd lived here, and he had no conscious memory of it. Just a weird, certain knowledge that this place had once, long, long ago, been his home.

The smell of the place was so damned familiar, another blow. He was glad Jilly's back was to him—he wasn't certain he could manage to keep his expression imperturbable. He knew the hallway, knew the long, curving staircase, and he followed her wordlessly as she cataloged the details of the house in a rapid, bored voice that slowly, reluctantly turned to warmth and fascination. She loved this house, he thought, loved it with a lover's passion. She would be an easy woman to use—her heart was on her sleeve. She loved the house, her brother and her sister, and all he'd have to do would be to apply a little pressure on one of those three things to get her to do what he wanted.

They wandered through drawing rooms, dining rooms, salons and breakfast nooks. Whoever had built this place had spared no expense, and the thing rambled for what seemed like acres. It was sparsely furnished, the few shabby pieces looking like lost remnants of a once grander time. "Brenda de Lorillard hired a set designer to decorate this place," Jilly was saying, "and unfortunately she picked someone who'd done a lot of work for Cecil B. DeMille. Some of it looks more like an opera set than a house."

She was right—it was gloriously tawdry, from the Italianate wallpaper to the gilt-covered furniture. The huge kitchen was a monument to impracticability, with not even a dishwasher in sight. There seemed to be no air-conditioning in the house, but the place was comfortably cool, anyway. He wondered if that was because of the supposed ghosts.

"What about upstairs?" he said, when her chatter had finally wound down.

"Bedrooms," she said.

"That's logical. Is that where it happened?"

She looked startled. "Where what happened?"

"The murder-suicide? Or does this place hold other scandals, as well?" He knew the answer to that, but he wasn't sure whether she did.

"The master bedroom. Trust me, there's nothing to see. All the blood was cleaned up."

"Show me, anyway."

"No. It's my bedroom now and I don't like strange men traipsing through it."

"Why?"

"I like my privacy."

"And you don't have any problem sleeping in a murder scene? A haunted one?"

"I told you, I don't believe in ghosts," she said.

"Don't believe in them? Or just don't see them?"

She glowered at him. She had a very impressive glower. "I'm getting tired of this."

"And I'm getting hungry. Show me the murder scene and then I'll ply you with fast food. Unless you've changed your mind and want to go someplace better."

"I told you I don't want to go anywhere with you," she snapped.

"But then your brother's left to sink or swim on his own."

She didn't say a word; her expression was with-

ering enough. But Coltrane wasn't easily cowed—
he was getting more reaction out of Jilly Meyer
than most people usually got, he was certain of it.
And he knew just how much to push, and when to
back off.

"All right," she said. "You can ogle the murder
scene, and then we talk." She turned and headed
out into the hallway, and he followed after her,
taking the steps two at a time until he caught up
with her, walking beside her. Now that he'd re-
gained his equilibrium he was more curious to see
her reaction. Did she really sleep in a room where
a murder occurred and not mind it? Would he recognize the room himself?

He almost laughed when he saw it. It was absurd, the ultimate in faded kitsch, from the swan-
shaped bed with its filmy draperies to the voluptuous, oversize furniture that littered the room.
There was a dressing table that looked as if it had
seen no use at all. He stepped past her, walking
into the room, looking out the French doors, across
the wide balcony that ran the length of the house
to the overgrown lawn below. He could see the
dark rectangle of a lichen-covered swimming pool
halfway down the row of trees, and an odd, stray
shudder passed over his body.

He turned to glance at Jilly, who still stood in

the doorway, arms folded across her chest, a stubborn expression on her face.

"Are you certain they died here? In that bed?"

"It's common knowledge. Hollywood loves its scandals, and this was one of the best ones."

"So Brenda de Lorillard killed her married lover and then herself, right? Any reason ever surface?"

Jilly shrugged. "Maybe he was growing tired of her. Men have a habit of doing that, you know."

"Do they?" He kept the grin from his face, but just barely. Someone needed to teach Jilly Meyer a few more effective defenses. She was as vulnerable as a kitten, spitting and scratching and pathetically easy to manipulate.

"How many other bedrooms?" he asked curiously, changing the subject.

"Seven. Rachel-Ann's in one, Dean's got his own apartment behind the kitchen. The rest are closed up."

So there was plenty of room for him. Assuming he didn't move right in with Rachel-Ann. He smiled briskly. "I've seen enough. Let's go find some food."

For a moment she didn't move, staring at him across the room.

"I don't like you," she said abruptly. "And I don't trust you."

"I know," he said with unexpected gentleness.

"Give me a reason why I should."

"I can't think of one."

"Are you going to help me?"

Lying was second nature to him. He didn't even hesitate. "Yes," he said.

And for a moment it looked as if she might make the desperate mistake of believing him.

5

The sky over Los Angeles was streaked with lavender and orange, the smog thickening the sunset into iridescent stripes. Jilly sat on the steps leading down into the tangled garden, an icy bottle of beer in her hand, waiting for Coltrane.

She had no idea what he was doing in the house. He said he'd needed to use the bathroom, and she could hardly dispute it. Nor could she wait outside the door of the ornate powder room with its pink swans and gilt faucets for him to reappear. She went back to the kitchen, took two beers and headed out for the terrace.

Not that she wanted to encourage the man. But it had been a long day, and she needed something from him. She was refusing to go out with him— she could at least offer him a beer without compromising her position.

What could he be doing in there, besides the obvious? Surely she was being paranoid—what possible interest could a stately old wreck like La Casa have for a man like him?

Her beer was half gone by the time he appeared. He'd taken off his jacket, his sleeves were rolled up and his tie was off. His streaked blond hair was rumpled, and he looked good enough to eat. Jilly ignored him.

"I don't suppose you have another beer, do you?" He leaned against the balustrade.

She handed it to him without a word, and he took a long swig of it. She watched the line of his throat, the condensation dripping off the bottle onto his skin, and she turned to concentrate on her own beer.

"So, what are we going to do about your brother?" he asked in a casual tone.

She glanced up at him. "You wouldn't feel like quitting your job and going back to New Orleans, would you?"

"You've been checking up on me." He sounded faintly pleased, and she could have kicked herself.

"I believe in knowing one's enemy."

"I'm not your enemy, Jilly," he said softly.

"Anyone who threatens my brother is my enemy."

"That's going to keep you pretty busy. Your brother threatens easily. Why don't you let him take care of his own business? If he thinks your father doesn't appreciate him then he should tell him so."

"Oh, Jackson would just love that," she muttered. "He'd probably tell him to stop whining."

"Dean does whine," Coltrane observed.

She glared at him. She was at somewhat of a disadvantage sitting at his feet, but she wasn't about to move. She didn't want him down on her level, either—she didn't want him anywhere near her.

"I don't think you're going to be able to save him," Coltrane said. "He's going to have to pull his head out of his computer and deal with life himself."

Jilly jerked her head around. "I could help if you'd just stop…stop…"

"Stop what?" He seemed genuinely interested.

"Stop being the paragon. Maybe screw up now and then. It's hard for Dean to compete with you around as the golden boy."

Coltrane looked out over the lawn, an odd expression on his face. "I suppose I'll just have to be less golden." He glanced down at her. "What do you really want me to do? Short of packing my bags or absconding with the company's assets, I'm at your disposal. You want me to have your father transfer some of the biggest accounts over to him? I can tell him I'm overloaded and need some help. I can tell him your brother's the best man for the job. I have no trouble lying."

"You're not very nice, are you?"

"Nope. I ordered some pizza. There's a place near here that delivers New York-style pizza that can make a grown man weep. I got enough in case your sister comes home."

Again she felt that extra shot of unease wash over her. "Why are you so curious about my sister?"

"I told you, I've heard stories."

"Don't believe the half of them. And I don't like pizza."

"You're not nearly as good a liar as I am."

It was true, she'd never been good at lying. "Maybe I don't need your help. Maybe all Dean has to do is stand up to Jackson."

Coltrane shrugged. "It's possible. Did it work for you?"

"What makes you think I stood up to him?"

Coltrane merely smiled, draining his beer and setting the bottle down on the stone railing. "Did it work?" he asked again.

"No. Jackson likes his children docile."

"Dean's practically a doormat, and Jackson doesn't seem any too fond of him," Coltrane said. "There's our pizza."

She hadn't even noticed the young man coming up the walkway, but the sudden rich aroma of tomato sauce and cheese wafted toward her, and her stomach leapt. She watched as Coltrane traded the pizza for cash, trying to school her wayward stomach.

He came toward her, carrying the box, and Jilly kept a stalwart expression on her face. "Real New York pizza," he said in a seductive voice. "No sprouts, no broccoli, no goat cheese or tofu. Do you realize how rare this is?"

It took her a moment to find her voice. She could resist a man that gorgeous, she knew she could. Real pizza was another matter.

"I'm not hungry," she said, her voice wavering slightly.

"Of course not. But then, neither am I. I'm afraid I have to leave."

She almost dropped her empty beer bottle. "Leave?" she repeated idiotically.

"I know it breaks your heart, but something's come up. We can talk about your family later. Maybe your sister might have an idea how we can help Dean. In the meantime, why don't I just leave the pizza here? Even if you don't like it maybe your ghosts would."

"I doubt it."

"Or maybe you'll consider trying it. Have you ever even had an honest-to-God real Italian pizza in your upscale California life?" His words were gently mocking.

"I went to Princeton," Jilly said. "They have great pizza in New Jersey."

"But you don't like pizza, right?" He set the box down on the step beside her, then moved away. "Think about what I said. Sooner or later your brother will have to fend for himself. Did he even ask you to go to your father?"

"Not in so many words, but..."

"I rest my case. He doesn't want you interfering. The more you try to fix things for him the worse things will get."

"Hi, my name is Jilly and I'm a codependent," she said flippantly.

"If you want my help you know where to find me."

She waited until he'd disappeared down the pathway beneath the overgrown trees, waited until the sound of his car faded away. Waited until the smell of pepperoni and cheese got too tempting, and then she tore into the box. Much good she was against the forces of darkness, she thought, dreamily shoving the pizza in her mouth. He was right— it was *great* pizza. She could stand firm against any onslaught and then be seduced by food.

"What are you eating?"

Jilly jumped, startled, and looked up at her sister. Rachel-Ann looked pale, sad and as beautiful as always, with her gorgeous pre-Raphaelite curls and her huge green eyes.

"Pizza," Jilly replied, her mouth still full. "The best pizza I've had in decades. Have some."

"I'm not hungry." Despite her words Rachel-Ann sat down on the steps beside Jilly and took the slice she offered. She stared at it for a long moment, as if she'd find the answers to the secrets of the universe in the thick topping. "Besides, I'm a vegetarian."

"Take the pepperoni off. I'll eat it for you," she offered generously.

Slowly, almost automatically Rachel-Ann picked off the circles of pepperoni and dropped them in the box. "Where did you get this? You're usually too cheap to call for take-out."

Jilly didn't even bother to correct her. Due to the complicated terms of Julia Meyer's will, the three siblings had possession of La Casa on equal terms, with money to support it. Rachel-Ann had gone through her share of the money in a record amount of time, but then, cocaine was an expensive habit. Jilly had no idea how much Dean had left, but she expected it wasn't much. Certainly neither of them contributed a penny to the massive upkeep of the old place. "It's my Scots blood," she said cheerfully. "And I didn't pay for it. Jackson's golden boy had it delivered."

"Really?" Rachel-Ann's interest perked up, and she took a tentative bite of the pizza. Her eyes closed in a moment of luxuriant bliss. "Is he as gorgeous as they say he is?"

"Yup."

"Are you sleeping with him?" She seemed no more than idly curious.

"No. I've been here every night, alone. You would have noticed if I was having an affair."

"I don't pay much attention to those things," Rachel-Ann said, taking another bite, and Jilly had to concede she was right. Rachel-Ann barely noticed if it was raining or sunny, she was too caught up in the foggy world she was battling to escape. Other people tended to flit through her life unnoticed. "Mmm," she said. "If he can provide pizza like this maybe I'll sleep with him."

For some reason Jilly found the notion deeply disturbing. It wasn't as if her sister didn't go through men like a hay-fever sufferer went through Kleenex, and while she'd remained celibate since she'd gotten out of treatment this time, it was unlikely to last. At least Coltrane would be a safer choice than some of the ones Rachel-Ann had made in the past. He wasn't a drug dealer or an addict, as far as Jilly could tell. "I don't think that would be a good idea," she said in a neutral voice. "I think he's dangerous."

Wrong words, Jilly thought, when Rachel-Ann's eyes lit up with a trace of their old spark. "Dangerous, gorgeous and he brings pizza? How irresistible."

"Resist him," Jilly said sourly.

At least Rachel-Ann didn't bother being coy. There was no question that Coltrane would want her—most any man did. And already he'd seemed far too interested in her older sister. It was fairly easy to guess why.

It was common knowledge that Rachel-Ann was Jackson's favored child. An ambitious man would use that to his advantage. Jackson was clearly disappointed in his own son—maybe he needed a smart and devoted son-in-law to inherit the business. And it didn't hurt that Rachel-Ann was sweet, beautiful and deeply wounded. She'd be dead easy to manipulate. Jackson was a past master at it, and Jilly had already seen enough of Coltrane to know he had a natural talent for it, as well.

Rachel-Ann smiled. "I'm doing my best to resist temptation. Just how pretty is the boy?"

"Too pretty," Jilly muttered. "We don't need to think about him or talk about him. If I have my way he won't be coming back to La Casa, ever. It's an easy enough matter to order pizza on our own—the phone number's on the box. Even a cheapskate like me has her weaknesses."

Rachel-Ann's answering smile was listless, and Jilly felt her heart twist.

"Listen, why don't we go upstairs and watch an old movie like we used to? Something trashy and romantic and weepy?"

"I'm not sure if I feel like weeping," Rachel-Ann said. "And I'm definitely not in the mood for romance. As for trash, I've been living that recently and it's no longer a vicarious pleasure." She rose, slim and delicate and graceful as always, and Jilly tried to hide the worry that filled her.

"Is there anything I can do, love?"

Rachel-Ann simply shook her head, drifting toward the house like the ghosts she insisted she saw.

Jilly leaned back against the stone railing, watching her go. Coltrane was right about one thing—she needed to learn to let go and let her siblings rise and fall on their own strengths. But right now Rachel-Ann looked so frail and easily crushed that only a monster could turn her back on her.

Hi, my name is Jilly and I'm a codependent. And it breaks my goddamn heart that I can't fix everything.

Rachel-Ann moved through the house carefully, keeping her eyes straight in front of her, never glancing to the right or left, or even looking over-

head. That was the safest way. She never saw them
head-on—it was always a shift in the shadows, a
whisper beneath the wind, a hint of perfume on the
air or the scent of Turkish tobacco in a house full
of nonsmokers.

They didn't want to hurt her, the ghosts of La
Casa, she was sure of that. But she had too much
going on in her life to make room for them. Back
when she was younger she'd see them sometimes,
and never think twice about it. But in the past few
years she'd grown increasingly unable to deal with
them, watching her, judging her, their pale, trans-
parent faces full of sympathy.

They were dead, she reminded herself. A fig-
ment of her drug-damaged, overactive imagination.
Brenda de Lorillard and Ted Hughes had been buried for close to fifty years—they weren't roaming
La Casa, watching her.

By the time she reached her bedroom door she
was practically running, and she slammed it shut
behind her, leaning against it, trying to control the
panicked shudders that washed over her. At least
she was safe in here. They never came in here—
she didn't need garlic braids or crucifixes to keep
them at bay. For some reason her room was the
only place she'd never seen them, and she took a
deep breath, letting the sense of safety wash over
her.

She turned on The Weather Channel, her constant companion, stripped off her clothes and lay down on the twin bed. Jilly had removed her old, king-size one when she was in treatment last time, which was a good thing. Too many memories in that bed, too many men. And too much blood.

She looked down at the scars on her wrists. Three different sets—you'd think she'd finally learn to get it right, she thought. Her father wanted her to have plastic surgery to cover the marks, but she'd stubbornly refused. A major victory, since she seldom refused Jackson Meyer anything. But she liked her scars. To her they weren't a sign of defeat, but of victory, a part of who and what she was and what she'd survived. She couldn't imagine wanting to get rid of them. She only hoped she wouldn't come to the point where she had to add to them.

The hurricane season was in full force, and The Weather Channel reporters were speaking in hushed, awe-filled tones about the devastating force of Hurricane Darla. Stupid name for a hurricane—it made her think of *The Little Rascals,* that old black and white serial with the precocious children.

She lay on the bed and watched, rapt. She had no cash, but her credit cards had been paid up. She could get a cash advance, take a plane and fly to the middle of the hurricane. She'd never experienced that kind of storm, wind and rain lashing all around, the sea climbing higher and higher, taking everything in its wake. She wanted to be there, naked, arms outstretched to the heavens, letting the storm howl around her.

But she was too tired to go anywhere.

Tired of meetings, where everyone talked in platitudes that made no sense. Let go and let God. What if there was no God? Or if God found you so unworthy He'd abandoned you years ago, and there was no way you could find your way back? The God of Rachel-Ann's childhood was Catholic, inflexible and unforgiving, and she had too many mortal sins on her soul to ever hope for comfort.

It didn't help that she'd seen Skye at the meeting tonight, looking disgustingly happy. She'd been in detox with her some five years ago, and she'd known immediately that Skye wouldn't make it. She'd overdose the next time, or the time after that.

But the Skye at the meeting had been clean and sober for five years—unless she'd lied, she'd never had a slip since that time in the hospital. And Rachel-Ann had been back in three times.

It wasn't that she was competitive. She was truly, deeply happy for Skye. Skye looked years older, but the lines around her eyes were from laughter and sunlight, not from squinting through the smoke in dark bars. If someone as strung out as Skye could make it, what the hell was Rachel-Ann still doing, bouncing from hospital to home to clubs and back again, on a never-ending cycle?

She glanced at the television screen, watching as the wind whipped pine trees and traffic lights in the torrential rain, and she closed her eyes, burying her face in the pillow. She could still taste the pizza, and she wondered whether she ought to go into her bathroom and make herself throw up. She hadn't been bulimic in ten years, but maybe that was a better problem to deal with than addiction.

No, the pizza was too good to waste. And what about the man who'd ordered it? Did she need a new man in her life, someone to distract her from her cravings? Someone to think about, dream about, be young and silly and giddy with as she hadn't been in what seemed like most of her life?

She'd started noticing the men at the meetings. Or at least one man in particular. The dark one, probably Mexican, with the rumpled clothes and the handsome, weary face. Not that it did her any good. As far as she could see, AA was full of rules. One of which was no major changes in your first year of sobriety. No new lover, no new job, no new life. If she had to have a year of sobriety before she had sex again then she might as well enter a convent.

At least Coltrane wouldn't know the rules. Somehow Rachel-Ann got the feeling that Jilly wouldn't be too happy about it if she went for Coltrane, which surprised her. Jilly was almost virginal when it came to men—and Alan Dunbar hadn't made things any better. Alan was a shit, a gorgeous, romantic, egotistical, uncaring shit. Much more Rachel-Ann's type than Jilly's. And while he was energetic enough in his lovemaking, it was performance art, devoid of any kind of caring or communication. Which had suited Rachel-Ann just fine, but left Jilly feeling empty and used.

Rachel-Ann had no idea whether Jilly knew at the time that she and Alan had been having an affair through most of her sister's short-lived marriage, though she knew now. Rachel-Ann had told her, repentant. If frenzied quickies, spiced with the thrill of almost getting caught, could be called an affair. And Jilly had forgiven her, because she loved her unconditionally. She was the one person who did.

So maybe Rachel-Ann would keep her hands off Coltrane, even if he was as cold-bloodedly gorgeous as Dean said he was. Jilly would have enough sense not to want him, but for some reason Rachel-Ann got the very strong impression that her sister didn't want anyone else to have him, either.

So be it. Small enough penance for the crime of sleeping with Jilly's husband.

Besides, it was probably moot. Jilly had said if she had her way Coltrane wouldn't be coming back to La Casa. And Jilly was notoriously stubborn.

It would be a cold day in hell before Jackson's pet lawyer set foot on La Casa property again.

6

By the time Jilly arrived home from work the next afternoon Coltrane had already moved into La Casa de Sombras. She'd kicked off her shoes, shaken her long hair free and grabbed an iced tea from the refrigerator, pausing a moment to stare into the suddenly replenished depths. And with sudden dread she knew what had happened, even before she went out on the terrace to find Dean, immaculate in white linen, laughing uproariously at something Coltrane had said.

"What are you doing here?" she demanded abruptly, not even bothering with a greeting.

Dean frowned at her, his blandly handsome face creased with disapproval. His thinning blond hair was swept back off his high forehead, and he looked like the clever dilettante that he was. "Where are your manners, darling? Coltrane's living here."

The pit of her stomach felt like ice. Dean was fairly cavalier about his relationships, equally involved with both women and men, and she'd known he'd found Coltrane attractive, but she'd assumed Coltrane wasn't interested. It shouldn't matter, but it did. Desperately.

She sat down in a chair, abruptly, hoping they wouldn't notice how shaken she was. Coltrane was watching her, an enigmatic expression on his face. "I didn't realize you two were a couple," she said finally in what she hoped was a breezy voice.

Dean looked amused rather than offended, fully past his sulks. "We're not, darling. Coltrane's town house had a fire and Jackson suggested we had more than enough room to put him up for a few weeks until his place gets repaired. Surely you couldn't have any objections."

Surely she could. Ignoring the wash of relief that spread through her, she met Dean's eyes, ignoring Coltrane. "We may have room, Dean, but this place is falling to pieces. I don't think any of the empty rooms are habitable." `

"He's already moved into the room at the far end of the hallway. The one that looks like it's underwater."

"The Sea-moss Room," Jilly said flatly. "There's a reason for it looking like that—the roof leaks in three places."

"It never rains in L.A., Jilly. If it does he can always come down and bunk with me." Dean cast a lazy glance in Coltrane's direction.

"I don't think it's a good idea. Jackson must pay him enough that he can rent a place on his own...."

"Jackson does pay him enough," Coltrane said in his deep voice. "But since Dean and I are going to be working closely on several important legal projects this seemed like a reasonable solution."

"And it's just as much my house as it is yours, Jilly," Dean added in a languid voice. "I don't see why you should get to say who stays here. You're the one who's always complaining about money. Coltrane can help. And I expect Rachel-Ann would agree with me. I was telling Coltrane all about her, and he's completely fascinated."

Rachel-Ann again. That sense of unease built once more, and Jilly sat very still, considering it. Why did the thought of Rachel-Ann and Coltrane bother her, as much as the thought of Coltrane and Dean? Was she jealous? Was she self-destructive enough to actually be attracted to a man like him? She'd learned to keep her distance from charming sharks like Coltrane—surely she wasn't going to lose her self-control now. Hadn't she learned her lesson with Alan?

Except that Coltrane was no Alan Dunbar. He was far more dangerous. "Rachel-Ann doesn't need to get involved with anyone right now," she said in a cool voice.

"Don't you think that's up to her, darling? And what is it to you?"

Typical of Dean to draw her into such an awkward conversation, while Coltrane watched and listened. She turned to him, a bland, polite expression on her face. "Wouldn't you be more comfortable in some place a little more...modern?" she asked, grasping at straws.

"I like it here. It has character. And, of course, I plan to contribute financially."

"I don't need your money."

"I thought the roof leaked."

"I doubt you're willing to front me that much."

"You never know. I can be very generous."

He had such green eyes, such very dangerous green eyes. Those eyes were oddly familiar, and yet she'd never been involved with a green-eyed man before.

And wasn't now, she reminded herself sharply.

"Besides," he added, "I told you, I've had to turn over some important clients to Dean, and it would be good if I was available if he had questions. I don't think you'd have a problem with that, would you?"

He knew he'd gotten her, and there was nothing she could do. He'd given her what she wanted—a chance for Dean to win Jackson's love and approval. Well, perhaps that was going too far—

Jackson wasn't ever going to shower affection and approval on any of his children but Rachel-Ann. Nevertheless, Dean could earn Jackson's attention and respect, instead of being shuffled aside for a golden protégé like Coltrane.

"I don't know why you're being so crabby, Jilly," Dean added. "It's not like we haven't had all sorts of people staying here over the years. The place is huge, even if it's an eyesore."

"It's beautiful!" Jilly protested.

"It ought to be bulldozed and you know it. But then, if it were up to you you'd save every tumbledown shack that had ever been built in the San Fernando Valley. I don't know where you get your sentimental streak—it certainly isn't from our father. Maybe you take after Edith, after all."

"There's nothing wrong with that." She rose to the bait. "Our mother was a good woman. You just don't remember her very well...."

"How could I? She died when I was eight, and before that she was never around. She never could stand up to Jackson, but then, who could? It's past history, Jilly."

"Let's not do this, Dean," she said wearily. "Not in front of company."

"Oh, just consider me part of the family," Coltrane offered.

"I'm going to get another drink," Dean said, rising abruptly. "You want one, Zack?"

"No, thanks." Coltrane watched as Dean disappeared into the house, leaving the two of them together, alone on the terrace. Then he turned to look at her. "So don't mince words. What have you got against my living here? I promise, I'm relatively harmless."

She allowed herself a hoot of laughter. "I don't know if you manage to convince other people of that, but you're not going to convince me. I grew up with Jackson as my father—I know a snake when I see one."

"You think I'm like Jackson?" He didn't like that—she could see it quite plainly.

"Ruthless, ambitious, capable of cold-blooded charm when you need it. Yup, I'd say you're exactly like Jackson Meyer. It's no wonder he's chosen you as his protégé over his own son. After all, most men want someone in their own image to carry on. I'm afraid he failed with me and Dean and Rachel-Ann, so now he's gone on to looking outside his little family for validation. But you're smart enough to know that, aren't you? I wouldn't ever make the mistake of underestimating you." She stopped, half shocked at herself. She'd been taught to shield herself with a veneer of politeness, but somehow Coltrane had managed to shatter it without making an effort.

"I really get under your skin, don't I?" he said after a long moment, seemingly unaffected by her hostility. "Why do you suppose that is?"

"You threaten everything I care about. You threaten my brother, you're far too interested in my sister when what she needs is peace and quiet, and you—you bother me. Now you've invaded my house, as well, so there's no escaping you."

"My house?" he echoed. "I thought it belonged to all three of you. At least for now."

"It does," she said, ignoring the stab of guilt. Just because she was the only one who loved it, the only one who took care of it, didn't make her the only one who owned it. As Dean had just reminded her. And in the end, if they ever left it, it would revert to Meyer, who'd have it razed in the blink of an eye.

"So, how do we work out a truce, Jilly?" Coltrane asked lazily. "This is a big house—you might not even know I'm here."

"I'd know."

"Why? Why do I bother you? Or is it more like 'hot and bothered'?"

"Don't flatter yourself, Coltrane," she snapped. "You're not my type."

"True enough. I'm not a long-haired pretentious son of a bitch like Alan Dunbar, now am I?"

"No, you're a bleached blond rapacious son of a bitch," she shot back. "And you shouldn't take my father's opinion of my ex-husband as gospel."

"I don't. I've dealt with your ex on any number of occasions. Every time he tries to get more money out of Meyer."

It felt like a punch in the stomach. She'd been divorced from Alan for two and a half years, and Coltrane had only been in town half that time. It was a pain she thought she was over. No longer the pain of betrayal, it was now merely the pain of her own needy stupidity. "I hope you make sure he doesn't get any," she said in a deceptively cool voice.

"Depends what kind of evidence he has. I can't say much for your taste in men. You might consider bleached blond rapacious sons of bitches for a change of pace."

"I don't think so."

"Don't think what?" Dean was back, handing a tall glass to Coltrane before he took his seat opposite. "What did I miss?"

"Jilly and me coming to a peaceful agreement," Coltrane said. "As long as I keep out of her hair she'll let me stay."

Dean raised an eyebrow. "Don't be ridiculous,

Coltrane. This is a democracy, even if Jilly's the alpha wolf in our little pack. I say you can stay and so will Rachel-Ann. Even if she disagrees, Jilly's opinion should be immaterial.''

''If I were you, Dean, I wouldn't ever make the mistake of thinking Jilly's opinion didn't matter,'' Coltrane said softly.

He made her absolutely crazy, Jilly thought with sudden despair. Maybe she'd throw herself on Jackson's mercy to get him out of there.

Except that Jackson didn't have any mercy; she'd learned that the hard way. It was all moot, anyway—Rachel-Ann would come home and Coltrane would be smitten, and apart from the occasional nauseating displays of affection followed by screaming fights, he'd no longer be her problem. Not until Rachel-Ann freaked out and started drinking and using again.

''Speaking of alpha wolves, you haven't heard from the vet, have you?'' She changed the subject to one of more import.

''Oh, yeah,'' Dean said. ''You can pick Roofus up any time. Though I think the office is closed by now.''

Jilly resisted the impulse to throw her iced tea at him. ''When did they call?''

''Yesterday. You should have asked.''

She glared at him. ''Maybe someone's still

there.'' She rose, pushing the old iron chair away from her, making a shrieking noise on the old flagstones.

''Who's Roofus?'' Coltrane asked idly.

''Her damned huge dog, that's who. You'll be as unobtrusive as a ghost compared to that great galumphing beast.''

''But then, I gather your ghosts aren't that unobtrusive, are they?'' Coltrane said. ''What was wrong with the dog? Getting him fixed?''

Dean snorted in brotherly amusement. ''You know Jilly pretty well already, don't you?''

She let the ornate metal screen door slam behind her as she went in search of a telephone, cursing all men under her breath.

For once fate was on her side. Dr. Parker's office was still open, and when she got there, Roofus was gloriously happy to see her, slobbering over her with great affection before bounding into the front seat of the Corvette.

Dean's disdain was probably as much for Roofus's lineage as his size. A probable cross between an Old English sheepdog and a Saint Bernard, with perhaps some other errant canine strains mixed in, Roofus was huge, shaggy, cheerful and enthusiastic. He shed like mad, drooled and growled at Dean at regular intervals. Dean refused to allow him into his spartan quarters and Roofus refused to enter them. Unless he happened to have muddy paws.

Despite Dean's insistence, Roofus was a very intelligent dog.

The Range Rover was gone when she pulled back up to the house, and she breathed a sigh of relief. It was too much to hope Coltrane had taken the hint and left. It had been more than a hint, actually, she admitted to herself. It had been outright hostility. Something she was going to have to deal with if he was really going to stay with them for any length of time. She couldn't live in an armed camp.

Roofus leapt out of the car, happily marking everything in sight, paying particular attention to the tires of Dean's Lexus. And then he was off, making cheerful barking noises as he scouted the property, looking for rodent intruders.

By the time Jilly had fed him and herself the night had closed in around the old house like a velvet wrap. She sat at the scarred old kitchen table, which had once seen the makings of feasts for movie stars, and ate cold pizza and iced tea, while Roofus lay happily at her feet. The faint trickles of anxiety were still gnawing at her stomach, and she went back over the day in a vain effort to calm herself. It was an old trick, one she'd learned in school, where she'd lie in bed and look ahead to the next day and try to guess where disaster lurked. Which teacher would pounce, which would discover she hadn't done her homework, which friend would be angry with her.

As far as she could tell, no real disaster hovered on the near horizon. Coltrane had moved into the house, to be sure, but he was doing exactly what she wanted, all without much effort on her part. He'd gotten Meyer to give Dean more responsibility, and with Coltrane leaning on him, Dean was unlikely to get distracted and screw it up.

Rachel-Ann was clean and sober, one day at a time. Roofus was lying at her feet, snoring faintly, and for now La Casa de Sombras wasn't falling to pieces. Life was never easy—she should just take each day as it comes, and this day could, in fact, have been worse.

By the time Rachel-Ann walked into the kitchen Jilly had worked herself into a relatively good mood, considering that a snake had taken up residence at La Casa. Her sister looked pale and tense, a sure sign she was sober, and Jilly breathed an unconscious sigh of relief.

"Who's here?" Rachel-Ann asked by way of greeting, stopping to rub Roofus's shaggy head. Roofus adored her as much as he disliked Dean, and he rolled on his back happily, a huge puppy enjoying the attention.

"What do you mean?"

"There's a Range Rover in the driveway and Dean's got someone in the dining room. I can hear the two of them laughing. Has he got someone new?"

"Not exactly. We do."

Rachel-Ann sat down. "What's that supposed to mean?"

"We've got a guest. He got burned out of his apartment and he'll be staying with us for a while."

"Is he cute?"

"Don't be adolescent, Rachel-Ann," Jilly said in exasperation. "He's not your type."

"Then he's Dean's?"

"Not that, either. He's too much like Jackson—you wouldn't want to get anywhere near him, no matter how gorgeous he is."

"Gorgeous?" Rachel-Ann perked up. She'd always had a weakness for beautiful men. Hell, she'd always had a weakness for any man, Jilly thought mournfully.

"Not your type," she said again.

"Is he yours?" Rachel-Ann leaned over and took the last piece of pizza from her plate.

"How well do you know me?"

"Better than you know yourself, sweetie," her sister said. "Is this all the pizza we have left?"

"Yup. But you can ask Coltrane where he ordered it from. He's the one who had it delivered last night."

"Oh, that one! Why didn't you say so? A gorgeous man who knows good pizza and has Daddy's approval?" Rachel-Ann murmured. "What more could a girl ask?"

Her tone was flippant, but Jilly felt her stomach sink. Her brain began its whispering litany of disaster as her stomach knotted.

"Do you have a meeting tonight?" she asked, changing the subject.

"Don't interfere, Jilly." Rachel-Ann's reply was flippant again. "I went to a noon one. Now I'm ready for a little relaxation."

Jilly could hear the sound of their voices, cheerful, intrusive male voices heading for the kitchen, and the anxiety rose into full-fledged panic. She wanted to take Rachel-Ann's fragile hand and drag her out the back door. Roofus had lifted his head with a warning growl, recognizing the approach of his nemesis. He disliked Dean, and doubtless a dog of his discernment would hate Coltrane, as well.

"Let's go for a walk," she suggested desperately. Roofus looked hopeful, but Rachel-Ann, her intended companion, ignored her, sliding off the table with a faint gleam in her eyes. Jilly remembered that gleam, and her heart sank.

"I want to meet the pizza man," she said.

Jilly watched in fascination. She'd seen Rachel-Ann do it a thousand times, any time a good-looking man was in her vicinity. Actually he didn't have to be good-looking—any man got the full, glorious treatment. She was small, frail, almost girlish when she was relaxed, but when a man came in sight she tossed her red-gold hair, squared her shoulders, and a seductive gleam came into her green eyes. She turned from a wren into a peacock within seconds, and by the time Dean and Coltrane entered the kitchen she seemed to glow with sensuality.

Jilly didn't move, a helpless voyeur at an accident site. Coltrane had a beer in one hand, paying only scant attention to Dean's lazy anecdote, and his eyes went directly to Jilly, meeting her gaze. And then they swerved over to Rachel-Ann as she positively radiated heat.

It was even worse than Jilly had imagined. It seemed as if Dean broke off his chatter and a sudden silence filled the room, though Jilly supposed it could have been her imagination.

But she didn't imagine the sudden tension between Rachel-Ann and Coltrane, so intense that she could practically see sparks fly. Even Roofus felt it. He lumbered to his feet, a low growl in his throat, just as Coltrane's beer bottle smashed on the old slate floor.

Rachel-Ann was used to having that kind of effect on men. Usually she simply turned up the wattage to blistering levels, but this was different. As Jilly watched, Rachel-Ann closed in on herself, going from a peacock to a wren. She slid back on the table, ran a taming hand through her red-gold hair, and muttered, "Hi."

Roofus was growling, Dean was petulant and Coltrane looked as if he'd been hit in the face with a shovel. Rachel-Ann often had that effect on men. What was surprising was that he didn't have the same effect on Rachel-Ann.

Jilly forced herself to break the awkward silence. "Hush," she said to Roofus, and the dog collapsed back beneath the table, a glowering expression on his face. "Dean, introduce Coltrane to Rachel-Ann while I go find something to clean up the broken glass." And a moment later she escaped, no longer willing to witness the odd, charged dynamics between her family and the snake.

By the time she returned with dustpan and broom the awkward moment had passed. Rachel-Ann was laughing at something Dean had said, Coltrane had taken her seat, and most astonishing of all, he was rubbing Roofus's huge head. Jilly paused, frozen, watching his long, clever fingers rub Roofus's shaggy nape, and then gave herself a little mental shake.

So Roofus liked him. It was unusual but not unprecedented. Roofus occasionally liked the male of the species, though not very often. He despised both her ex-husband and her father, which seemed to indicate a fairly good judgment of character.

But not if he was lapping up Coltrane's attentions. She started toward the broken glass, then stopped, disconcerted. It was already cleaned up, and neither of her siblings had ever lifted a finger to clean up a mess in Jilly's memory.

Rachel-Ann looked edgy, frenetic, almost manic. "I'm going out," she said abruptly. "Anyone want to come with me?"

Jilly assumed the invitation was for Coltrane alone, but for a moment she contemplated disrupting everything by saying yes. Except that Rachel-Ann didn't want her sister tagging along, watching her out of anxious eyes while she sipped club soda at some of her dangerous old haunts.

Fortunately Dean forestalled her. "Coltrane and I have a long day tomorrow," he announced. "And you look like you've been burning the candle at both ends, precious. Why don't you be wise and make an early night of it yourself?"

Rachel-Ann's smile was forced. She was positively vibrating with tension. "I thought I was looking rather good. What do you think, Coltrane?'' Her voice was a sexual purr, but it sounded odd, almost forced to Jilly's ears.

His face was completely unreadable as he looked at her, and Jilly had to admit he was good. There was nothing that egged Rachel-Ann on more than indifference. ''Gorgeous,'' he said lightly, his long fingers still kneading Roofus's head.

It was the final straw for Jilly. ''I'm the one who's feeling haggard. Come on, Roofus. Bedtime.'' She snapped her fingers, and for one shocking moment Roofus didn't move. And then he lumbered to his feet, coming toward her, then glancing back at Coltrane to see if he was coming, too.

Fat chance, Jilly thought. He was still sitting at the table, seemingly relaxed, watching Rachel-Ann from beneath hooded eyes. While Dean chatted on, supremely unaware of the tension surrounding him.

And Jilly made her escape.

7

It was very late by the time Coltrane finally retired to the waterlogged room at the back of the house. He walked past Jilly's silent room, picturing her lying in that swan bed. Most likely not wearing a diaphanous negligee like the original movie stars who'd once lived here. She probably slept in sweats. She'd be curled up in a tight little ball, her arms wrapped around her body to ward off all dangers.

Rachel-Ann's room was next to Jilly's, and it, too, was silent. Hers was unoccupied—she'd taken off soon after Jilly had gone to bed, and it was clear that despite her edgy flirtatiousness she didn't want anyone going with her.

He wondered if she knew the truth that had hit him so hard.

He didn't think so. She wouldn't have any reason to guess, any knowledge to make that inevitable leap. She'd only known her gut instinct and run.

He shut the door behind him, turning on the dim

lights. The room filled the end of the hallway, and there were windows on two sides, with a set of French doors leading out onto the balcony that ran along the back of the house. The wallpaper was a murky green, peeling in places, and the brown water streaks from the leaking roof added to the sense of being trapped underwater. He'd never been particularly fond of algae.

The bed was a mess, the box spring half collapsed. He simply pulled the mattress off and set it on the floor, shoved the old frame and box spring up against the wall, and opened the windows to the balmy night air in a vain attempt to rid the place of the musty smell. There was a private bathroom off to the left, and the toilet worked, but the sink and bathtub were supposedly beyond repair. He could share with the girls, Dean suggested. Or come down and use his palatial bathroom. And anything else he might feel like using.

Not bloody likely, Coltrane thought. So one plan was shot—he couldn't get to Meyer through Rachel-Ann. That didn't mean he couldn't come up with an alternative that was equally pleasing and didn't involve cozying up to Dean. If he couldn't sleep with Rachel-Ann and bring her father down that way, then there was another sister in the house, one who was already clearly susceptible to him, whether she wanted to admit it or not.

He wasn't about to waste his time trying to develop a conscience.

He leaned against the wall, looking at the room. The carpeting had been torn up, and the floors were marble, cracked and stained, but marble nonetheless. Cold as hell in the morning, but at least the mattress would have good support. Most of his clothes had suffered smoke damage, but it hadn't been difficult to arrange for replacements, and by the time they'd arrived he'd at least managed to fumigate the closet. He wasn't crazy about the smell of mildew, either.

It had been a simple matter, setting his apartment on fire. But then, he had a talent for a number of unusual things. He'd long ago scoped out where the fire hazards were, who the secretive smokers were. In L.A. it was more socially acceptable to beat your wife than to smoke cigarettes, and even in the privacy of their own apartments his neighbors went out of the way to hide their secret vice, making accidental fires almost inevitable. It had been arranged easily enough, and as far as anyone knew he'd been at work when the flames broke out. There was no way it could ever be traced to him. Then it had been only a matter of a carefully orchestrated suggestion and he'd ended up ensconced in La Casa.

With a different victim, he reminded himself.

Rachel-Ann Meyer was off-limits. He only hoped she'd listen to her instincts and keep away from him. He really didn't want her coming on to him. This situation had suddenly gotten very tricky, and that was one complication he wasn't going to deal with.

No sheets, no towels, and he hadn't thought to bring any. He was in shirtsleeves, and he pulled his shirt free, unbuttoning it to hang loose, kicking off his shoes so he could move silently through the house. He should leave Jilly alone, but he was restless, ready to move, and Jilly had become his obvious target. She wouldn't want him showing up at her door shirtless, but this was the next best thing. She was reluctantly fascinated by him, and he had every intention of exploiting that fascination right into her bed. Maybe even tonight. He was in that kind of mood.

Not that he really had any particular reason to seduce her. Getting to Rachel-Ann had made sense, since she was the only one Jackson Meyer cared about. He didn't need to sleep with Jilly Meyer to gain entrance into the house—he was already safely ensconced. Her father wouldn't give a damn whether he was screwing her or not—Jackson had already given him his blessing—and he was reasonably certain she didn't know a thing about her father's business affairs or the dark secrets of his past. She'd taken a step away from the old bastard, unlike her siblings, and there was very little to gain from sleeping with her.

Well, maybe he wasn't going to do it for gain. Maybe he'd do it simply because he wanted to. Because she looked at him with those huge eyes of hers, curled her lip in anxious contempt, and kept as far away from him as she could. He found that wariness oddly irresistible.

Besides, if he was sleeping with Jilly, maybe her brother and sister would consider him off-limits. It was probably a vain hope—Alan Dunbar had been getting payoffs from Meyer for months to cover up some of Rachel-Ann's more extreme behavior, and a lot of it stemmed from back when he was still married to Jilly. Apparently Rachel-Ann wasn't too conversant with the aspects of monogamy and loyalty, at least when she was drinking.

Still, it might slow her down a little. And it would give him an excuse to keep his distance from both Dean and his older sister, one that wouldn't offend their pride. Though if history had it right and Rachel-Ann started drinking again she'd probably suggest a threesome. And not have any problem with his real objections.

Most of the hall lights were either burned out or broken. He knocked on Jilly's door in the shadowed hallway, grinning to himself as he heard the muffled growl of her huge dog. Of everyone in this motley household, he'd decided he liked Roofus the best. Roofus accepted things at face value, and he accepted the snake in their midst. Coltrane heard the clicking of his nails on the floor, and the growl turned into a kind of whine once he realized who was on the other side of the door. All it had taken was knowing the right place to scratch and Roofus had been his.

He wondered if Jilly was going to be as easy to manipulate. If she'd let him get close enough to find the place that itched.

He knocked again, and Roofus whined miserably, scratching at the door. He heard the rustle of bedclothes, and he could picture her, rumpled and grumpy, staggering toward the door, ready to blister him with a few well-chosen words.

She opened the door a crack, peering out at him, and her thick brown hair hung down around her face, making her look surprisingly childish. She wasn't wearing sweats. In the shadows behind the narrow crack of the door he could see her long legs and not much else, but they weren't covered with sweatpants.

"Go away, Coltrane," she mumbled in a sleepy voice.

He knew the sentiment came from the heart, but he wasn't giving up that easily. "You don't have any extra sheets and towels hanging around this place, do you? That old mattress has seen better days."

"Fastidious, aren't you?" She was waking up, against her will, he suspected. "I warned you this wasn't the Beverly Hilton. Stay there and I'll find you something." She started to close the door in his face, but Roofus proved the invaluable friend Coltrane had known he'd be. He pushed through the door to greet Coltrane with slobbery affection, leaving Jilly standing there in a tank top and boxers and nothing else.

He squatted down, busying himself with Roofus, with the express purpose of staring at Jilly's endless legs. "I don't know why he likes you," Jilly said irritably. "He's usually an excellent judge of character."

He looked up, past her long, long legs, and laughed. "Maybe he's a better judge of character than you are, darlin'," he said lazily. "I'd trust a dog over most humans."

Bingo. She looked startled, as if considering an unexpected possibility. "So would I," she said, staring at him. And then she shook her head. "But even dogs can make mistakes."

"So can stubborn young women." He was astonished at how long her hair was. It reached her elbows, a thick mane of chestnut waves. He wondered what it would feel like, flowing around him. He intended to find out. Soon.

"Sheets?" he reminded her. Not that he wasn't enjoying himself thoroughly, watching her, but there was no way in hell she was going to let him get any closer. Not so fast.

"Yeah," she said in a tone of resignation. She glanced back into her shadowed room, hesitating.

"Did I come at a bad time?" He rose, keeping one hand on Roofus's head, scratching absently. "I didn't realize you weren't alone."

"I'm alone, damn it," she said through gritted teeth.

"Well, you don't need to be so irritable about it. I'm more than willing to keep you company."

"When there's snow in L.A.," she said grimly. "I was wondering if I had a bathrobe."

"I'll control myself and not leap on you. You're wearing more than you wear on the beach. Just find me a sheet and I won't bother you again."

"Promises, promises," she muttered, pushing past him and starting down the hall in the direction of his bedroom. Roofus immediately bounded after her, and Coltrane allowed himself a fond moment of speculation. Maybe she'd make the bed and then lie down on it for him. It had been known to happen that easily.

But not with someone like Jilly Meyer. He was

going to have to work for her, and he had nothing in particular to gain from it. If he had any sense he'd look for sex on the side, away from this decaying household. But he liked living dangerously. And God, he loved the thought of those long legs wrapped around him and all that hair beneath them.

She'd disappeared through a door he hadn't noticed before, and a moment later came out with a pile of sheets and towels on her arms. "I only have one bed, Jilly," he said in his most reasonable tone of voice when she thrust the load into his arms.

"Everything in this place is falling apart. Some of those bed linens date back to the forties and fifties—you'll be lucky if they don't shred in your hands."

"What do you use on your bed?"

"Three hundred count Egyptian cotton, and I'm not sharing," she snapped. "You can go buy your own if these won't do. Not that I expect you'll be staying very long, but you'll probably need new sheets when you get back into your apartment."

He simply smiled at her, not bothering to correct her. By the time he was ready to leave he'd be going far away, and he wasn't going to bother with transporting bed linens.

"Come on, Roofus," she said, snapping her fingers. The dog looked up at him longingly, then swung his huge head back toward Jilly, clearly torn.

"He's having a hard time choosing between us," Coltrane murmured, resisting the impulse to suggest the obvious solution.

"Traitor," Jilly said darkly. "Roofus!"

In the end she won, and who could blame the dog? He suspected that all Jilly had to do was snap her fingers and he'd trot after her, as well, if it meant he could sleep with her.

He half expected her to slam the door behind her, but she closed it quietly, and there was no sound of locks clicking. Maybe the locks didn't work. Or maybe she wasn't sure she wanted to keep him out.

His room looked murkier than ever. He had a hell of a time wrapping a flat sheet around the thin mattress—Jilly was right. Most of them were so fragile they simply ripped in his hands. By the time he'd managed to cover the mattress he'd stripped to his shorts and stretched out on the thin, hard surface. No pillow, but he could do without. He'd slept in worse places in his life. Besides, he kind of liked the decaying grandeur of La Casa de Sombras. The House of Shadows.

He stretched out on his back, tucking his hands beneath his head. There was that faint, teasing scent on the air, overriding the mildew and mustiness. The warm breeze blowing through the French doors must have carried it in, though he'd been aware of it on a number of occasions. So few people smoked nowadays that the scent of tobacco was unmistakable. None of the Meyers smoked, at least not openly, and the odd scent of tobacco wasn't the lingering odor that clung to clothes. It was fresh, quite pleasant, actually. Different from the cigarette tobacco people used nowadays. Not cigar smoke, certainly a far cry from the acrid sweetness of marijuana. It had to be something very old, still lingering from the house's heyday in the thirties and forties, when everyone smoked.

Odd, but the smoke smelled fresh, as if someone were in the room.

"Ghosts," he muttered out loud, just to hear the sound of his voice in the stillness. He waited, half expecting an answer from the darkness. He didn't believe in ghosts, but he never ruled out any possibility.

"Well," he said lazily into the darkness, "if you're still haunting this place then you're not doing a very good job of it. Why don't you just move on to the next level or whatever it is you're supposed to do?"

No answer, of course. He chuckled to himself. "I might be inclined to believe you if you'd do more than just smell like cigarettes. I'm in the mood for an apparition, if you feel like obliging.''

Nothing, of course. He rolled over onto his stomach, burying his face in the thin mattress. He would have taken any kind of distraction right then, anything to take his mind off Jackson Meyer's two dissimilar daughters. Jilly, tall and luscious and truculent and desirable, with her wary brown eyes and her rich mouth.

And Rachel-Ann. Who looked at him with his mother's green eyes, from his mother's face. Rachel-Ann, the sister he never knew he had.

Life had just thrown him a curve he'd never expected. He had a sister.

And she wasn't going to like what he had in store for her father.

"You're naughty, darling," Brenda said, removing the unfiltered French cigarette from Ted's mouth and taking a long, elegant drag on it. "You shouldn't tease the poor man."

Ted Hughes snorted in gentle amusement. "He's not a poor man, honeybunch. He's after something, and I don't like him in our house, bothering our girls."

"They aren't our girls, Ted," Brenda said calmly.

"No, I suppose not." He took the cigarette back

from her, inhaled and then blew it out directly at the man's prone figure, clearly distrustful.

Brenda was perched on the dresser in the Seamoss Room, her negligee draped elegantly around her trim ankles. "Thank God you died in that gown," he said unexpectedly. "If there's one outfit I'd like to see you in for eternity, that's it."

A shadow crossed Brenda's porcelain complexion. "I don't like to talk about it, darling. You know that."

"I know," he said gently.

"It's really too depressing," she added with a little laugh, sliding down off the dresser. "We're dead and nothing will change that. It's best not to dwell on such things."

"I suppose so," Ted said doubtfully.

She paused, looking down at the nearly naked man lying on the old mattress. "He's quite good-looking, isn't he?" she said.

Ted shrugged, tossing his cigarette stub out the open French door. "If you like that sort of thing. What do you think he's after?"

"What makes you think he's after something?" Brenda questioned. "And as a matter of fact, I do like good-looking men. That's why I'm here with you."

"You're here with me because we died together

and something's trapped us in this house," Ted grumbled.

"Ted!"

"Forgive me, honeybunch. I'm just in a lousy mood. I know it upsets you to think about it." He leaned over and kissed her perfect little nose. "So we won't think about it. It doesn't matter why we're here—sooner or later it should be obvious. In the meantime, I like the way things are. Just you and me, together, with no one to interfere. The way it should have been."

"You and me," she echoed.

"Forever. As I always promised you, honey-bunch."

"Forever," she said in a hollow voice. And then she smiled brightly. "I think Rachel-Ann's finally arrived home. Shall we go see what she's doing? If she's brought someone home we can scare him away."

"That's my girl," Ted said fondly. "Let's go raise some hell."

8

Rachel-Ann held her breath as she stepped inside the huge front hallway. She never knew when the ghosts would be waiting. She never had much warning. Somewhere she'd read that ghosts made everything cold. Maybe that accounted for the natural air-conditioning at La Casa, she thought without real humor.

She shut the door behind her, locking it carefully. It was so much easier when she was drinking—when she was loaded she didn't see ghosts. Or if she did, they didn't frighten her.

But here she was, stone cold sober and not very happy about the fact. She'd gone out with the intention of getting drunk. She was already past her previous record of sobriety, but for the past couple of days she'd felt strange, upset, and she had no idea why. She'd been perfectly ready to seduce the handsome man who'd somehow ended up at La Casa and knew where to find great pizza. She'd given up alcohol and drugs—surely she didn't have to give up sex, as well. And Coltrane was just as gorgeous as Dean had told her.

But she'd taken one look into his cool green eyes the night before and felt oddly, faintly repelled. She couldn't imagine why—there was very little she considered repellent, and if he was as amoral as Dean thought he was, it would be no worse than a number of other people she'd been involved with. At least he didn't look like the type who hit.

But he made her uncomfortable, and no amount of rationalization could change her mind.

So she'd gone out last night and again tonight, looking for something to divert her. Someone young and strong and healthy, to fuck her to distraction and back again with no responsibilities, no names, leaving nothing but a smile and a memory in the morning.

She'd headed for the Kit-Kat Klub, but for some reason she never made it there. She'd ended up down at the Unitarian church, at another AA meeting, and she'd sat through it, numb, silent, listening to the words wash over her and seething with resentment underneath. She didn't want to be there. Other people could drink and drug themselves into oblivion and then walk away from it. Why did she have to be trapped by an addiction she couldn't control?

After the meeting a group of them went out for coffee, and Rachel-Ann went with them, as she always did, silent, sipping the bitter, too sweet coffee sludge and saying nothing. No one forced her to talk. They let her come with them, a silent, sad-eyed ghost as haunted as the house she lived in.

He was there again. She didn't remember when she'd first noticed him, but he'd been at the last three meetings at the Unitarian church, he'd joined them for coffee and he'd watched her.

He was tall, almost too thin, with hair that needed cutting and clothes that needed pressing. She had no idea what he did for a living, only that he was "Hi, my name is Rico and I'm an alcoholic." Hispanic, probably Mexican.

She couldn't bring herself to talk to him. To meet his eyes. He shouldn't be watching her—he'd know as well as she did that one of the major rules of recovery was not to get involved with anyone for the first year. She was having a hard enough time staying sober—if sleeping with someone managed to distract her from her need for a drink then she'd do it gratefully.

She didn't want to sleep with a recovering alcoholic, though. He'd probably lecture her, drag her to meetings when she was sick and tired of them. She didn't know why she still went when she hated them so much. Probably because she didn't have anything else to do, and the alternative was to stay home alone with the ghosts.

She'd sat next to Rico, squeezed into a booth with a group of people whose lives she knew better than she knew her siblings'. Susan had been a hooker on Sunset Strip, and not the gorgeous Julia Roberts version. She was well over two hundred pounds, almost as tall as Jilly, with a foul mouth and the kindest eyes. Then there was Maggie, a divorced mother of three. She'd lost her children, she'd lost everything, and people kept telling Rachel-Ann that that was the only way you could recover. You had to hit bottom.

It seemed to Rachel-Ann that she'd hit bottom so damned many times she couldn't get any lower. So why didn't she have that fucking blissed-out serenity the rest of them had?

It must have been her frustration over Coltrane that had made her react to Rico. She wanted someone, anyone, and he was warm, strong and available. It would have been easy enough to ask him for a ride home, or offer him one. Any excuse not to be alone, not to come home to this shadowed house with the ghosts who watched her.

But in the end she hadn't said a word, she'd simply watched as he climbed into an ancient Plymouth and driven off into the Hollywood night.

She moved through the house like a ghost herself, half hoping they were sleeping. Ghosts had to sleep sometime, didn't they? She knew perfectly well who they were—the stories about the murder-suicide were the stuff of legends. Brenda de Lorillard had shot her married lover in the back of the head and then killed herself, rather than lose him. Her career had faded, Ted Hughes's wife was making demands, and like something out of *Sunset Boulevard* she'd taken a gun and killed both of them. And now they watched and waited, trapped in the mansion that had once been the site of their grand passion.

Rachel-Ann had almost made it to the foot of the stairs when she smelled it. The scent of Ted Hughes's imported cigarettes, mixed with a trace of Brenda's French perfume. It was a combination of smells like no other, and there were times when Rachel-Ann woke with the scent of them in her nostrils and felt comforted.

And then she'd remember who and what they were.

She glanced nervously over her shoulder as she started up the stairs, but there was no sign of them, just the telltale trace of perfume, the lingering hint of tobacco. She should have brought Rico back with her. He would have come, she knew it. He stared at her too much not to want her. If she'd brought him back to the old house the ghosts wouldn't dare come closer, and for a night she wouldn't have to be afraid.

Except that in the morning, or even sooner, he'd leave. She'd kick him out, and she'd be alone again, alone with the truth of what really terrified her. Not the ghosts of Hollywood.

But her own empty life.

As usual, Jilly couldn't sleep. It was an annoying fact of life that she'd been troubled with insomnia ever since she was fifteen years old, and nothing, not sleeping pills, not biofeedback, not meditation, had any effect on it. She could even remember when it started, and she wished she didn't.

She'd been staying with her grandmother. She was never sure why her grandmother chose to live at La Casa when she could have lived almost anywhere. It was only recently that Jilly had decided she'd lived there for the express purpose of keeping her son away.

Jilly's parents had divorced in the late seventies, and for some reason Jackson had maintained custody of the children. In retrospect Jilly couldn't figure out why he bothered—he never paid attention to any of them except Rachel-Ann. She'd assumed it was simply spite on his part, that Edith Walker Meyer had dared to leave him.

But when Edith had died in a car accident up near San Simeon Jackson had simply shipped his three children off to live with his mother at La Casa de Sombras. Jackson and Grandmère had a strained, hostile relationship at best, but Julia Meyer was one of the few people who got her way with him. She'd gotten his children for a few, important years, and she'd manipulated the legal system enough to keep La Casa out of his greedy hands for as long as possible. The house had remained empty for more than a decade after the murder-suicide. Then her grandmother had moved in, dispossessing the squatters who'd taken up residence, sinking far too much money against the inevitable decay of time. She'd lived there for a number of years in the early 1980s, pouring her energy and her money into the place, and when the three children had gone to stay with Grandmère, as she liked to be called, even though she didn't have a drop of French blood in her, it had become the first real home Jilly had ever known.

Jilly had fallen in love with La Casa the first time she'd seen it. She'd always thought of it as Sleeping Beauty's castle, surrounded by tangled growth, magic inside. While Dean had busied himself at school and Rachel-Ann had simply seemed unnerved by the place, young Jilly had thrown herself into Grandmère's restoration projects with a full heart, looking for something, anything, to expend her love and energy on.

She'd lived there from age twelve to age seventeen, when she'd been sent off to college, and they'd been some of the best years of her life. Until the night at the swimming pool.

It had been a liability even back then. All the chemicals in the world hadn't been able to keep it clear, and Grandmère had been ready to give up on it. But Jilly had been young, thoughtless, and the summer days in L.A. were hot. So were the summer nights.

It had started with a bet from Rachel-Ann. Jilly had been sitting in her sister's bedroom, cross-legged on her water bed, watching Rachel-Ann get ready for a date. If you could call it a date—she was sneaking out with the son of one of the servants, meeting him in the pool house. Jilly didn't even want to think about what she did there—she was already preternaturally worried about her siblings, since no one, not even Grandmère, seemed that concerned about their well-being.

"If you're so hot go for a swim," seventeen-year-old Rachel-Ann had said carelessly. "Grandmère just had the pool service in today so it should be relatively free from slime. I don't see why she doesn't just bulldoze the thing and have a new one dug. That pool is absolutely disgusting."

"And you think that'll make me want to go swimming?" Jilly had responded.

"Well, if you're too chicken," Rachel-Ann taunted. Her sister had been stronger then, confrontational. Not the fragile, wounded creature she was now. "No one's seen the ghosts at the pool, y'know. They were found in the house, not on the grounds."

"There aren't any ghosts," Jilly maintained.

"Just because you haven't seen them doesn't mean they don't exist. Haven't you smelled that tobacco-y smell? Or the perfume?"

"If I were you I wouldn't call attention to any strange-smelling smoke." Even at fifteen Jilly had been outspoken. "And everyone who walks into this house wears perfume, even Consuelo."

"You'll learn to be more discerning when you're older. That's French perfume, a very rare and costly blend, and it's a far cry from anything a housekeeper would wear."

"I thought you liked Consuelo," Jilly protested. In the last few years Consuelo had been the closest thing to a mother Jilly could find, and she was devoted to her.

"I do. I just wouldn't make her fashion choices." Rachel-Ann had stepped back from the mirror, admiring her reflection. She'd dyed her red-gold hair a tawny brown, and she was even wearing brown-tinted contact lenses. She was more voluptuous back then, and the thin lace dress molded to her body like a second skin. "How do I look?"

"Gorgeous. Does Consuelo know?"

"Know what?"

"That you're sleeping with her beloved son Enrique?"

"Richard," Rachel-Ann corrected sharply. "He likes to be called Richard. And Consuelo's plans aren't necessarily his. She's hopelessly hooked on the American dream, where her son becomes a doctor. Richard doesn't want to be a doctor."

"What does he want?"

"Me," Rachel-Ann said calmly. "So, are you going for a swim?"

"What's it to you?"

"We'll be in the pool house and we'd like a little privacy. Keep your distance if you don't want your precious innocence sullied."

"Rachel-Ann, are you sure you know what you're doing?"

"Don't start with me, Jilly. I'm a big girl now. I can take care of myself."

But she couldn't, Jilly thought. Couldn't then, couldn't now, and yet no one seemed able to help her.

Of course Jilly had had no intention of going swimming that night. She knew that her sister was sleeping with Consuelo's son, but that didn't mean she wanted to walk in on them, or even be anywhere near them. But the night was stiflingly, sufferingly hot, and the house was too old to come equipped with central air-conditioning. Grandmère had a window unit in her downstairs suite, as did Consuelo in the spacious servants' quarters, but the rest of them were supposed to make do with whatever breezes the L.A. nights could come up with.

There were none that night. Jilly lay on the bed in her shorty pajamas, feeling a coat of sweat cover her body like slime. She tried a cool shower, she tried a fan, she tried cold washcloths and ice cubes. By the time she heard Rachel-Ann tiptoe back up to her room she couldn't stand it anymore.

The pool was clear, clean and definitely refreshing. A few laps would cool her off and tire her out enough to sleep.

Back then the gates were kept closed, and Consuelo's husband and son did a decent job on security. Of course, Enrique—Richard—would be tired out after his tryst with Rachel-Ann, but his father, Jaime, was a responsible man. There would be no one lurking in the underbrush, waiting to grab her. This was La Casa de Sombras, the place she loved. She was safe there.

At least, until she passed the hedgerow of tangled roses and reached the top of the path leading to the pool. There was only a sliver of moon that night, and right then it hid behind a cloud, making the path barely visible. The water looked thick and black, even though common sense told Jilly it was fine. She could no longer smell the chemicals they'd dumped in that very afternoon. No stench of chlorine—instead there was the smell of rotting vegetation.

When she reached the edge of the pool she paused, suddenly unnerved. Even up close the water was dark, threatening and impenetrable. But the air surrounding her was like a cocoon of humid heat, and if she chickened out she'd be even hotter, sweatier, more miserable.

She took a step forward, ready to dive into the water, cotton pj's and all, when the moon slid out from behind a cloud. Suddenly it was another time, another night, long ago before she'd ever been born. Just as Jilly dived, a face appeared in the water beneath her, a face from a dream. It was the face of her sister.

She screamed, but it was too late. She twisted in the air, hitting the water with a belly flop, and the water was warm, thick, fetid around her. She went under, swallowing some of the dank stuff, and then pushed herself to the surface again, swimming toward the edge with a panicked strength. It felt as if the water were full of weeds, clinging to her, wrapping around her wrists and ankles, tangling in her hair, trying to pull her under with the woman who lay beneath the water. The woman who was Rachel-Ann, and yet who wasn't. With a final burst of terror Jilly reached the side of the pool, vaulting out of it with a strength she never knew she had.

She didn't dare look back. She simply ran, screaming, up to the house, no longer caring whom she frightened, who was torn out of a deep sleep. Her sister was dead in the pool, someone had tried to kill her, and a stranger was in the house.

The lights were flooding the wide stone terrace as Jilly stumbled toward the house, and Grandmère was already standing in the doorway, with a rumpled Consuelo and Jaime beside her. Jaime had a gun, and for a brief, hysterical moment Jilly thought he looked like something out of *Viva Zapata!* with his bristly mustache and his pajamas.

"It's Rachel-Ann," she sobbed, stumbling into the house. "She's in the pool. She's dead...."

"I don't know what you've been smoking, Jilly, but I'm right here." Rachel-Ann moved from behind Grandmère's disapproving figure. "And you're the one who looks like a drowned rat."

With a cry of relief Jilly threw her arms around her sister, who immediately shrieked and shoved her away. "You're alive!" Jilly cried.

''And you're cold and wet!'' Rachel-Ann said.

''You saw someone in the pool, Jilly?'' Grand-mère demanded. ''Jaime, you'd better go down and check. I can't imagine who could have gotten on the grounds—you locked the gates, didn't you? But stranger things have been known to happen. I hope to God we don't have a corpse floating in the swimming pool. This house has seen enough scandal.''

Her grandmother's prosaic tone had its usual bracing effect, but Jilly discovered she was still shivering, whether from the damp cold of her soaked clothes or the memory of that face. ''She wasn't floating, Grandmère. She was lying on the bottom of the pool, trapped in the weeds.''

''There are no weeds in the swimming pool, Jilly,'' Grandmère said patiently. ''No bodies, either, I expect. It's simply not possible. You must have been dreaming. I want you to go upstairs, take a hot shower and get into dry clothes. I'll bring you a sleeping pill to help you calm down.''

''I don't need a pill.''

''It's that or a glass of brandy. I don't fancy having my sleep disturbed by another of my impressionable granddaughter's nightmares.''

''It wasn't a nightmare,'' she said. No longer trusting her own memories. It hadn't even felt real at the time, no matter how horrifying. And yet she'd been there, in the pool. Her clothes were still wet.

"Take her upstairs, Rachel-Ann, while I check with Jaime."

Rachel-Ann had said nothing as she took her sister's arm and half dragged her up the winding marble staircase. It wasn't until she'd shoved Jilly into the bathroom that she'd spoken. "You tell Grandmère about me and Richard and I'll never forgive you. She'd fire Consuelo, for one thing, and she'd probably kick me out of the house, as well. And I don't want to go and live with Daddy."

"I didn't think we had that choice," Jilly said, her teeth chattering.

Rachel-Ann looked at her strangely. "I don't know if you do," she said, oblique as ever. "All I know is the only person who was in the pool tonight was you. Don't you think we would have noticed if anything was wrong? As far as you're concerned, you're the only person who left the house at all. Understood?"

Jilly nodded, shivering.

There was no body in the pool. Jilly made herself walk down there the next morning in the blistering heat, knowing that if she didn't go on her own her grandmother would force her. The water was crystal clear, the smell of chlorine was strong in the air. No weeds, no drowned faces, no fetid odor. If anyone had ever drowned in that pool it had happened in another lifetime, another reality.

But Jilly never went near the swimming pool again.

It came to her, though. In her dreams, she'd see her sister's drowned face, the eyes wide and staring, the mouth open in a silent cry for help. Slime-covered branches would reach out of its murky depths for her, trying to pull her in. And she'd wake up screaming, as she did this night, the sound muffled in her pillow, as she was suddenly, blindingly awake in the pitch darkness of her bedroom.

Roofus lay on the floor, whimpering in sympathetic distress, and she reached down a hand to pat him automatically, rubbing behind his ears. Coltrane had known just where to rub him, as well. She'd always thought you could trust a man who liked dogs. Obviously she'd been mistaken in that basic belief.

Alan had hated Barkus, Jilly's previous dog, and the feeling had been mutual. When Barkus had been found poisoned Jilly's husband had said all the right things, but she couldn't rid herself of the notion that Alan was secretly relieved. And once she'd accepted that fact, she knew there wasn't any way she could stay with him.

But Roofus liked Coltrane. Maybe Roofus simply didn't have any taste. Or maybe Coltrane wasn't as bad as she thought.

Two days he'd been living at La Casa de Sombras. Two nights, sleeping just down the hall from her. He'd had a bed delivered sometime today, and she'd had every intention of confronting him and demanding what right he had to start buying furniture. In the end he hadn't shown up at the house by late evening, and she'd gone to bed, deprived of her confrontation, both relieved and disappointed.

She climbed out of bed, piling her sweat-damp hair on top of her head. She wouldn't be sleeping again that night, she thought wearily. It was 2:33 in the morning, and she knew from bitter experience that the rest of the night was shot. She pushed open the French doors and stepped out onto the balcony, into the cool night air, and stared down at the grounds.

The pool was hidden by the overgrown tangle of roses. She really should do something about it, she thought again. As long as it lay there, a veritable algae farm, then it had the power to haunt her dreams. If she just had it filled in then maybe the dreams would stop. She should have gotten over it by now.

She shook her hair free, feeling it settle down around her back like a curtain. She ought to go and have it all cut off, but for some reason her father hated it. Told her she looked like a hippie chick from the sixties. And Jilly merely smiled and let her hair grow longer. She'd always told herself her father's approval or disapproval had no effect on her any longer. But she still didn't cut her hair.

She leaned on the railing, staring down across the lawn, the Spanish tiles cool beneath her bare feet. The second-floor balcony ran along the front of the house, but Rachel-Ann, with her pale, freckled complexion, eschewed sunlight, and it had always been solely Jilly's own.

She glanced down to the darkness at the end of the balcony. At least Coltrane was asleep—he wouldn't trouble her during her bouts of insomnia. And if he intruded on her privacy she'd kick him out, no matter what Dean or Rachel-Ann said.

"Can't sleep?" Coltrane murmured, far too close for comfort.

9

"**Y**ou frightened me!" she snapped.

Coltrane moved closer. He'd heard her moving around on the balcony, known instinctively that it was Jilly and not her sister. Not *his* sister. After more than twenty-four hours the knowledge still made his head spin.

"No, I didn't frighten you," he drawled. "Not this time. You already knew I was there. That doesn't mean I don't frighten you in general, of course. But you weren't shocked to see me."

She didn't bother denying it. "It's two-thirty in the morning. Why should I expect to run into you?"

"Kindred spirits? I have trouble sleeping on nights like this. Maybe I'll go for a swim. I presume like all L.A. houses you have a pool...."

"Don't!" There was a ragged edge of panic in her voice, one that surprised him. Maybe he'd scared her, after all. "The pool isn't usable," she continued in a shaky voice. "It seemed like low priority when the roof was leaking and the electricity was dangerous.''

"I could pay for a pool service."

"No!" she said, sounding as if he'd suggested having sex with a goat. "I don't like having a pool. Besides, there's something wrong with the ground there. Some kind of toxic seepage. It would cost a fortune to have it repaired."

He would have dropped it, except that she was so unexpectedly vehement. "Your father pays me a fortune," he said. "I could afford it."

"You could afford to live somewhere else."

"But then I wouldn't be able to help you, would I? And you want my help, don't you? Much as it galls you to admit it."

"I want your help," she said. "With my brother. But I want you to leave my sister alone."

Now she'd managed to surprise him. "What makes you think I'm interested in your sister?"

"Most men are. And you've been asking about her, talking about her since you first showed up here. I don't know why you're so interested, and I don't care. Leave her alone. She's fragile, and she doesn't need her life complicated right now."

"You really do take your family responsibilities seriously, don't you? I'm not interested in sleeping with your sister."

"Good."

"I'm interested in sleeping with you."

Even in the dark he could sense her reaction. He'd never had a woman hit him, though he'd deserved it more than once. Jilly Meyer might be the one to do it.

"Yeah, sure," she drawled after a moment. "If you think that's the way to my father's heart then you're not as smart as I thought you were. Jackson doesn't give a damn who I sleep with, any more than he cares about Dean. You'd be wasting your time."

"I don't think having sex with you would be a waste of time. I think it would be quite... pleasant." He chose the word deliberately, knowing it would enrage her.

"Pleasant?" she practically sputtered. "I don't do things because they're pleasant."

"Then maybe you should," he murmured. She couldn't know how close he was to her on the night-shrouded stone balcony, or if she did, she wasn't wise enough to realize he could reach out and touch her, quite easily. "What have you got against pleasure?"

"I don't trust it. And I don't trust you," she said sharply.

"What do you think I'm going to do to you, Jilly?"

She didn't answer, but then, he didn't expect her

to. He knew exactly what she was afraid of. Being vulnerable.

He took her hand. She jerked, obviously startled, but he held on, not letting her pull away. Her hand was strong, chilled beneath his.

"I'll tell you what, Jilly. You're so worried about your fragile older sister, so concerned about your family. Why don't you sleep with me to keep me away from Rachel-Ann? You can keep me so busy I won't even look at your sister. Maybe you can even distract me enough that I'll stop doing my job at Jackson Enterprises and Dean will have to fill in, winning your father's love and approval at last. It's a small enough sacrifice, isn't it? Your body for the well-being of your family."

"You're disgusting."

"Actually I'm quite good. Probably a hell of a lot better than you've ever had, if Alan Dunbar is anything to go by."

"How would you know? Did you sleep with Alan?" she retorted. She'd stopped trying to pull her hand free, but she hadn't given up fighting.

"No, but your sister did."

"Is that the best you've got for a trump card? I already knew that. Rachel-Ann doesn't keep secrets from me."

"Maybe she should."

"Maybe you should let go of me. I'm not inter-

ested in having sex with you, Coltrane, no matter
how talented you are in bed. I don't want to end
up some pathetic, needy love slave who's so desperate for affection that she'll do anything."

"Hey, I'm good," he said lightly, still holding
on to her. "But I'm not that good. I haven't had a
love slave in years."

"Leave me the fuck alone," she said bitterly.

"Now that's just what I'm not going to do." He
tightened his grip on her hand and pulled her toward him in the darkness. He knew exactly how
she'd respond, her other hand coming up to push
him away, her hand touching the bare, hot skin of
his chest so that she drew back in surprise, long
enough for him to wrap her tightly against his
chest, trapping her hand between them. He knew
she'd try to jerk her head away when he slid his
hand into her hair and tilted her face back for his
kiss. And he knew she'd open her mouth for him.

What he hadn't guessed was what it would feel
like. She was almost as tall as he was, her strong,
ripe body wrapped in his as they stood on the terrace. Her hair was like a curtain down her back,
reaching almost to her hips, and her breasts were
soft and full beneath the thin layer of cotton as they
pressed against his naked chest.

He hadn't known a mouth could feel like that.
That a woman, an argumentative, reluctant woman

could feel so hot in his arms, so incredibly right that his monumental control could start to slip. In a moment he'd be on his knees in front of her, using his mouth, and she'd let him, he knew it, even as she hated herself for it.

She wanted him, which was no real surprise. All that hostility usually came from somewhere deep inside, and it was just as likely to be sparked by attraction as anything else. What shocked him was how much he wanted her. On a deep, growling primal level that made him want to howl at the moon.

He knew how to kiss; he was quite skilled at it because he knew women liked it. But he'd never realized until that moment how much he liked it, too. He could push her against the stucco wall and kiss her for hours, quite happily. Or he could unzip his jeans, pull off her skimpy nightclothes and fuck her in the moonlight. Just lose himself in her, body and soul, so that he didn't need to think about anything but the touch and taste and scent of her, her breath in her mouth, her heart pounding against his.

But he wasn't going to do it. The only thing he wanted more than Jilly Meyer was his self-control, and he set her away from him, carefully, holding her at arm's length, wondering if she was going to hit him.

"Go away," she said, but her voice wasn't much more than a raw whisper.

He looked at her for a long moment in the moonlight, and then he nodded. "All right."

"I mean it. Go away. Leave this house," she said, her voice shaking. Maybe with fury, maybe with something else.

"I'm staying and you know it," he said.

"Then keep away from me."

He hesitated. "We both know I won't. We both know we'll end up in bed together, sooner or later. Why fight it?"

"Because I don't want it."

"You almost sound like you believe that."

"You arrogant bastard, I—"

He moved swiftly, coming so close to her that she fell back against the wall. He didn't touch her this time. He didn't have to. "I'm not deluded enough to think everyone wants me. But you do."

"I don't even like you."

"What's that got to do with anything?"

She looked pale in the moonlight, and she closed her eyes for a moment, looking even more vulnerable. He should have felt remorse. He simply felt desire.

"Please," she said in a weary voice.

"Open your eyes and tell me to go away, Jilly.

Put your hand on my cock and then tell me to leave.''

Her eyes flew open in shock and there it was between them. Desire, lust, fierce and mutual. Too soon, he thought dazedly, but it didn't matter. She was looking at him with a wary intensity that was going to lead them straight to her swan-shaped bed, and he was going to screw her senseless at the scene of a murder, and none of it mattered. All that mattered was the creamy warmth of her skin, the sweet taste of her mouth, the fact that all he had to do was reach out and take her....

''Jilly?'' The glass door behind him swung open, and Rachel-Ann stepped onto the terrace. ''What's going on out here?''

He'd stepped back, automatically, and the moment between them had vanished. It wasn't going to be tonight, after all.

As if nothing had happened, Jilly laughed lightly. ''Nothing, Rachel-Ann. Coltrane and I were just talking about...the pool.'' The hesitation in her voice was almost imperceptible.

Rachel-Ann moved closer, glancing up at him with decidedly frank interest. ''That goddamn pool. I don't know why you don't do something about it. You've never gotten over that time when you were fifteen—''

"I don't want to talk about it!" Jilly said quickly.

Fascinating, he thought. Something about the pool. The first free time he had he was going to have to go for a little stroll around the grounds, see what there was about an overgrown swimming pool to inspire such fear. "I'd better turn in," he said with an extravagant yawn. "I've got a full day's work tomorrow. Thanks for keeping me company," he said lightly.

Rachel-Ann moved past them to the railing, and Jilly glared at him behind her back. In response he mouthed a kiss at her, unable to resist the temptation.

"Good night, Coltrane," Rachel-Ann said calmly, keeping her back to him.

"Night, ladies."

He wasn't under any foolish impression that Rachel-Ann had just happened to wake up and come out onto the balcony. He went back into his bedroom, closing the French doors noisily behind him, then silently opening one just a crack so that he could hear the sisters talking.

"Are you out of your mind?" Rachel-Ann said flatly.

"Sssh. He'll hear you."

"No, he won't. He's gone to bed, and trust me, you can't hear anything from that far room. God knows I've tried. What were you doing with him? In another minute I thought you were about to do the nasty.''

"Lovely way to put it.''

"Would you prefer 'getting your brains fucked out'? He looks capable of it. Which would make him more my type than yours. You prefer them respectful and civilized, don't you? Coltrane's a little too *muy hombre,* if you know what I mean. I don't think you can handle him.''

"Keep away from him, Rachel-Ann.'' Jilly's voice was different when he wasn't around, he thought, resting his forehead against the cool pane of glass. Softer, more vulnerable. "You know he'd be the worst thing in the world for you.''

"And when have I ever let that stop me?'' Rachel-Ann's self-mockery was chilling. "I had a sudden ghastly thought. Please don't tell me you're throwing yourself at the man to save me. It won't do any good. You know I'll take him if I want him, and your sacrifice will be for nothing.''

"I'm not that noble,'' Jilly said wryly.

"Aren't you?'' Rachel-Ann mused. "He's very good-looking. Maybe you've just decided it might be fun to play with the bad boys for a change. I can't say I blame you, but I don't think you're quite up to the game. Someone like Coltrane would eat you whole.''

Just what he had in mind, Coltrane thought. Starting at her toes and moving up, slowly, lick by lick....

"Rachel-Ann, you're jumping to conclusions," Jilly said wearily. "We were just out here talking. He's not really interested in me at all."

"Not really? As in, he's pretending he's interested? This sounds worse and worse. You've got it backward, little sister. I'm the one who does self-destructive things, sleeps with the wrong men, makes a mess out of my life. Not you."

"What do you consider my marriage to Alan?"

"An aberration," she said flatly. "You're too smart to make that same mistake over again."

Silence, and he strained closer to listen. "Would it be the same mistake?" Jilly asked in a very soft voice.

"Not the same. Far worse. Alan's a prick, and a not very adept one at that. Coltrane strikes me as a man who knows how to please women. He could break your heart."

"Not likely," Jilly said.

"Likely," Rachel-Ann corrected her. "Keep away from him, Jilly. I will if you will. Leave him for Dean."

"I don't think he's interested in Dean."

"Then let him figure out some other way to get what he wants. And he wants something, have no doubt about that. Don't let him use you. Been there, done that, got the T-shirt. It doesn't feel good, and I don't want it to happen to you. Promise me.''

"Promise you what?''

He heard Rachel-Ann's deep sigh. "I won't ask you to promise not to sleep with him. I know human nature, and I know you, sometimes better than you know yourself. That would just make him irresistible. Sleep with him if you want. As far as I know you haven't had a man since Alan, and I can tell you from experience he wasn't very good.''

"Thanks for sharing,'' Jilly said dryly.

"Oh, no, dear, thank you for sharing.'' Rachel-Ann said with a rough laugh. "God, I shouldn't be making jokes about it. Have I told you how sorry—?''

"We don't need to talk about it, love. It's past.''

"I don't want to see you get your heart broken.''

"Alan didn't break my heart.''

"But Coltrane could. If you let him. Don't.''

Coltrane pushed the door shut silently, moving away. For some reason he didn't want to hear any more. He'd found out enough. Jilly was as vulnerable as he thought she was. And if he was as big a bastard as he prided himself on being he could manipulate Rachel-Ann without sleeping with her.

But he wasn't quite sure if he really was that

big of a bastard. Could he deliberately cause pain to his sister, someone who'd battled more than a few demons already, even if all he shared with her was bloodlines? Jilly Meyer was another matter—he owed her nothing, and if she provided him a way to get to Jackson then he'd take it, take her.

Hell, maybe he'd just take her, anyway, whether he had a good reason or not. Maybe wanting her was reason enough.

He had to remember why he was there. To bring Jackson Meyer down. But first he wanted answers. He wanted to know how he ended up with a sister he'd never known about. It didn't take much to guess who her father was—Jackson Meyer's adopted daughter was as much the old man's blood as Jilly and Dean were.

The question was, what was Coltrane going to do about it?

Right now he was going to sleep. He was going to stretch out on his brand-new bed, all alone, and try not to think about anything. Particularly not about Jilly Meyer's soft, sweet mouth. And what he could talk her into doing with it.

"We're going to have to get rid of him. I don't like what he's doing to our girls."

"Honeybunch, they're not our girls," Ted corrected her patiently.

"We've watched them since they were children. They feel like my daughters, and since neither of us had any children there's no reason why I can't think of them as mine. After all, their mother is dead," Brenda said in a cranky voice.

"So are we, my sweet."

Brenda would have blushed, but she didn't think she was capable of it. "I hate it when you talk about us like that," she said. "I don't like to think about it."

"Sorry," Ted said, flicking the end of his cigarette over the railing into the trees below. For the first few years she'd cautioned him about the fire hazard, before she realized that, in fact, there was no flame, no cigarette. No them. "I just wish we had some answers. I want to know what happened."

Brenda squashed down the shiver of guilt. "We're better off not knowing."

"Not knowing how we died? Don't you think we have a right to know that?"

"Most people don't. They die, and they're gone. For some reason we've been left behind, and I'm not about to argue. It means I can spend eternity with you, my love." She leaned forward and kissed his mouth. His mustache tickled her delicate skin, and she nibbled at it lightly.

"But why?" he said, putting his strong hands

on her arms and holding her a few inches from him. "Why did their grandmother die and simply disappear? And what about the other woman? Why are we still here?"

Brenda looked up at him. She was a much better actress than they'd ever given her credit for, and even a talented director like Ted couldn't see through her performance. Not when he never suspected her of lying. "I have no idea," she said. "And after all this time, I doubt that we'll ever know."

"We could find out. People still talk about us. If we could get down to the tour buses we could find out what they're saying."

"We can't leave the grounds. Besides, I'm not even sure the buses still come here."

"Then we should listen. Every time someone starts talking about us you start feeling amorous. Just once I'd like to stay and listen to what people have to say."

"They don't have the answers, either, darling. You've heard enough to know that. No one knows what happened that night. Including us." The lie was so familiar it almost felt like the truth, and she looked up into his eyes with a clear conscience.

He shut his eyes for a moment, his dear, beloved eyes behind the wire-rimmed glasses. And then he opened them and smiled, a crooked, accepting smile. "You're right, honeybunch," he murmured. "Why argue with destiny? Particularly when it gave me you."

And Brenda's answering smile was blindingly, falsely bright.

10

It was harder than Coltrane thought it would be, facing Jackson Dean Meyer. He drove Dean into work in his Range Rover—he really had no reason to object when Dean asked for a ride in to work, and Coltrane was adept at giving people the impression he was actually listening to what they had to say. People, particularly overbright computer nerds like Dean Meyer, tended to be so absorbed in their own interests that they seldom noticed when someone else was barely paying attention. The sound of their own voices was music enough.

Very few people, including his own children, could approach Jackson without prior arrangement. Coltrane was one of the chosen few. He went directly to the thirty-first floor office, not even bothering to knock.

Jackson Dean Meyer was accounted to be a good-looking man, and Coltrane had no doubt he'd been irresistible to women when he was young. Even now, with the carefully preserved patina of age upon him, he still managed to ensnare almost any female he took a passing fancy to. His young wife, Melba, had to be aware of it, but since he had as little real interest in his love affairs as he had in his marriage she was content with the status quo. And the money.

Meyer was leaning back in his chair in front of the windows, the city spread out behind him like a panorama of his own personal possessions. Everything about him was polished and perfect, from his artificial tan to the creases at his eyes. He'd had the best plastic surgeon, a doctor clever enough to leave character in an older face that didn't deserve it.

"No one's supposed to know I'm here," Meyer greeted him in an irascible voice when Coltrane walked in on him. "Everyone thinks I'm in Mexico."

"I'm the one who's been spreading that lie, boss," he said in a deceptively genial tone.

"I thought you were going to keep Dean busy at home. I don't need him wandering around asking questions. This is a very delicate time for me. The Justice Department is breathing down my neck, and as far as I can tell you've done squat to take care of things."

"You underestimate me," Coltrane said smoothly, taking a chair without being asked. "I've got everything under control."

Jackson made a disbelieving noise, his eyes narrowing. "I couldn't find the Sanderson records."

"Were you supposed to? I thought the whole point was that no one would be able to find them. They're gone, boss, vanished without a trace, and no one will be able to find them without going through me."

"And why should I trust you?" he demanded in a fractious voice.

"You'd be a damned fool not to, after putting this little matter in my hands," Coltrane said lazily. "If the Justice Department catches wind of it, your entire house of cards is going to come tumbling down. I doubt it would have lasted this long without your knowing who you can and can't trust."

Meyer was glaring at him, unconvinced. "I don't trust anyone completely. Not even you."

Coltrane smiled at him. "Neither do I."

Meyer stared at him for a moment longer, then nodded. "How's that damned mausoleum? Falling down yet?"

"It has a certain gothic charm. It would really be quite spectacular if it were fixed up as it was in its prime."

"Can't be done." Meyer dismissed the notion. "Sooner or later that crazy daughter of mine will realize it's a lost cause and abandon it. And then I'll have the place razed."

''Why don't you just kick them out now?''

''I would if I could. My goddamn mother left it in trust to them. She knew I'd tear the place down, and she was as sentimental as Jilly is. They'll cling to it as long as they can, but sooner or later they're going to have to give in. I'll even help them out financially when they get resettled, which I'm not obliged to do. But then, I'm a generous man where my children are concerned.'' He didn't even blink.

''Why did your mother leave the place in trust to them rather than you?'' Coltrane asked, taking advantage of Meyer's uncharacteristically chatty mood.

''You know mothers,'' he said with a harsh laugh. ''Bitches, all of them. We never got along. She thought I was a conscienceless son of a bitch. Which, of course, was exactly what I was.''

Coltrane didn't react, wondering what would happen if he threw Meyer through those heavy plate glass windows. He'd probably bounce rather than go crashing through. Patience, he reminded himself, as he looked at the man who'd stolen his mother.

''You ever live there?'' Coltrane asked.

''At La Casa? No way in hell. That place was a ruin for as long as it was in the family. Mother bought it while I was in college, and by the time

I got back I was engaged and setting up a place of my own.''

Coltrane said nothing, letting Meyer continue with his lies.

''I had no use for decaying grandeur. Jilly gets a kick out of it, for some twisted reason. Can't imagine why. Her mother hated it, I hated it, and it's been nothing but an albatross. If it were up to Dean he'd give the damned place to me, and so would Rachel-Ann.'' His voice softened slightly, ''Rachel-Ann would do anything I ask of her. But not Jilly. She'd see me in hell before she let me take that monstrosity off her hands.'' He sat up, swiveling around to stare at the cityscape. ''What did you think of her?''

Coltrane didn't move. He knew by the oddly caressing tone in his voice that Meyer wasn't talking about Jilly, but he chose to deliberately misunderstand. ''Quite the Amazon. Have you made up your mind whether you want me to sleep with her or have her killed?''

''I was talking about Rachel-Ann.'' Meyer's voice was icy.

''I thought you didn't want me to sleep with her.''

''Don't be an asshole, Coltrane. What did you think of my daughter? Beautiful, isn't she? Sweet and fragile and helpless.''

Meyer sounded almost abstract as he described his eldest child, but Coltrane wasn't fooled. He'd known all along that Rachel-Ann was the only child he cared about. He still wasn't sure just how deep that attachment went. Or how healthy it was, for either of them.

"Gorgeous," he said briskly. "She doesn't look much like you."

"She's adopted," Meyer said stiffly. "You knew that."

"I forgot. For that matter, Jilly doesn't look like you, either, though Dean does. Are you sure Jilly's mother wasn't playing around on you?"

"I couldn't care less. I'm not the paternal type— I don't really give a damn about my children."

"Except for Rachel-Ann," Coltrane said.

"Yes. Except for Rachel-Ann. Are you passing judgment on me, Coltrane?"

"None of my business, boss," he murmured. "So what is it you want me to do?"

"Keep Dean occupied. You told me you were giving him the Wentworth project. That's perfect busywork. Between that and his computers he'll be so tied up he'll have no time for snooping into what doesn't concern him. As for you, I want you to concentrate on keeping Jilly out of my way. She's far too nosy for her own good."

"What would she be nosy about?"

Meyer frowned. "You don't need to know everything, Coltrane, just enough to protect me. I've got some stuff in the works that I don't want complicated. You do as you're told. Keep Jilly occupied. Someone with an agenda could do a lot of damage, and Jilly's someone with an agenda."

"Which is?"

"The stupid house, for one thing. And her brother and sister. She thinks they need protecting from me."

"Do they?"

Meyer shrugged. "Dean's harmless. As long as he keeps out of my way he doesn't bother me. And I wouldn't let anything happen to Rachel-Ann. That's a warning, Coltrane. You cross me and you won't know what happened to you."

"Got it," he said dryly. "Sleep with Jilly, distract Dean, keep away from Rachel-Ann, keep the Justice Department off your back. Anything else while I'm at it? Any seas to part, water that needs turning to wine?"

"You can handle it. Jilly's probably easier than she looks. She fell for a pretty boy like Alan Dunbar, she'll fall for you if you put a little effort into it."

"And Rachel-Ann?"

"Leave her to me. I'll look out for her. I always have. In the meantime, why don't you make yourself scarce around here? Take a few days off, enjoy the luxuries of La Casa de Sombras,'' he murmured. ''Make sure Jilly and Dean know I'll be out of town.''

''Will you?''

''Maybe,'' Meyer said. And he smiled his affable, charming smile. That had never fooled Coltrane for even a moment.

Rachel-Ann left the house before nightfall. Her BMW wasn't running smoothly, and if she'd gotten it together she would have dropped it off at Meyer's mechanic to have it overhauled. She had almost no cash, but Jackson would pay the bills without complaint. He always did.

She wanted a drink. Quite badly. It had been another in an endless line of endless days, and she wanted it over before it got any worse. The house was deserted when she woke up, early that afternoon, but the scent of perfume and tobacco followed her wherever she went, until she wanted to scream. She tried to call Jilly at her office, but she was out on a site, probably trying to save another lost cause, and she must have turned off her cell phone. Jilly had spent her life on lost causes, Rachel-Ann thought, including her older sister. Sooner or later she'd have to give up.

The one thing Rachel-Ann didn't want was to

be home alone when Coltrane returned. He gave her the creeps, there was no other word for it. If she had to choose between the ghosts of La Casa and the tall, gorgeous, available Coltrane, she'd take the ghosts. There was something about the man that disturbed her, roiled her stomach and scratched at her veins, and she was afraid to look too closely at why she found him so disturbing.

It wasn't lust. The very thought was unsettling, and if there was one thing Rachel-Ann was comfortable with, it was lust. She recognized it when she saw it, recognized it when she felt it. And it had nothing to do with whatever was going on between her and Coltrane.

Not that anything was, she reminded herself shakily. He was after Jilly, which wasn't much of an improvement. Maybe that damned, unwanted gift that enabled her to see the ghosts and know things that people shouldn't know was telling her that Coltrane was trouble. Maybe her instincts were screaming at her to get Jilly away from him.

But that was the trouble with instincts. You could never tell if you were just being paranoid, or if it really was some kind of message. And she'd look like a hell of a fool if she got between Coltrane and Jilly without offering herself as live bait.

And she didn't want him. Odd as it was for her to believe, she most definitely didn't want him.

Belatedly she realized she'd ended up near the Unitarian church on Sunset. She glanced at the digital clock on the dashboard—a meeting would be starting in another fifteen minutes. An hour and a half of platitudes and guilt. Just what she needed.

She found a parking spot, pulled over and turned off the car. The church was just up ahead, it would only take her a moment to cross those few yards. All she had to do was open the door, get out and walk. And maybe this time she could say, "Hi, my name is Rachel-Ann and I'm an alcoholic."

Or maybe not. Maybe she should just turn the car back on, put it into Reverse and get the hell out of there. The Kit-Kat Klub would be in the full swing of Happy Hour, and no one would pay any attention to her if she sat in a corner and got quietly loaded. She'd end up with someone, anyone, it didn't matter. Just so long as she didn't have to be alone.

She kept her hands on the leather-covered steering wheel, not moving. Three months and five days since she'd had a drink. Meetings every goddamned day. Ninety and ninety, they told, another of their endless rules. Ninety meetings in ninety days. If she walked into another meeting she'd go postal.

Maybe she'd just drive. She didn't have to get drunk any more than she had to go to a meeting. Life didn't always have to be composed of extremes. Maybe she'd take a drive along the ocean, watch the moonlight on the water. And when she walked back into La Casa and the damned ghosts started looking at her she'd ignore them.

Or maybe she'd…

She saw the face in her window out of the corner of her eye, and she screamed, panicked, before she turned and realized who it was. She tried to lower the window but the power was off and the electric window stayed shut. With shaking hands she reached forward and turned on the car, and the window slid down in one smooth move.

"You coming in to the meeting?" Rico asked. It was the first time he'd ever spoken to her directly, despite all the meetings, and now, looking into his dark-brown eyes, she had the oddest sense of déjà vu.

"I don't know," she said honestly, then could have kicked herself. Give a recovering alcoholic an inch and they'd take a mile. He'd preach to her until she had no choice but to follow him numbly into the meeting and sit through another endless round of qualifying.

"Do you want to?"

"No. I want to go out and get drunk."

"What do you want me to do?"

It was a simple question, and she knew what the answer should have been. She should tell him she wanted him to stop her. But she was so tired of giving the expected response. So tired of it all.

"You want the truth?" she asked.

"Yes."

"I want you to come with me."

He rose, and she couldn't see his face any more, just the rumpled clothes, the bottom of his jaw rough with five o'clock shadow. He walked away from the door, and she breathed a sigh of relief. Until he came around the other side of the car and got in beside her.

He put on his seat belt. She hadn't bothered to wear hers. "Where are we going?" He seemed no more than casually curious.

"Does it matter?" Her hands were still shaking, and she turned the key, forgetting that the car was already running. The starter shrieked in protest.

"No," he said. "Put on your seat belt."

"Why? Because it's the law?"

"No," he said. "Because I want you to keep yourself safe."

She glanced at him doubtfully. The interior of the car was filled with shadows, and she could barely see him. "You're not going to tell me you've suddenly fallen in love with me, are you?"

His laugh was soft, unexpectedly charming. "No."

"Then you can come with me."

"I thought you wanted me to."

"I don't have any idea what I want."

"Yes," he said gently. "I know."

She drove into the L.A. night, and because she could think of nowhere else to go she took him to the Kit-Kat Klub, the most decadent public place she could think of. He followed her in, watching her quietly as she ordered a margarita. And then she sat there staring at the glass, not touching it.

"Am I cramping your style?" he asked with an unexpected trace of humor. The club was very noisy, and she had to lean forward to hear him. She could smell the tequila, and the odor made her sick.

"Aren't you going to stop me?" she asked him. "Lecture me?"

"If you want."

"What if I want you to drink with me?"

He shook his head. "Now that I won't do. Do you want to drink it, Rachel-Ann? Or do you want to leave this place?"

There was something odd about the way he said her name. Something familiar about it. She picked up the margarita, her eyes meeting his defiantly.

His eyes looked familiar, too, in a face that was weary, lined and oddly appealing. He looked like a man. She usually didn't bother with men, just good-looking boys.

178					Anne Stuart

"Who are you?" she asked, still holding the salt-encrusted glass. "I know you, don't I?"

"Do you?"

"Stop answering my questions with questions. You're like some damned therapist. I must have run into you in my drinking days," she said. "Or drugs. Were you also into drugs?"

"Yes."

"But now you're clean and sober," she mocked him. "We probably slept together and I've forgotten all about it."

He didn't say anything, just kept looking at her out of those enigmatic dark eyes.

"Well, did we?" she demanded.

"What do you think?"

She took a deep breath, oddly shaken. She'd had a nagging sense of familiarity bothering her for days, and it seemed to reach out and touch everyone she ran into, including Coltrane. Maybe it was simply this forgotten face from the past that had triggered it.

"Well, Rico," she said defiantly, "aren't you going to take this drink out of my hand?"

He shook his head. "You need to put it down yourself, *chica*. It has to be your decision."

Chica. No one had called her that in years, at least that she could remember. Consuelo used to called her that when she fed her chocolate chip cookies and milk.

She set the drink down, untouched. "Okay," she said with a crooked smile. "My decision. Let's blow this pop stand and we can relive old times. Your place or mine?"

She'd managed to startle him, a good thing. "It's up to you," he said finally.

She rose, tossing the car keys in front of him. "Your place," she said. "You can drive." And she walked out of the night club, certain he was following her.

11

Rico reached over and fastened her seat belt, then slid the driver's seat back to accommodate his longer legs. Rachel-Ann hadn't realized he was so tall. She leaned her head back and closed her eyes. She didn't want to think about it. It didn't matter. She had someone to keep the darkness away, she didn't have to go back to La Casa and dodge the ghosts, and she might make it through one more day of sobriety. All good things, right?

So why was she closing her eyes, hiding from him as if he were the threat?

He drove smoothly, but she didn't want to see where they were going. She knew it was a mistake—she didn't have the best sense of direction, and when she left later she might have a hard time finding her way home.

It didn't matter. The longer she spent driving the mean streets of East L.A. the longer it would take to get home.

Of course, she had no idea whether they were heading into East L.A. or not. It was probably just latent prejudice on her part, to assume that because the man she'd picked up was Hispanic that he'd live in East L.A. For all she knew they'd end up in a condo in Century City.

She opened her eyes a tiny bit, to glance at him in the reflected light of the dashboard and the city lights. Good profile. A strong nose, high forehead, silky black hair in a widow's peak. Nice mouth, as well. If she tried very hard maybe she could convince herself he was dangerous. Going off with a stranger wasn't half as effective if the stranger was safe.

"What are you thinking?" He must have realized she was watching him, but he kept his gaze on the crowded streets, driving with a casual self-assurance in the insanity of L.A. traffic.

"You're a good driver," she said.

"It's a family trait. My father was a chauffeur."

"And what do you do? Besides go to AA meetings and pick up women."

"I don't make a habit of picking up women," he said calmly, avoiding a Lexus bent on destruction. "And I work for Los Angeles County Hospital."

"Doing what?"

"In the emergency room."

"Are you an orderly?"

"If you want."

He was beginning to annoy her. "Are you always so agreeable?" she said in a cranky voice.

"No. Ask my mother—I can be a pain in the butt. I just happen to be in a good mood."

"Why?"

He glanced at her then, just a brief look before he turned back to concentrate on the heavy traffic. "Because I'm with you."

She grimaced. "I told you, I'm not interested in someone who's going to fall instantly in love with me."

"Not a problem, *chica*," he murmured. "I promise."

There was something going on, some undertone she didn't quite understand, and she sat up, casting a suspicious look at him. "You aren't a sicko, are you? I'm not into D and S, S and M, or any of those other initials. I just want oblivion. I'll take it with sex if I can't use drugs or alcohol, but I don't get off on pain."

"Neither do I."

"Then why do you work in an emergency room?" she shot back, distrustful.

"Because I can help," he replied calmly. "Isn't it a little late to be having second thoughts about coming with me?"

"Is it? What if I tell you to stop the car and get out, let me drive away? Will you do it?"

Without a word he pulled over, out of the traffic, and turned to look at her. "It's up to you. I'm not going to make you do anything you don't want to do, and I'm not going to hurt you. If you want me to leave I will."

And leave her alone, with nowhere to go but back to La Casa. Or the Kit-Kat Klub. She nodded. "Okay, I trust you," she said.

He laughed softly, putting the car into gear and pulling deftly back into the stream of cars. "No, you don't, *chica*. You don't trust anyone. But we'll work on that."

Great, she thought sourly. "What's your name? If I'm going to spend the night with you I ought to know your name."

"You know it. It's Rico."

"Your full name."

"Enrique Ricardo Salazardo de Martinez y Columbo." The Spanish syllables flowed off his tongue so smoothly she could barely follow them.

"Rico will do," she said wryly. She waited a moment, but he said nothing. "Don't you want to know my name? Or do you prefer to keep this anonymous?"

"'Hi, my name is Rachel-Ann and I'm an alcoholic,'" he quoted lightly.

"Except that I've never said that," she pointed out coolly.

"I know."

Of course he knew. That was why he'd said it. And why the hell had she chosen someone like him to find forgetfulness? He was far too observant.

Except, in fact, she hadn't chosen him. He'd simply appeared, available when she needed someone to distract her. To keep her sane. "My name is Rachel-Ann Meyer. Not nearly as exotic as yours, I'm afraid."

"Not as many ancestors," he said with a crooked smile.

"Not that want to own up to me. I was adopted."

He nodded, seemingly unsurprised. "But you have family?"

"A sister and a brother," she said.

"No parents? What happened to the people who adopted you?"

"My mother died years ago in a car crash. She'd already divorced Jackson."

"Who's Jackson?"

"My father. He's still alive."

"So you have a brother and sister and father...."

"I don't want to talk about it. We're sleeping together, not getting married," she snapped, uneasy.

"You don't like talking about your father?"

"Drop it, Rico," she said. "Or you can get out and walk."

Once more he pulled up to the curb, into a parking space, and he turned off the car, plunging them into a darkness lit only by the streetlights and the passing cars. "So will you," he said. "We're here."

She craned her neck to look out the window. She wasn't quite sure what she expected—certainly not the working-class neighborhood that looked more like New York than L.A. "You live here?"

"My apartment's just down the block." He took her hand, and for a moment she tried to jerk away, suddenly nervous. He held on, putting her keys in her palm and closing her fingers around them before releasing them. "Your decision, Rachel-Ann," he said calmly. "But I'm going in."

He slid out of the car, coming around to her side. It would be easy enough to push the lock, to slide over into the driver's seat and get the hell out of there. He'd given her that choice—he wouldn't try to stop her. He didn't open the door for her, either. Not out of a lack of courtesy, she realized. But because he wanted her to make the choice.

She unfastened the seat belt, reached for the door and opened it. She didn't take the hand he held out for her, climbing out on her own instead, and she glanced back at her BMW for a doubtful moment. On a street full of low-riders and ancient sedans it stood out, even in its current less-than-stellar condition.

"Will my car be here in the morning?"

"There are no guarantees. If people know you're with me though, it'll probably be safe."

"Why? Are you that strong an influence in this neighborhood? Are you a drug dealer? Is that where I know you from?"

"If I'm Hispanic I'm either an orderly or a drug dealer? Not very politically correct, *chica*," he chided her, unoffended.

"Sorry," she muttered, oddly ashamed of herself. It wasn't often that that happened—her behavior was usually so reprehensible that regret was a waste of time. But for some reason this man had her doing all sorts of unexpected things, feeling unexpected feelings.

He lived in a second floor walk-up in an old building that smelled of spices but shone with cleanliness. He preceded her into the apartment, leaving the lights off, and she wondered if he was just going to jump her in the dark. So much for old-fashioned courtesy.

A moment later the lights came on, and she saw she was in a small, tidy studio apartment, slightly shabby, oddly comfortable-looking. She looked

around her, surveying her surroundings. There was
a sofa with a brightly colored afghan thrown over
it, a wall of books and stereo equipment and a
television. A desk and computer by the window
that faced the fire escape, a kitchen in an alcove,
equally spotless.

"It's very nice," she said weakly.

"It's a good thing my cleaning lady was in today, or you wouldn't be so overwhelmed by my
luxurious living quarters. Are you hungry?"

"You're going to cook for me?" She was oddly
uneasy. She wasn't used to doing this stone-cold
sober, and he wasn't making much effort at moving things along. He should have backed her
against the wall, pulling up her sweater so he could
touch her breasts.

But she didn't want him to touch her breasts. Or
maybe she did—he was very attractive in a loose-
limbed, rumpled sort of way. But he wasn't coming any closer, and she wasn't sure she wanted to
start things.

"I could order pizza."

Which made her think of Coltrane and her weird
reaction to him. "No pizza," she said. "I'm not
hungry. Got a drink?"

"Diet Coke."

"That's not what I meant."

"I know. But if you wanted to drink you

wouldn't have come home with me, would you?'' he said reasonably, locking the door. Locking her in, she thought, wondering if she should be even more nervous. Locking out the night.

She shrugged. "Where's the bed?"

"In a hurry? The night's young. Why don't we—"

"Sit and talk?" she suggested. "Get to know each other? Maybe have a little AA meeting on our own? I didn't come here to talk. Where's the bed?"

Without a word he went to the sofa and opened it, laying the brightly colored afghan on his desk with a certain reverence. "Clean sheets," he said with a crooked smile.

"I don't care." She began unbuttoning her sweater, afraid that if she hesitated she wouldn't do it, that she'd start crying. Then she'd have to run away. And she had no place to run to.

She pulled off her sweater, dumped it on the floor, then slid out of her jeans, standing in her skimpy silk underwear. She took a handful of brightly colored condoms out of her purse and put them on the table beside the bed, just as Rico came back into the room carrying pillows and a duvet. He glanced at the stack of condoms with a faint smile. "You think I'm going to need all of them?

That's a little overoptimistic, isn't it?'' he said, then turned to look at her.

She was too thin and she knew it. Heroin chic, they called it. That was the one drug she'd managed to avoid, but she was still waif-thin, and she didn't want him looking at her, passing judgment.

''Would you turn off the lights?'' she said in a deceptively calm voice.

''If you want.''

''Are you always so agreeable?''

''If you were looking for abuse I'm afraid you picked the wrong man.''

The wrong man. Too many times the wrong man. ''Turn off the lights,'' she said again, and the room was plunged into darkness.

She heard the rustle of clothes as he stripped and got into the bed, and she reached for the front clasp of her bra, ready to do what she'd done countless times before. At the last minute she changed her mind, slipping beneath the pillowy duvet with her underwear still on. She lay on her back beside him, rigid, trying to control her racing heart, her shallow breathing.

He was nothing more than a shadow in the room, lying beside her. She couldn't see him; he wouldn't be able to see her. It was a small comfort. She waited for him to touch her, but he was in no

hurry, seemingly content to watch her in the shadows, when he couldn't really see her at all.

"You have a lot of books," she said.

She didn't have to see his smile to know that
she'd amused him. "Yes, I do. Do you want me
to turn the light back on so you can read them?"

"They looked a little too heavy-going for me.
What are they?"

"Medical texts. And you're right, they're pretty
heavy-going."

"Why do you have medical texts?" she asked.

"Oh, even an orderly gets curious. Actually my
interior decorator thought they'd dress up the room
a bit…"

"You're not an orderly."

"Nope."

"You're not a nurse, either?"

"Nope."

"Paramedic?" she said hopefully. "Medical
technician?"

"Why does it matter?"

She already knew the truth. "I don't like doc-
tors."

"Then stay out of the ER and you don't have
to see me at work."

Not good enough. "Shouldn't a doctor have
more sense than to sleep with a stranger who has

a history of drug and alcohol abuse? Ever hear of AIDS? HIV?''

"You brought condoms. And what makes you think I'm safe?''

"Are you?'' And would she leave if he said no?

"Yes.''

"Aren't you going to ask me?''

"Stop arguing with me, *chica*," he said softly. "If you're sick I'll take care of you. But I don't think you are. You wouldn't have come home with me. You like to think you're so bad and cruel, but you wouldn't go around picking up strange men and making them sick.''

"I don't know why you think you know me so well,'' Rachel-Ann said bitterly.

"Because I do. Come here.'' She felt his hands on her, pulling her against him, his hand cupping her head, and without thinking she let him tuck it beneath his chin. He was naked, as she expected him to be, and he was hard. She waited for him to do more. To reach down and push the rest of her clothes off. To kiss her mouth, hard, to make her touch him.

But he didn't. He seemed perfectly content to hold her. "You may as well relax, Rachel-Ann,'' he whispered in her ear. "We're not going to do anything you don't want to do.''

"And if I don't want to do anything but lie here?"

"Then that's fine, too."

"That's not what your body is saying."

"No," he agreed. "But my body doesn't rule me. Here." He turned her around, so that she was cuddled against him, spoonlike, his arms hard and secure around her, holding her, demanding nothing. "Stop shivering. I'm not going to hurt you."

She was so cold, he was so hot, and all she wanted to do was lie in his arms and weep. She wouldn't do that. She stared sightlessly at the wall of books, trying to absorb the heat from his body, the strength, and slowly, imperceptibly, the tension began to drain from her body. "So many books," she murmured sleepily.

"So many books," he agreed. "Go to sleep, angel."

"Not an angel," she whispered. "Don't want to sleep."

"Yes, you do. You're tired of fighting. I'll keep you safe."

"What makes you think you know what I want? What makes you think you know anything at all about me?" She could see the gilt outline of picture frames up on the bookcases, tipped facedown. Strange, she thought sleepily.

"I know you. Trust me and sleep."

"No," she said. And slept, safe in his arms.

12

Rachel-Ann hadn't come home. Jilly lay face-down on her bed, wide-awake, listening. No sound of the omnipresent Weather Channel filtering through the walls, no footsteps racing up the front stairs in a panic. Rachel-Ann had been gone by the time Jilly got home, and she hadn't returned.

The fact that Coltrane was missing, as well, shouldn't have been a problem. Any day spent without having to face him was a blessing, particularly after last night. Why in God's name had she let him kiss her? Why in God's name had he done it? He had to have some ulterior motive—there was no way he was simply swept away by passion. He'd backed her up against the wall and kissed her, and what was far, far worse was that she'd kissed him back. If Rachel-Ann hadn't interrupted them she would have taken him into this bed, and then she'd have no haven left.

No, if it hadn't been Rachel-Ann then it would have been something else. She'd watched her sister and brother fill their lives with self-destructive mistakes. Alan was a big enough one to last her a lifetime—she wasn't going to make a habit of sleeping with good-looking, heartless men who didn't even want her. Who wanted her sister.

She rolled over onto her back. She couldn't remember being jealous before. Not that she was jealous now—there was certainly nothing to be jealous of. When she found out that Rachel-Ann had been sleeping with Alan it had filled her with both rage and relief. Rage that Alan would betray her. Relief that she didn't have to pretend any longer.

She'd never felt anger toward Rachel-Ann. Her sister harmed herself more than anyone else, and Alan had been a mistake from the very beginning, a delusion at best. Jilly should have known when the worry of leaving La Casa had been more overwhelming than her excitement of a marriage that it hadn't been a match made in heaven. And Alan had never been that exciting.

She couldn't stop thinking about sex, and it was all Coltrane's fault. She'd never been prey to her hormones—she used to think Rachel-Ann had been overloaded with sexuality and she'd been short-changed. She'd had her share of crushes as a girl, dates as a teenager. She'd slept with the ones she thought she'd loved, the ones she should have wanted to sleep with. And none of it had ever made much of a difference except in her self-esteem.

At one point she'd even pondered whether she was gay. It was an entirely acceptable life-style, and it probably would have made Dean happy to know his sister chose it. But for some reason she couldn't summon up even stray lustful feelings for another woman. Even if she preferred women socially, they just didn't appeal to her as sex objects.

Neither did most men, leading her to the logical conclusion that maybe she was, if not frigid, perhaps a bit lukewarm. She and Alan certainly hadn't caused any major conflagrations—she'd known all the right moves, made all the right noises, but what had started out as mildly pleasant soon turned into a chore.

Which was why she hadn't been involved with anyone in the three years since she and Alan had separated. Why she hadn't even been tempted, until someone totally inappropriate had pushed his way into her life.

She rolled onto her side, punching the soft feather pillow. She was too hot, even in boxers and a tank top. She'd started out wearing sweats—the night was cool, and she didn't want to remember what her body had felt like, up against Coltrane's through the thin layer of cotton.

But she'd lain in the bed, twisting and turning,

half awake, half dreaming, until she'd given in and stripped off the enveloping sweats. It wasn't as if she had to worry that Coltrane would saunter into her bedroom uninvited. He wasn't even home. And if he was, as long as she stayed in her room she'd be safe.

Safe. A strange notion. Why in the world would she think Coltrane wasn't safe? Granted, he had the delicious bad-boy streak that Rachel-Ann had always found irresistible and Jilly had always been too wise to succumb to, but he wasn't a real danger to her. Was he?

She rolled onto her stomach, punching the pillow again. And why couldn't she just put him out of her mind? Maybe it was a sudden upsurge of hormones. She was almost thirty—maybe she was just a late bloomer, and she'd soon become as voracious as Rachel-Ann had been in her heyday.

And there were other men, good-looking men who'd been attentive in the past. Sam Bailey and Mark Fulmer and that lawyer down at the Preservation Society…no, she didn't want lawyers. And she couldn't seem to summon up even a trickle of yearning for any of those strong bodies, handsome faces, pleasant souls.

It was beginning to look like she had more in common with her sister than she'd ever realized.

Including an irresistible attraction to exactly the wrong man.

She sat up, kicking the tangled covers away from her feet. It was four in the morning—typical of her usual sleep patterns. Maybe she should follow her sister's example even more closely. She had no idea whether Dean was home or not—his quarters were removed enough that sound didn't carry, and he often spent the night away. Besides, his drink of choice was vodka, just as Rachel-Ann's was tequila, and Jilly hated both.

Alcohol would help her sleep, though. A nice glass of brandy would burn its way down her throat and warm the pit of her stomach, and she'd be able to snatch another few hours of sleep. Besides, it didn't matter if she was late for work—there was nothing on the agenda.

It probably wouldn't matter if she never went to work again. The historic preservation of Los Angeles was a joke. She couldn't even keep her own house from falling in, much less save any other place. The salary she was paid was pitiful—surely there was something else she could do that would bring in enough money to support La Casa. If not restore it, at least keep it from falling into complete ruin.

Roofus slept soundly on the floor beside her bed, and she tiptoed past him out of the room. If he heard her and followed he'd be full of his usual bounding energy, leaping with joy, and there'd be no way she'd ever get back to sleep. If she could just manage to creep downstairs to the kitchen, find the brandy and pour herself a glass she might be able to make it back upstairs before dawn.

The brandy snifters were long gone, of course. She ended up pouring a healthy dose of Calvados into a small juice glass with Wile E. Coyote on the side. She leaned against the iron sink as she took a tentative sip, letting it trickle a fiery path down her throat.

She might as well accept it—Rachel-Ann and Coltrane were off somewhere together. There was something between them, something powerful. Even the most unobservant person in the world would have to recognize it, and Rachel-Ann had never been shy in expressing her interest.

Nor did Jilly have any delusions about Coltrane. He wanted something from the Meyer family, and he had no qualms about how he got it. He'd probably sleep with both of them if it served his purpose. She only wished she knew what the hell his purpose was. What he wanted from them.

She drained the glass, then on impulse refilled it. Too much, when she wasn't used to drinking, but who would it hurt? There was no one around, and she'd simply crawl back in bed and sleep as long as she could. It was the least she deserved.

It was a relief, really, she thought, switching off the overhead light and plunging the kitchen back into darkness. She'd been more unsettled by that kiss than she wanted to admit. Unsettled enough to consider kissing him again. To consider just saying the hell with it and…and…

And do what? Sleep with him? She wasn't that crazy, was she? And now, of course, it was out of the question. He'd gone off with Rachel-Ann, and she wasn't going to take her sister's leftovers. Despite her best efforts, her self-esteem wasn't that strong.

The cognac was soothing her jangled nerve endings. She was finally relaxing, that bone-tightening tension draining from her. Who the hell cared who Rachel-Ann was sleeping with? The last man had been a physically abusive drug dealer—even Coltrane was a step up from that.

As for Coltrane, well, he was clearly no good for Rachel-Ann, but she'd tried to warn him off. Obviously it had been a waste of time. So be it. She wouldn't worry about it. About him. About them. Maybe they could live happily ever after and Jilly wouldn't have to worry any more.

And pigs could fly.

There was a faint light coming from the living

room, and Jilly halted at the foot of the stairs, momentarily startled. It wasn't a room anyone used much—if the three siblings actually spent time together it was usually in the Tropicana Room, an art deco room sporting a huge curved bar, shag rugs and a big-screen television, a present from Jackson when he was in one of his more generous moods.

As far as Jilly knew there were no lights in the living room, and yet the glow was palpable. The furniture was draped with Holland covers and pushed against a wall, the place was coated with dust. Who the hell would be in there?

The ghosts. There could be no other explanation. The unearthly light, the eerie silence, the sense of some…presence, just beyond. Maybe she had to be half-loaded to finally see them. It didn't matter. After eighteen years Jilly was finally going to see the famous ghosts of La Casa de Sombras, and nothing was going to make her go back to the dubious safety of her bed without making the most of the long-awaited opportunity.

She peered inside the arched doorway, half-empty juice glass of brandy clutched in one hand. The place looked deserted, except for the glow of light in the far corner, behind the high-back sofa. The cover had been thrown off in a heap on the dusty floor, and Jilly felt a moment's misgiving.

Maybe she should go upstairs and get Roofus. Maybe she should go upstairs and stay put.

She stood motionless, listening. She'd been told the ghosts of La Casa were particularly noisy ones—if they were there on the sofa she should hear something. Come to think of it, what would they be doing on the sofa? There were rumors that Brenda de Lorillard and her lover had been seen frolicking, nude, decades after they'd been found dead. While Jilly had a strong interest in finally seeing her purported ghosts, she didn't fancy catching them in the act.

Nothing. Not a sound. The light was a steady glow, creating a small pool of warmth, and she moved toward it, unable to resist the pull, like a moth.

She was halfway across the room when she realized it was no unearthly ghost illuminating the corner. Someone had taken a table lamp from one of the unused rooms and plugged it in. The bare lightbulb was probably not more than a forty watt, making little dent in the cavernous shadows. But at least there was a perfectly logical explanation for the light.

It wasn't until she came around the other side of the high-back sofa that she realized logical explanations were not particularly what she wanted.

Coltrane lay there stretched out on the sofa,

shirtless, unshaven, barefoot and gorgeous. Alone. There was no sign of Rachel-Ann anywhere.

She took an instinctive step backward, stumbling into another one of the sofas. His eyes opened, but she suspected he already knew she was there.

"Wile E. Coyote?" he murmured. "What are you drinking?"

"Brandy."

He scooted back on the sofa, sitting up, and leaned against the overstuffed armrest. In the dim light of the bare lamp the ripped damask looked ivory against his golden skin, golden hair. He held out his hand for the glass, and without thinking she handed it to him. She'd never seen someone so completely comfortable with his body. Alan had always preened, expecting admiration. Coltrane seemed oblivious, accepting his body for what it was, a tool.

An incredibly beautiful tool, Jilly thought, sinking down on the sofa opposite him. The cover was still draping it, a small defense against the ravages of time. She'd forgotten just how comfortable the sofa was.

"Where's Rachel-Ann?" she asked.

"I haven't seen her all day. Is she missing? Should we be worried?"

She ignored the *we*. It was a slip of the tongue.

"She didn't come home last night. I assumed she was with you."

"Why?"

"Because you seemed so interested in her."

"I told you, I'm interested in you." He slid down a little bit, eyeing her over the juice glass. "Any particular reason why you don't want to believe that? Don't try telling me you're not used to men wanting you—I wouldn't believe it."

"Not more than my sister." Jilly couldn't believe she'd actually said that out loud. She hated even thinking it, but to have spoken it was far, far worse. Especially to him. It must be the brandy. If she'd known she was going to run into him she would have stayed put. It was too high a price for sleep. "I thought you were the ghosts," she said, quickly changing the subject.

"I didn't think you believed in them." He was watching her, but she couldn't see his expression. Maybe it was just as well.

"I didn't say I didn't believe in them. I've just never seen them."

"And how long have you lived in this house?"

"Seventeen years, off and on."

"You'd think you'd have run into them by now if they existed," he said reasonably.

"You'd think so. What are you doing down here when you've got that wonderful new bed?"

"Thinking. And it's not that wonderful." He took a sip of the brandy, then offered the glass back to her. There was no way in hell she was going to put her mouth where his had been, so she shook her head.

"I've had enough," she said. "I'm not used to drinking much."

There was no missing his slow, wicked smile. "Don't tell me you're wasted, Ms. Meyer?"

"Only very slightly," she said with great dignity. "What were you thinking about?"

"That maybe I should leave here."

"Leave?" she repeated stupidly. It was everything she'd prayed for, the answer to her current problems. It was the last thing she wanted.

"Leave," he said. "You know, git, skedaddle, vamoose, take a hike, get the hell out of Dodge."

"You've been watching too many westerns."

"Maybe it's the house that does it to me. Though Brenda de Lorillard wasn't famous for westerns, was she? She was big in those weepy women's movies of the forties."

"I don't know," Jilly said. "I don't really care. Why are you leaving?" She centered in on what was important.

His eyes narrowed, and his smile was wryly self-deprecating. "Does it matter?" he said. "Maybe I ought to get out of here before I become what I hate.''

''And what do you hate?'' She knew the answer with sudden, illogical certainty. He hated Jackson Dean Meyer, her father. His deep-pocketed mentor.

He didn't answer. She didn't expect him to. He drank the rest of the brandy, then set the empty juice glass down on the parquet floor. He looked up at her, a lazy smile on his face. ''Then again, maybe I don't give a shit. So why don't you want me to leave?''

''I want you to leave,'' she said immediately.

''Then why don't you come over here and say goodbye?''

She didn't say a word, leaning back in the sofa and stretching her long bare legs out in front of her. He liked her legs—she had absolutely no doubt about that. He really liked her legs.

Fair enough—she liked them herself. They were her one true beauty. Not even Rachel-Ann had end-less legs like she did.

''You don't know me nearly as well as you seem to think you do,'' she said.

''I don't?''

''You think I'm a shy, fragile little flower, don't you? Terrified of big strong men like you, afraid of sex, afraid of life?'' Her voice was mocking.

''I don't know if you're afraid of all big strong

men, sugar. You're certainly scared shitless around me.''

She didn't even hesitate. She rose with one fluid movement, crossed to the sofa and calmly straddled him, putting her arms around his neck and looking down into his eyes. "Who's afraid of the big bad wolf?'' she mocked him. He shifted, and she could feel his erection. It startled her so much she started to pull away, but he caught her arm and pulled her back.

"Don't leave now that it's getting interesting,'' he said. "You started it this time. Let's see how brave you really are.''

Part of her wanted to pull away, run away. She had no idea whether he'd let her go if she struggled, and she wasn't sure she wanted to find out.

The other part, centered between her legs, wanted to call his bluff. He was so mockingly sure of her.

But she hadn't survived her family by being a coward. Or by hiding from what she wanted, even if she knew perfectly well it was bad for her.

And she wanted the man beneath her. At least a taste of him. "You'd be surprised how brave I can be,'' she said. And she leaned down and put her own mouth against his chest, her hair falling around them like a curtain of night.

"Jesus Christ,'' he gasped, his hands reaching

up through her hair to cup her face. She ran her mouth down the thin line of hair on his chest. She wanted to kiss his stomach, but she couldn't reach without moving from her perch astride him, and she liked the feel of him, hard and full between her legs. She rocked slightly against that ridge of flesh, and the sensation was exquisite, overwhelming, unnerving. She froze, but his hands caught her hips. "Don't stop, sugar," he murmured. "If it feels half as good to you as it feels to me then you can't stop."

It was the most erotic experience she'd ever had in her life. The layers of cloth between them only increased the friction, and when he reached up to touch her breasts he did so through the thin cotton, not touching her hot flesh. The barrier of cloth was incredibly frustrating, incredibly arousing.

"You like that, don't you, Jilly?" he whispered as her hair flowed around them. "Nice and safe, all that clothing between us. Nothing touching, no skin, just safe. Distant. Strangers." She was moving slowly, back and forth, sliding against the ridge of flesh, and she was hot, cold, panting, moving.

He was talking to her. Hot sex words, telling her what he wanted to do to her, how he wanted to touch her, taste her, take her, as his hands caught her hips, controlling the rhythm, arching against her, and she heard the words in a blind flurry of shame and desire. This was wrong, this was bad, this was indecent, and there was no way she was stopping, no way she could stop. But she needed more, she needed his flesh, she needed him inside her as she'd never needed anyone before, and she was sweating, trembling all over.

"No," she said in a choked voice. "I can't..."

"Sure you can. Just try it," he mocked her, arching up against her sensitive body, and she wanted to punch him, to bite him, for tormenting, teasing her like this when she couldn't...

He was right, she could. One moment she was fighting it, the next she was convulsing, her entire body exploding in a fast, fierce orgasm.

And he was with her. She heard his harsh groan, felt the heat and wetness that flowed between them, and she slid down slowly, sensuously, pressing her face to his chest, her breasts against his stomach, letting the wetness soak into her T-shirt.

It took her long, shocking moments to realize what she'd done. What he'd done. With a start she scrambled away from him, landing on the floor in a sprawling, ungainly heap.

He rose on his elbows, looking down at his body with a slow, wry grin. "Well, that hasn't happened in a hell of a long time. You're a dangerous woman, Jilly Meyer."

She couldn't look at him, couldn't look at herself, as waves of mortification swept over her. It was growing light outside—she didn't even have the mercy of the night to cover her embarrassment.

So she did what any brave, self-respecting woman would do. She ran away. Hearing the sound of his laughter echoing in the distance.

13

"I need a cigarette," Brenda said breathily, leaning back against the sofa.

Ted passed her one of his, a grin on his face. "You always had a voyeuristic streak, honeybunch."

"You have to admit that was a lot more inspiring than some of the stuff we've seen over the years. Those disgusting creatures who filled this place in the sixties used to pile on each other like dogs," she said with a sniff.

"Rachel-Ann hasn't proved to have much taste where men are concerned. And I'm not sure if I approve of this Coltrane character. Jilly deserves better."

Brenda smiled serenely. "You're just jealous. There's no reason to be. He's very good-looking but he's not my type."

Ted looked at her with mock affront. "You mean you prefer your men ugly like me?"

"Don't be silly, darling. You know I'll worship you till the day I..." She let the sentence trail off.

She couldn't worship him until the day she died—that day had long passed. "I think Coltrane will be perfect for Jilly. That was definitely the best orgasm I've ever watched her have."

"Voyeur," Ted said again lazily.

"You, too, darling. We have our own real-life television show here, and it's a lot more interesting than some of the things the girls watch. Why would someone be obsessed with weather?"

"At least it makes more sense than street addresses. Melrose isn't even in a decent neighborhood. Stop trying to distract me, honeybunch. I don't trust Coltrane."

"Well, of course not," Brenda murmured. "I never said he was trustworthy. Some of the most interesting men are far from trustworthy. But I think he's got potential. Just a little redemption and he'll suit Jilly very well."

"Not Rachel-Ann?"

Brenda shook her head. "Not Rachel-Ann."

"Should we do anything about Jilly?"

"She's upstairs sitting in the shower, crying. She does that sometimes, when she thinks no one can hear her."

"Maybe I ought to go see…." Ted suggested, and Brenda hit him.

"You keep your filthy mind off her, darling. I

know you're infatuated with her, but I've already claimed you.''

He smiled at her. ''So you have. Just teasing, my precious. I don't want to see anyone curled up in the shower.''

''Besides, she's still in her nightclothes.''

''They'd cling quite nicely. I always liked a statuesque woman.''

Brenda, a full five feet tall, hit him in the shoulder. ''Behave yourself. Jilly will be fine in the shower. In a few minutes she'll turn off the water and throw herself into bed, where she'll probably sleep for hours.''

''And Coltrane?'' He jerked his head toward the man who was still sitting on the sofa, watching the sun rise past the windows, a distant expression on his face.

''Oh, he'll be fine, as well. He's just got something to think about. Things aren't going according to his plan. I love it when that happens.''

''Tell me, honeybunch, are you privy to his plans?'' Ted asked dryly.

''I can't read minds, darling. I only know that when he came into this house he had a clear agenda, and that's been shot to hell. It makes things even more interesting.''

''A little too interesting, if you ask me,'' Ted

said. "I think I liked it best when the place was deserted. Then I had you to myself."

Brenda smiled at him. "You still have me all to yourself, darling. You always will." And she leaned down to kiss him, nibbling lightly on his mustache.

The light was filtering in through the miniblinds, sending stripes of sunshine across the mattress. Rachel-Ann didn't want to wake up. It seemed as if she'd never been so comfortable in her entire life. She felt cushioned, cradled by the mattress. The temperature was perfect, neither too hot nor too cold; the scent of coffee on the air gave an added aura of comfort.

She opened her eyes, unmoving, focusing on the details of the apartment. She was alone in the bed, and in the kitchen she could hear someone moving around. Rico.

She closed her eyes, trying to will herself back to sleep. She usually left after she'd had sex, slipping out of the apartment or hotel room without a word the moment her partner had fallen into an exhausted slumber.

But this time she was the one who'd slept like the dead. And, in fact, they hadn't had sex. They hadn't even kissed. She'd slept in the safety of his arms, and for some reason she felt more raw and exposed than if she'd danced naked on his coffee table.

She didn't want to face him. She'd pretend to sleep, wait until he left and then sneak out. She wouldn't ever have to see him again—she hated those AA meetings, anyway, and if she ever decided to go to another one she could avoid the ones at the Unitarian church, head farther west and find other ones. God knows AA meetings were like rabbits—they multiplied like crazy. You couldn't walk two feet without tripping over one.

She heard him coming out of the kitchen, and she quickly closed her eyes, feigning sleep. Then she smelled the coffee even more strongly, and she knew she couldn't fake it any longer.

''Wake up, Rachel-Ann. I've got to go to work, and I don't want to leave until you're safely in your car. It's a rough neighborhood without me to look out after you.''

She opened her eyes, reluctantly. He was dressed, he'd even taken a shower and shaved. He smelled like soap and shampoo, he looked clean and rumpled and the best thing she'd ever seen in her life.

She managed a shaky smile. ''I'll be out of here in a minute,'' she said, pulling the duvet up around her. There was no particular reason to be modest—she was still wearing her underwear, the same fancy underwear she'd stripped down to last night in front of his watching eyes. The pile of condoms still lay on the bedside table, unused, and she could feel color flood her face.

"You're not going anywhere until you've had something to eat. I've made you a good breakfast and if you don't eat it I'll be offended."

"I don't eat in the morning." It smelled divine, though. The wonderful smells of a huge breakfast and coffee, things she hadn't smelled since she'd been an adolescent and Consuelo ruled the kitchen at La Casa.

"You will today. The bathroom's over there. I left towels for you. Take a shower if you want— by the time you finish, breakfast will be ready."

"I don't eat—"

"In the morning," he finished for her. "Did I ever tell you I'm incredibly stubborn?"

She waited until he'd gone back into the kitchen, for some reason oddly loath to prance around in front of him. Her clothes were folded neatly beside the bed. She grabbed them and dashed for the bathroom, slamming the door behind her.

The shower went a long way toward making her feel half human, and she liked the smell of his soap, his shampoo. She'd smell like him when she came out, she thought absently.

She didn't bother putting her underwear on

again, simply tossing it in the trash before she opened the bathroom door a crack, half hoping she'd be able to sneak out the front door while he was in the kitchen cooking.

No such luck. He was waiting for her, and he had her car keys in his hand. She hadn't noticed his hands before. In fact she hadn't looked at him clearly at all—she preferred to keep these things impersonal.

But not having sex with him had suddenly made it very personal, and she looked first at his hands, elegant, long-fingered, quite beautiful. Deft, clever-looking hands. Hands that would know how to touch a woman.

She looked at his face. Bony, interesting, attractive rather than handsome, with astonishingly beautiful brown eyes. She looked at him in the bright daylight and that strange sense of comfort washed back over her.

It was the smell of food, she told herself, reminding her of her safe childhood. The untold benefits of an uninterrupted night's sleep, though she supposed she ought to be offended that he hadn't interrupted it.

Except she remembered the feel of him, wrapped around her, and she knew it hadn't been lack of interest that had kept him from making love to her.

Making love—that wasn't a term she used often. But somehow, with this man, she sensed that was what it would be. Making love. And it was the last thing she wanted.

She tore her eyes away. "Okay, feed me, Seymour," she said flippantly. "And then I've got to get home."

He'd made *huevos rancheros*. She couldn't remember when she'd last had them, and the sight of eggs and salsa so early in the morning should have made her stomach revolt. Instead she found she was starving.

It was heavenly, rich and spicy and perfect, and the coffee was exactly the way she liked it, strong with cream and tons of sugar and just a hint of cinnamon. She was practically at the point of licking her plate when she realized he was watching her.

"You don't eat breakfast?" he said gently.

She shrugged nonchalantly, reaching for her coffee. "What can I say, it was delicious. Who taught you to cook like that?"

"My mother."

She set the coffee down hard on the table in sudden shock, jerking her head up to stare at him. A simple, clicking into place when she hadn't even begun to guess.

He was wearing a loose white T-shirt. She stood

and yanked the back up before he could stop her. Not that he would have. The tattoo was on his shoulder blade, faded slightly with the years. A heart, split by a lightning bolt with her name etched into it. Into his skin.

She let the T-shirt drop, suddenly chilled. He didn't move, just sat there looking at her.

"Richard," she said in a hoarse voice.

"Rico," he corrected her gently. He held out his hand, his beautiful hand that had touched her all too well in the past. "Rachel-Ann…"

But she backed away, stumbling into the doorway that led to the rest of the apartment. "You lied to me."

"I didn't."

"You didn't tell me who you were…."

"I told you my name. I should have realized you wouldn't know it. I was Richard the Cook's son, the Mexican son of the chauffeur. I didn't need a last name." He didn't even sound bitter about it, just accepting.

"You were stalking me."

"No. You walked into a meeting and I knew you immediately. Unlike you, I hadn't forgotten."

"For God's sake, I haven't seen you in more than fifteen years," she said. "How the hell was I supposed to recognize you?"

"You weren't," he said calmly. "Don't be so

upset about it, *chica*. There's no reason you should have known who I was, and I didn't want to spook you by mentioning it. As you said, it was a long time ago. It's not important. I'm not the first man you slept with and I wasn't the last.''

"Nicely put," she said in a cool voice.

"You know what I mean. You've been married twice since then...."

"You're behind the times. I just divorced my third husband. No, you weren't the first and you most certainly weren't the last. I can hardly keep track of my husbands, much less my adolescent fucks...."

"Don't," he said softly.

"Don't what? Say *fuck?* That's what we did, isn't it? Everywhere, every time, every way we could think of. That's what you do when you're seventeen. Sorry you've lost interest in it recently, but I still enjoy myself every chance I get.''

He was supposed to be hurt, offended by her hostile words. Instead he just smiled at her with great sweetness. "You have such a happy life, Rachel-Ann?''

"Go to hell," she muttered, pushing her way out of the kitchen. Her sandals were by the sofa with the brightly colored afghan draped over it. Consuelo must have made that afghan. Somewhere, packed away in her bedroom, was a similar one she'd made for Rachel-Ann for her sixteenth birthday.

He didn't try to stop her, though he stood in the doorway of the kitchen, watching her. He was leaner than he'd been as a teenager, more wiry. He'd been strong and young and gorgeous as a teenager. He was devastating as an adult.

She shoved her feet into the sandals, grabbed her car keys from the table, accidentally knocking over the stack of condoms. She looked at them littering the floor. "I suppose I should take those with me," she said lightly. "I imagine I won't have much trouble finding someone who wants to use them."

She'd finally managed to get to him, break through his gentle calm. He took a step toward her, then halted, visibly getting himself back under control. "You have a talent for pushing buttons, Rachel-Ann," he said lightly. "Leave the condoms. We'll use them next time."

"Fuck you," she said deliberately.

"Next time."

She slammed the door on her way out, racing down the narrow flight of stairs to the street with complete disregard to her safety. In daylight the neighborhood looked worse, and there were three teenagers leaning on her BMW, peering inside. They looked up as she approached, keys in hand,

and it took all her self-control not to hesitate, just to keep walking.

She'd just reached the car when one of the boys removed himself from it to stand in front of her. He was taller than she was, beefy, wearing gang colors. He had three teardrops tattooed on his cheek, and he couldn't have been more than sixteen years old. Or been more frightening.

Then a voice rang out, and he turned, all danger dropping away from him, as he answered, in Spanish. Rico was standing on the sidewalk, barefoot, calm, in charge.

The other two boys immediately backed away from the car, but the boy who'd confronted her argued for a moment with Rico. Rachel-Ann's Spanish was rusty, but it would have taken a fool not to realize they were talking about her. And that Rico was warning him away from her in cool, implacable tones.

Finally the boy shrugged, lifting his hands in a helpless gesture before reaching for her car door. And then he stood there, the perfect gentleman, holding the door for her as she quickly scrambled inside, closing it behind her with a mocking little bow before stepping away.

Her hands were shaking as she shoved the key into the ignition, and at first try it wouldn't start. She almost burst into tears. If worse came to worst she would stay locked inside her car until they all went away or she died of starvation, which, considering the breakfast she'd just wolfed down, would be quite a while. The food should have made her sick, especially given the shock that had followed it, but for some reason it had settled nicely into the pit of her stomach, warming her.

The car roared to life, a sudden blessing, and she pulled into traffic, narrowly missing an oncoming truck.

It was far too easy to find her way out of the neighborhood, onto Sepulveda. It would be simple to find her way back. She turned the radio on, loud, only to switch it off immediately when Ricky Martin started singing in Spanish. She didn't want to think about Spanish and sex, and with Ricky Martin the two were inextricably entwined.

She was overreacting, she told herself, as she drove through the morning traffic back toward Sunset. There was no way she could even begin to remember everyone she'd slept with. It probably wasn't the first time she'd ended up back in bed with someone she'd tried earlier. She'd never been one to learn from her mistakes.

Except that Richard…Rico…hadn't been a mistake. He'd been young and strong and passionate and deeply devoted to her, and she'd loved him. For a while, at least.

Hell, she couldn't even remember what had broken them up. They'd had to sneak around, of course. Consuelo and Jaime had been completely disapproving. They'd loved her, but they'd wanted a good, Catholic virgin for their only child. Rachel-Ann had been nominally Catholic, but she'd lost both her virgin and good status a long time ago.

Grandmère wouldn't have noticed, and Jilly was childishly thrilled to be an accomplice to Rachel-Ann's midnight rendezvous. Had she just lost interest, gone on to someone new and broken his heart? What had happened?

With a sudden chill it came back to her. Something she hadn't wanted to remember, and her stomach twisted for a moment, rebelling against both the memory and the *huevos rancheros.*

It had been Jackson, of course. She had no idea how he found out, when even the people living at La Casa, Jaime and Consuelo and Grandmère, hadn't the faintest idea. She used to think he hired people to spy on her. She knew Jilly wouldn't have betrayed her, and Dean was away at military school and hadn't the faintest idea what kind of trouble his sister was getting into.

But Jackson had found out, and his icy rage had been horrifying. He'd summoned her to his office—he wouldn't come to La Casa, claiming the place depressed him. He'd been very calm, very

detached as he'd detailed the times she'd met with
Rico, the things they'd done. He'd rattled off the
particulars in his cool, clipped voice, and she'd sat
there, mortified at the words he used. She was being taken away from La Casa—from then on she
would live with him in his town house. She
wouldn't see or talk to her sister or brother, she
wouldn't go anywhere without her father guarding
her.

She'd run away once, hitchhiking to La Casa
late one night. The gates had been locked, but
she'd always known where she could scale the
walls, and she'd gotten in without trouble. Only to
find that Consuelo and Jaime had been fired
months before, without warning. That they'd disappeared, with their son.

She used to wonder if Jackson had ordered them
killed. She had no doubt he was capable of it—
unlike her siblings she had no illusions about how
ruthless Jackson really was.

She wasn't fool enough to ask. She wasn't fool
enough to care. Ever again.

And now the earth had turned again, and he was
suddenly there. Richard. No, Rico, with his beautiful hands and his gentle voice.

She'd learned her lesson, long ago. But he'd
tricked her—if she'd known who he was she would
have kept far away from him. She'd always known

the AA meetings would be nothing but trouble. She should have listened to her instincts.

Except, hadn't it been her instincts that had sent her out with him last night? Something deep inside that she thought she'd managed to destroy?

She wouldn't let it surface again. She didn't like that kind of pain—life was too short to put up with it. She liked forgetfulness. Oblivion. Peace.

She turned into the overgrown drive leading up to La Casa. If she wanted peace, La Casa de Sombras was the last place she'd find it.

But then, she'd come to realize, there was no place on this earth that would give her the kind of peace she craved.

No place at all.

14

Zachariah Redemption Coltrane was feeling like shit. He'd never had many illusions about his own nobility. Neither did he tend to feel sorry for himself. Sure, he had a few strikes against him from the start, in particular his family, though come to think of it, he'd take his long-vanished family over Jilly's all too present dependents. And his entire family hadn't vanished. He was still having a hell of a time coming to terms with the truth about Rachel-Ann.

He had a sister. He was torn between a sentimental streak and annoyance. This new-found knowledge had thrown a monkey wrench into his plans, and once they were skewed, Jilly Meyer had managed to get under his skin, complicating matters even more.

He'd planned to leave. He'd decided earlier that night, when he couldn't sleep and found his way downstairs to the abandoned living room. Meyer was already set up for a fall, the Justice Department was ready to make its move, and there was nothing more to be gained by staying there. Nothing was going to bring his mother back, and there was no guarantee he would ever find out the truth about her death. Maybe it was time to get back to his own life.

It seemed an obvious answer to a difficult situation. He couldn't seduce Rachel-Ann, and Jilly had no particular value in the scheme of things. He should just walk away.

If he were a decent human being that's just what he'd do, but he had no illusions about himself. He was a cold-blooded bastard, through and through, and he couldn't walk away from revenge, even for his fragile sister's sake. Word had it that she and her father were devoted. If he brought Meyer down then it might put Rachel-Ann over the edge.

He didn't want to be the one to destroy his own. He didn't particularly want to hurt Jilly, either, though why he should care one way or the other mystified him. Some latent decency that needed to be squashed, fast. Jackson Dean Meyer fought dirty, and there was no way Coltrane could bring him down if he played by the rules.

And he had to bring him down. If Jilly and Rachel-Ann were hurt, well, that was just their bad luck. He wasn't about to let latent, unnatural stirrings of decency get in the way.

He'd managed to get the shower working in his

bathroom, and by the time he came downstairs it was after eight. He expected Jilly wouldn't appear until she absolutely had to, and if she could manage it she'd keep out of his way for days. She wasn't going to manage it. He kept seeing that horrified expression on her face as she tumbled off him onto the floor, soaked and messy and dazed. He kept remembering the tight urgency in her body, the sound she made when she came. And he kept wanting to go upstairs and finish what they started.

She'd probably locked and barricaded the door, and he'd been sorely tempted to follow her upstairs, kick it open and finish things. She couldn't lock out what frightened her. It wouldn't do any good. He wasn't the one who'd horrified her. It was her own reaction, voluptuous, sensual, completely unexpected.

He'd never expected it to go that far. She was calling his bluff when she climbed on top of him, but he hadn't been bluffing. He'd intended just to take her for a little ride, get her hot and bothered and leave it at that. But things had spiraled out of control so quickly he hadn't been able to stop. Hadn't wanted to.

He found himself grinning wryly in the shadowy kitchen. He needed to learn not to underestimate

Jilly Meyer. Even more particularly, not to underestimate the effect she had on him.

He was on his second cup of coffee, sitting in
the peaceful stillness of the kitchen, when Rachel-
Ann walked in, looking a hell of a lot livelier than
he'd ever seen her. She halted in the doorway
when she saw him sitting there, and he suspected
that if she'd known he was there she would have
gone in the opposite direction.

"There's coffee," he said.

"I've already had two cups." She stayed in the
doorway, frozen.

"Have another."

"It'll make me too nervous."

Good point, he thought. She was already a visible bundle of nerves. "Suit yourself," he said.

It was the first time he'd ever been alone with
her, and it was oddly unsettling.

"Nervous has its uses," she said, coming into
the room and pouring herself a mug of coffee. She
sat down opposite him and he watched in fascination as she emptied huge amounts of sugar into
the mug so that it must have been a thick, sweet
sludge. "Anyway, I wanted to talk to you."

"Okay." He leaned back in the kitchen chair,
waiting.

"What did you do to my sister?"

It was the last thing he expected her to ask. "What do you mean?"

"I saw her driving away from here when I came home this morning and she didn't even see me. She had Roofus with her and she was crying."

"When was this? I thought she was still asleep."

"Not more than five minutes ago. What did you do to her?"

"Not a damned thing," he said, unblinking. He wasn't about to tell his little sister what he'd been up to on the living room sofa. "Besides, do you really think she needs you looking out after her? She's an adult—she can make her own choices."

"She's not as invulnerable as she likes to think she is. She's strong, but she can be wounded. Probably because she makes the mistake of caring too much about people."

"Maybe you should have taken that into account before you slept with her husband," he drawled.

Not the way to endear himself to his long-lost sister, he thought belatedly as her green eyes turned hard with anger. "I forgot," she said, "you're privy to everyone's little escapades, aren't you?"

"Is that what you call it? An escapade?"

"She already knows all about it. She's forgiven me."

"Of course she has. Didn't you just define her problem? She cares too much. It doesn't matter that you betrayed her on one of the most elemental levels—she still loves you and wants to protect you. Even when you're intent on killing yourself as speedily as possible and there's not a damned thing she can do to save you." His voice was surprisingly bitter, and he picked up his coffee cup, waiting for her inevitable explosion.

She didn't explode. In fact, the anger seemed to have left her, and she was staring at him in a kind of wonder. "Interesting," she murmured. "Who would have thought it?"

"Who would have thought what?" He was sounding more and more irritated, and he didn't care. Jilly irritated him, with her bleeding heart and her vulnerability. Rachel-Ann irritated him with her death wish.

And most of all, he irritated himself for even giving a damn what happened to either of them.

"You care about her," Rachel-Ann said. "Better not let Jackson know. He wouldn't like having his chief henchman having feelings about Jilly. He considers his children completely expendable."

"I'm his legal advisor, not his henchman."

"Same thing," she interrupted airily.

"And I don't care about her any more than I care about her damned dog. I just don't like to see people betrayed by people *they* care about. And, for that matter, I've been around your father long enough to know that he certainly doesn't consider you expendable."

An odd expression darkened her eyes for a moment. "No, he doesn't," she said in a lifeless voice. "But then, you probably know he isn't really my father. So any...attachment he might feel isn't necessarily, legally paternal."

The words were so simply, evenly spoken that it took him a moment to realize what she was saying. Before he could do more than stare at her she rose, taking the unfinished mug of coffee to the sink and draining it. Then she turned and smiled at him, and he realized with shock that her smile wasn't terribly different from the one he'd seen in a Christmas photograph from almost thirty years ago, on his very own face.

He didn't smile like that any more. And she looked far too cheerful for his peace of mind.

"Anyway, I'm glad we've had this little talk," she said breezily. "I'm feeling much better about the whole thing."

"What whole thing?"

"You and Jilly."

"There is no me and Jilly," he said in a perfect drawl. "Anymore than there's a me and Roofus."

Rachel-Ann raised an eyebrow. "I think the

three of you will be very happy," she murmured and floated away before he could protest.

She had a few more defenses than anyone gave her credit for, he thought belatedly, tipping the chair back and putting his feet on the scarred work-table. And she was more observant than anyone realized. She sensed that Meyer's affection for her crossed the paternal line, and Coltrane didn't think she liked it.

She really wouldn't like it if she knew just how taboo that paternal affection was.

Meyer knew. There was no way he couldn't. Rachel-Ann didn't just show up on his doorstep—he'd gone out of his way to get her, to bring her home and pass her off as a foundling. The old man was an even bigger bastard than Coltrane had even begun to imagine. Bad enough that he murdered Coltrane's mother. His sins were reaching the next generation and he had to be stopped.

"There you are, Coltrane!" Dean lounged in the door, deliberately languid as ever. "Whatever has gotten into my sisters? First Jilly goes driving away from the house like a bat out of hell, then Rachel-Ann ignores me and goes upstairs singing. Singing, for God's sake!"

"I can't imagine."

Dean shrugged his shoulders. "Not that it matters. Any sign of cheer is encouraging. I just wanted to tell you I'm throwing a little dinner party tonight, and I'm counting on you to be there. Don't disappoint me.''

''Why me?''

''It'll be just the family, I promise. I decided that since the four of us are such a motley crew, a group dinner might help us learn to get along. I've already been in touch with the caterers—no one has to do a thing but show up. You drink Scotch, don't you?''

Sitting down to a cozy dinner with the three Meyers was just about the last thing he wanted to do. Jilly would probably flat out refuse to attend if she knew he was coming. "I've got other plans."

''Cancel them.'' He followed the order with what he obviously thought was a winning smile. "You won't be sorry."

Coltrane resisted the impulse to snort in disbelief. "How are you coming on the Wentworth project?"

Dean held a silencing finger up to his mouth. "I'm learning all sorts of fascinating things, and not just about Wentworth. My father has unexpected depths. Amazing what kind of information you can dig up when you use a little imagination and a passing knowledge of computers."

Coltrane's eyes narrowed. He'd buried the Sanderson stuff in a file that Dean would never be able to access, no matter how adept he was at computers. But Dean still looked far too smug for Coltrane's peace of mind.

"Want to talk about it?" he asked casually.

"Not now. I'm still busy gathering information. You'll know when I'm ready to deal."

Coltrane stared at him, suddenly edgy. "I wouldn't underestimate your father if I were you. I don't know if he'd let family loyalties get in his way if he's feeling threatened."

Dean laughed. "Believe it or not, I know just what my father is capable of. And he'd be smart not to underestimate me. I've got the same ruthless genes. Too bad Jilly and Rachel-Ann didn't inherit them—it could have made their lives easier."

"How could Rachel-Ann inherit your father's genes? I thought she was adopted."

Dean's smile was like the Cheshire cat's famous grin, smug and secretive. "So she is. Sometimes I forget. Dinner tonight, Coltrane. I promise you an entertaining time."

Dean knew, Coltrane thought, staring at him. Knew about Rachel-Ann, at least. The question was, did he realize Coltrane's connection?

"Looking forward to it," he said idly. "Do you know where Jilly went?"

Dean shrugged. "Could be anywhere. It's Saturday, and she doesn't have to work. If I know her she went to the ocean. That's what she does when she wants to think. Why do you care? She's not your type. I thought you were hot after Rachel-Ann.''

So he didn't know everything. ''I'm not hot after anyone, Dean,'' he said lazily. ''Just curious.''

''Sure you are, Coltrane. What are you going to do with your day off? Or does Jackson have plans for you?''

''I'm planning to do a little plumbing.''

Dean looked as if he'd said he was planning a mass murder. ''Plumbing?'' he echoed in tones of deepest horror.

''One of the many talents I've picked up over the years. I don't touch electricity, though—at least plumbing can't kill you. As long as I'm here it would be nice to have a working sink and shower.''

''I told you you could use mine. Doing your own plumbing seems a little extreme.'' He shuddered.

''It'll keep me busy for the day. You'd be surprised at some of my talents, Dean.''

''I imagine I would. I wonder what other surprises you have in store for us,'' he said softly.

It was there between them, solid distrust overlaid with a veneer of charm.

''You never can tell,'' Coltrane replied.

* * *

Jilly always loved this stretch of beach, almost as much as Roofus did. He was racing down the deserted sand, leaping in the air and chasing seagulls, in doggy ecstasy, and for a moment Jilly was able to smile. It was a chilly day at the ocean— the wind was whipping up the surf, and the few hardy surfers didn't look as if they were having that good a time.

She took off her shoes, anyway, walking barefoot in the wet sand, letting the icy foam wash over her toes. She was half tempted to throw off her clothes and jump into the water, letting the chilly Pacific Ocean scrub away everything….

She wasn't going to think about it! Denial had its uses, and today was one of those days. She'd walk for miles along the beach, watching Roofus leap and frolic, and she wouldn't think about a damned thing but what a clear, clean, beautiful day it was. She'd ignored the strange knotted feeling in the pit of her stomach, the weird ache between her breasts. Ignored the intrusive memories, sensations.

Hell and damnation. It wasn't even sex. It was heavy petting, and it was nothing but an accident. She'd had too much to drink, she'd been feeling feisty, and she should have known that someone like Coltrane would take advantage of her.

It was also an unpleasant fact of life that the

longer you did without sex the less you needed it. Until something started your motor again. She'd been jump-started but good last night, and she couldn't stop thinking about it. About him.

She didn't want to see him again. The very thought of being in a room with him made her cringe. It would be one thing if she could count on him to be gentlemanly and ignore what had happened between them. But if she'd learned one thing about Coltrane it was that he'd do the unexpected.

She didn't want to go home. There were places she could go—she could drive all the way up to Berkeley and visit with her old friend, Margie, and her husband, or she could head down to San Diego to see Christie. She wasn't trapped at La Casa with the man.

But she also knew perfectly well that she wasn't going to let him drive her out of her home. La Casa meant too much to her—she'd fought for it for too many years, worked for it, to cede it to the first interloper who used sex as a weapon.

Not that he wanted the house, she admitted fairly. She didn't really know *what* he wanted. It wasn't Rachel-Ann, as she'd first suspected, and it wasn't her, thank God. She was sure of that—last night had been nothing more than an accident, an aberration. She never was much of a poker player.

She should have been wise enough not to try to call his bluff.

Maybe Coltrane was just trying to worm his way into Meyer's family, to make himself indispensable.

But a smart man would know that Meyer didn't give a damn about most of his family. And Coltrane was definitely a very smart man.

So what did he want? And how the hell could she get rid of him? By giving him what he wanted, whatever that might be? Chances were, it wasn't in her power to give it.

She sat down in the damp sand, watching the waves, while Roofus came and collapsed beside her, his tongue lolling happily. Her choice was simple. Turn tail and run, or go back and brazen it out.

It was really no choice at all. She wouldn't abandon her house, her siblings, or her life to him. Most importantly, she wouldn't abandon her self-respect, and if she ran she'd never be able to look herself in the mirror again.

She'd survived Alan, dealt with him. Coltrane was a piker compared to Alan's self-centered game playing. Wasn't he?

Except the unhappy truth was that half sex with Coltrane was more arousing than the entire act with Alan.

The sun was moving slowly toward the horizon, and there was nothing Jilly wanted more than to stay there, watching until it turned into a bright-red ball and sank into the roiling Pacific. But the longer she put it off the harder it would be.

She rose to her feet, and Roofus immediately took that as a sign to play. "Come on, baby," she said, starting back along the pathway to the car. "Time to go home and see that man."

And Roofus, undiscerning creature that he was, barked with cheery enthusiasm, racing ahead of her.

15

"I wish I knew why I was edgy," Brenda said, reaching for Ted's omnipresent cigarette.

"Honeybunch, you're always on edge on Saturday nights and you know it. It's your Catholic blood. You want to be going to mass."

She glared at him. "Hardly. I stopped going to mass once I got involved with you, you wicked creature. One can't very well confess to the sin of adultery, accept penance, and then go right back home and do it all over again."

"I've told you, I'm the one who was married, not you. I'm the one who committed adultery," Ted said gently.

"The Catholic church doesn't see things that way," she drawled. "There's not much bargaining room when it comes to penance. If you intend to keep repeating your sin then it's a waste of time confessing."

"I'm sorry, darling."

She smiled at him. "Don't be. You aren't a

wicked seducer, darling, I am. And I don't regret a moment of it.''

Not even the moment of their death, she thought.

They were sitting on the sofa in the living room, her feet in his lap, and he was giving her the most divine foot massage through her silk stockings. She'd seen their girls pulling on panty hose, and while they certainly looked convenient, they were hardly as erotic. Nevertheless, it might have been nice to live long enough to try them.

She'd be an old woman by now, Brenda thought. A very, very old woman, wrinkled and ugly. She should count her blessings—Ted would never have to see her as an old hag. She'd stay throughout eternity as she'd been in her prime. Well, to be truthful, not quite in her prime. At seventeen she'd been perfect. At twenty-three almost as glorious. She'd been thirty-three when she died, and if she'd looked very closely in the mirror she could see her firm, gorgeous skin was beginning to lose some of its elasticity.

They speculated that was why she'd killed him, of course. She'd heard them talking about it, those wretched, smug, filthy creatures who'd taken over La Casa and destroyed its beauty decades ago. They said she was afraid of losing her looks, her career and her man, and so she'd killed him and herself. And they'd laughed at her, at the silly vain movie star with her shallow values, and she'd screamed at them, tried to hit them.

But, of course, they didn't even know she was there.

At least Ted hadn't heard them. He was down watching the Bad Man, for what little good it did him.

And they said the dead were frightening. The Bad Man was far more terrifying a creature than Brenda and Ted had ever been, despite Rachel-Ann's silly panic every time she spied them.

He'd been so young, so handsome, so charming, and the group of gypsylike young people who sprawled all over La Casa adored him. Brenda had seen that kind of charisma in the past. She was too young to remember Valentino, but she'd worked with others who'd had it in spades. If the Bad Man had decided to use his acting talent he could have reached the top.

There was no question that he could act. They watched him manipulate his followers, lie and be-witch and trick them, all without them guessing what lay behind his charming façade.

Of course they were doing all sorts of drugs, which could have accounted for their absurd gull-ibility. They treated the Bad Man like he was the voice of God.

But they hadn't known what he could do. Most

of those poor, credulous fools hadn't watched him, as Ted and Brenda had. They never questioned what happened to the young man who'd played guitar and sung like an angel and used a hypodermic needle to inject drugs into his arms. And no one knew about the red-haired girl who'd come back to meet the Bad Man down by the pool house. The woman he'd drowned in that pool, while her desperate hands scratched at his face and arms. The baby he'd been ready to throw in after her mother without even thinking.

It made no difference that after a long, horrifying moment he'd stepped back from the edge of the pool, the baby still in his arms. Brenda had hidden her face against Ted's chest, trembling in horror at their helplessness. The woman was already dead, floating facedown in the pool, and there had been nothing they could do but watch. The baby was safe, but for how long? Maybe he just had a different plan to dispose of it.

It was the last time they'd seen him, thank God. While the baby had screamed blue murder he'd taken the woman's body out of the pool and dumped it in the trunk of his car. She and Ted had stood there, frozen and helpless, until she'd finally pushed away from him. "I can't stand it," she said and circled the pool to kneel by the tiny bundle lying on the ground screaming.

She already knew that no one could see her, no one could hear her. But she reached out and touched the furious, red face of the infant, stroking it gently, and to her amazement the screams began to quiet to dull sobs.

"Poor little one," Brenda had crooned, feeling her heart break. She'd never had children—the studio had forbidden her to get pregnant during her two short-lived marriages—but looking at the poor little bundle of humanity made her want to take it in her arms and hold it tight against her body, soothing it.

But she couldn't. There was no body warmth to calm the child, no voice to hear, nothing she could do.

The sobs shuddered to a stop, and the baby looked up at her, focusing intently on eyes she couldn't see. "Poor baby," she'd whispered, stroking its face, down the tiny, flailing arm to the baby's dimpled hand.

And to Brenda's astonishment, the baby's fingers curled around hers, holding tight.

The man had pushed right through her when he came back, and the baby started to scream once more. Brenda had beaten on his back, yelling at him, but he hadn't noticed. She might have been a fly, batting at his head. He walked away, with the crying baby in his arms, and she'd tried to follow, but once the car left the grounds she was trapped, bound to this place. All she could do was weep in Ted's gentle arms.

The Bad Man had never returned to La Casa de Sombras, a small consolation. It wasn't until the old lady came and took over, years later, bringing the girls and the brother, that Brenda and Ted began to feel cheerful again.

If there was punishment for their sins, that had been a major one, and it still haunted her. Bad enough that they were trapped on earth for their crime. Far worse to have had to witness murder and be unable to do anything about it. And to be unable to stop him from taking the baby, when she wanted it. She would have been a good mother if she'd been given half a chance, and the child had looked up at her with such trust in its eyes.

"Why the sigh, honeybunch?" Ted asked, massaging her toes.

"Just remembering," she said honestly.

"Don't, love. It's a waste of time. We can't change things. Isn't that what you've always told me? What does it matter what happened, how or why? It happened, we're here, and we'll make the best of it. As long as I have you then I'm happy. You're what I need."

But he hadn't had that choice. For almost fifty years she'd been able to keep it from him, the truth about their deaths. If he knew what had really happened, if he knew the truth, would he be happy? If he could leave, would he, abandoning her?

She didn't want to think about it. She glanced around the living room. In the fading sunlight it almost looked like the glory days when she and Ted had entertained the beautiful and the powerful. The Holland covers had been removed, and in the shadowy light the rips in the upholstery weren't as apparent. The two low-slung sofas faced each other across a large, glass-topped coffee table that had been a more recent acquisition, though Brenda approved of it, and she recognized the tall, tarnished silver candelabra. She'd stolen one of them from the set of her last movie, *The Runaway Heiress,* and Ted, her director, had stolen the other. She'd always loved those candelabra—it was sheer luck they'd been hidden away during what she tended to call The Occupation. They probably wouldn't have survived the gypsy hordes—they would have been smashed or sold for drugs.

But they remained, and while no one had bothered to light them yet, their presence was a gentle reminder of the past.

"What do you suppose that boy has in mind? I've never trusted him," Ted said.

"You're just being homophobic. He's harmless.

He spends all his time at that ridiculous computer. Besides, I do think he's rather fond of his sisters.''

"The dog doesn't like him. Neither do I."

"Hush," Brenda said, as a tall figure appeared in the doorway, silhouetted by the fading light.

"Don't be silly, honeybunch. He can't see us or hear us."

It was the man from the sofa. The good-looking one, Coltrane. Brenda wiggled her toes appreciatively as he approached their sofa. "Just as well. Do you suppose he'd be embarrassed if he knew we watched him last night?"

Ted looked at him. "Doubt it. He's a cool customer. And it looks like he's going to sit down on us."

"Come on." Brenda jumped up, pulling Ted with her, just as Coltrane threw himself on the sofa. He glanced around him, an abstracted expression on his face. And then a slow, wicked grin crossed his face.

"Not as cool a customer as you think," Brenda said, sliding on top of the piano, her negligee swinging around her long legs. "He likes her."

"He has good taste," Ted said. "But I don't think he's good enough for one of our girls."

"He's a step above their usual," she murmured. "Look at Jilly's husband. A major creep."

Coltrane leaned forward and lit the candles, filling the room with a soft, romantic light. He was quite attractive in the candlelight, though Brenda decided not to point that out to Ted. A little jealousy had its uses, but tonight she wasn't in the mood for games. Ted was right, she was letting the past get to her. As well as the future, when, sooner or later, he was going to find out what really happened. Whether she told him or not.

"Sun's going down, honeybunch," Ted said, taking her hand. She slid off the piano, into his arms. "And I want to be alone with you."

"Sweetheart, you're always alone with me," she said with a laugh.

"Humor me. Let's go up to the rooftops and dance in the moonlight."

"There's no music."

"I'll sing to you."

"You're tone deaf," she said fondly. "I'll sing. You just lead."

Then Brenda caught sight of Jilly and Roofus standing in the arched entryway to the living room. She hesitated for a moment. "Are you sure you don't want to watch?"

"We've seen enough, honeybunch. Allow them some privacy. Besides, I'm willing to bet you he's not going to be able to get within touching distance for days."

"Wrong," she said. "They'll be in bed by midnight. Dawn at the latest."

"Are you crazy? You saw her reaction after last night," Ted argued.

"I know my sex."

"That you do," Ted murmured.

She gave him a mock glare. "I mean I know my gender. She won't be able to resist him. If it's before midnight we might even be able to watch."

"Behave yourself, darling!" Ted said.

"Don't be a prude—we've been watching people have sex here for almost fifty years. It might be nice to see people do it with love for a change."

"You think the two of them are in love? Precious, you are naive!" Ted murmured.

"No, darling, I'm right. Call it my woman's intuition."

"They hate each other."

"That's always a sure sign."

"You did too many screwball comedies, honeybunch. When people hate each other it usually means they hate each other."

"You'll see," she said with a smug smile. "Let's go dancing."

And he lifted her hand to his mouth and kissed it.

16

The living room was a cavernous expanse of light and shadows, but Jilly could still make out Coltrane sprawled on the sofa, exactly where she'd left him the night before.

At least this time he was fully dressed, but the candlelight was even dimmer than the lightbulb that had illuminated the scene last night.

She would have backed up, disappeared, but even from such a distance he saw her, and she was torn between pride and panic. Roofus had no such qualms. He bounded across the room, his paws skittering on the parquet floor until he came to a sliding stop against the sofa, greeting Coltrane like a starving man at a banquet.

"Jilly!" Dean came up beside her, immaculately dressed in a white linen suit. He looked at her and sniffed. "You're dressing for dinner, of course." It was a statement, not a question.

"I'm not going to be here for dinner," she lied instinctively. "I have other plans."

"You can't!" Dean said in the distressed voice

she could never say no to. "I've gone to such pains to arrange this all. If you hadn't taken off at the crack of dawn I would have given you more notice. You weren't answering your cell phone, either. Really, Jilly, it's most inconsiderate of you not to think about the rest of us. I needed to get in touch with you! What if there'd been an emergency?"

Jilly softened. "I didn't mean to worry you."

"I wasn't worried. I know you're perfectly able to take care of yourself. But I went to a lot of trouble for this little dinner and I'm counting on you to do your part."

She glanced across the room toward Coltrane, but he was busy scratching Roofus's head, seemingly oblivious to their conversation. She wasn't fooled. Doubtless he was absorbing every word, the snake.

"What dinner party?" she asked warily.

"Just family. And Coltrane, of course, since he's part of our happy household right now. Very low-key and relaxed. I've had Emilio's cater it, to make things easier."

"Fine," she said shortly.

"I charged it to you, of course, since it's your month for household expenses."

It had been her month for taking care of the household expenses since 1998. "Fine," she said again, too weary to argue. "Let's get it over with."

She started into the living room, but Dean caught her arm.

"Aren't you going to change into something a little more…festive? You look like something out of LL Bean. Surely you have some standards."

Jilly glanced down at her faded jeans, bare feet and baggy sweatshirt and shrugged. Her hair hung in one long, thick braid down her back, her face was burnished by the late autumn sun and the wind off the ocean, and she didn't give a damn. She wasn't about to dress up for Coltrane's admiration.

"If this dinner is so laid-back then it shouldn't matter what I'm wearing," she said, moving past him into the living room before she could change her mind. With anyone else she might have worried that Dean was matchmaking, but in the case of her brother she knew that to be outside the realm of possibility. Dean was too focused on his own needs to even notice what his sister was doing, much less interfere in it. He'd have no idea she was the slightest bit attracted to Coltrane.

The two sofas faced each other across an elegantly set coffee table, and the candlelight flickered seductively. Jilly headed toward the opposite sofa when Dean interfered, pushing her toward Coltrane. "You sit there, Jilly, and Rachel-Ann can sit with me."

"I don't want—"

"Don't be a pest, Jilly," Dean snapped. "Coltrane doesn't have cooties. For God's sake sit down and stop making a fuss out of nothing."

At least Coltrane was ignoring her, concentrating on the perfect spot behind Roofus's ears. For one brief moment Jilly considered outright rebellion, then chickened out. If she made a fuss he'd assume last night mattered more than it did. It was nothing, an embarrassing little…experience…that was best ignored and quickly forgotten. If she tried hard enough.

"Fine," she muttered, sitting down beside Coltrane on the sofa. Roofus turned and shoved his big head under Jilly's hand, looking for her approval, as well. "Traitor," she said under her breath.

She wasn't going to look at Coltrane. He'd probably smirk at her, and if he did she'd take the candelabrum and bash him over the head with it, then upend the glass coffee table….

Pleasantly violent thoughts, but she wasn't going to act on them, and she knew it. She was cool, impervious, she reminded herself. And the longer she put off looking at Coltrane the harder it was going to be.

"What can I get you, Jilly? Brandy?" Dean asked helpfully.

"No!" She couldn't help her reaction. It was

brandy that had gotten her into that mess last night. "Just iced tea, thanks."

Too late she realized that Dean would have to leave to get it for her. Leave her alone with Coltrane. She opened her mouth to speak but Dean had already vanished, abandoning her to her fate.

"You shouldn't blame the brandy," Coltrane said.

Steeling herself, she turned to look at him. At least he wasn't smirking at her. "For what?" she said in a cool voice.

"Haven't you figured out yet that it's a bad idea to call my bluff, Jilly?" he said softly. "I'm not bluffing. It wasn't the brandy last night."

She leaned back against the far end of the sofa, pulling her feet up between them. "Do we really need a postmortem?" she said in an utterly convincing drawl.

Except that he didn't appear convinced. "No," he said. "We just have to finish what we started."

Lucky for him that Rachel-Ann appeared at that moment, or the candelabrum would have been destroyed. "Aren't you two cozy-looking?" Rachel-Ann said, curling up on the sofa opposite them. She'd dressed for dinner in a simple black sheath, and she looked livelier than Jilly had seen her in months. A momentary dread formed in the pit of her stomach, as she surveyed her sister anxiously.

But there was no telltale glitter in her green eyes, no imperceptible slackness to her mouth. Jilly had gotten so that she could tell if her sister had even touched a wineglass, and despite the fact that her sister looked unexpectedly cheerful, she also looked completely sober.

"You look gorgeous," Jilly said.

"Thanks, darling. I wish I could say the same thing about you. You look like something the cat dragged in. Did you spend the day at the ocean?"

"How'd you guess?"

"Isn't that where you always run when you get upset? I run to a bottle, you run to the ocean. Your answer is probably healthier."

Oh, God, don't go there, Jilly thought miserably.

"What upset you, Jilly?" Coltrane asked in a dulcet tone.

"I discovered there are rats at La Casa," she replied grimly. "I'm going to have to call in an exterminator."

He laughed, unmoved. "I think you're more than capable of getting rid of any unwanted rodents. If you really wanted to."

"I don't like rats," Jilly said.

"No one does, Jilly," Rachel-Ann protested. "Let's not talk about vermin—it's not very appetizing. Tell me, where do you run to, Coltrane? You must run somewhere when you're upset."

"I don't get upset," he said simply.

"And I don't believe you," Rachel-Ann returned. "Where do you go when things get too much for you? Drugs, alcohol, sex? Come on, don't be shy! Dean's arranged this little party so we can get to know each other better. After all, we're living in each others' back pockets—we might as well know what we're up against. What's your drug of choice, Coltrane?"

"Revenge." The reply was short, simple and faintly chilling.

Even Rachel-Ann looked taken aback. "Now how healthy is that, I ask you? And who are you wanting revenge on?"

"Anyone who's wronged me and mine."

"Me and mine?" Rachel-Ann echoed. "How wonderfully feudal. What fair damsel are you defending? Whose honor was besmirched?" She was mocking him, and Jilly wanted to stop her. There was an odd tension in the room, one that Rachel-Ann was ignoring, but even Roofus was whining slightly, upset at the undercurrents.

"My mother," Coltrane said softly.

Rachel-Ann's eyes widened, and she was momentarily silenced. Long enough for Jilly to jump into the breach, willing to do anything to change the subject. "What did you do today, Rachel-Ann? You were out late last night."

Wrong distraction, Jilly thought the moment the words were out of her mouth. It would sound as if she were cross-examining her sister, and that was the last thing she wanted. It didn't matter if she knew where Rachel-Ann was or not. She couldn't stop her from doing what she wanted to do, and knowing only made it worse.

A brief, almost girlish smile crossed her sister's face, and then vanished, as if she were ashamed of it. "Sorry if you were worried. I spent the night with…an old friend."

"I didn't think you had any old friends, darling," Dean said, setting a tray of drinks on the table. "I thought they either dropped you cold or succumbed to ODs."

"Don't be a pest, Dean," Rachel-Ann said lightly. "I'm in a good mood for a change—don't mess with it. By the way, does anyone know what happened to Consuelo and Jaime?"

"Grandmère's cook and chauffeur?" Dean said. "I remember Jackson fired them without any warning when we were staying here. I think Jaime died of a heart attack a few years ago, but Consuelo retired and is living in the Valley. I forget—did they have children?"

"A son," Jilly said. She watched with fascination as a faint stain of color tinged her sister's pale cheeks. "I don't know what happened to him—I think his name was Richard."

Rachel-Ann shrugged in a fine show of disinterest. "It doesn't matter. I was just thinking about Consuelo. She made the best *huevos rancheros* in the world."

"The very thought of eggs and chili in the morning makes me want to hurl," Dean said.

"Actually it's not as bad as you might think," Rachel-Ann murmured.

"Am I to presume you had *huevos rancheros* for breakfast after your night of debauchery?" Dean said with his usual lack of tact.

"I'm afraid my night was totally free of debauchery," she replied with surprising dignity. "Hate to disappoint you, brother dear."

"No disappointment, love," Dean said softly. For all his petty malice Jilly had no doubt that he truly loved both his sisters, almost as much as he loved himself.

And this little get-together would be just lovely if it weren't for the interloper sitting at the other end of the sofa, watching them as a scientist would watch mating cockroaches.

There was a definite limit to how long she was going to manage to sit here being sociable, Jilly thought. She'd told herself she wouldn't run, wouldn't let Coltrane drive her from her home and family, but that was when she'd been fool enough to think she had some defenses left. All it had taken was a few moments in his presence and she realized just how vulnerable she was.

"When's dinner?" she asked abruptly.

Dean frowned at her. "Were you thinking you might change out of that nouveau hobo apparel into something a little more flattering?"

"No, I was thinking I had things to do."

"They can wait," Dean said, taking a sip of his wine. "Aren't you interested in what the rest of us did to spend the day? Isn't that how a happy household unwinds over cocktails? Discussing the day's events?"

"We aren't a happy household and Rachel-Ann and I aren't drinking cocktails," Jilly pointed out.

"Details!" Dean dismissed them. "You'll never guess what Coltrane did."

"I don't really give a damn," Jilly said, no longer caring if she sounded rude. She had to get out of there, away from that assessing look in Coltrane's green eyes.

"Of course you do, darling. Since he spent the day messing with your beloved La Casa. Our father's chief of legal affairs has unexpected talents."

Coltrane wasn't saying a word, watching them all with distant tolerance.

"All right, what did he spend the day doing?" Jilly asked wearily, tired of the game playing.

"He can plumb."

"Plumb? Plumb what?"

"Pipes, darling. Faucets and drains and all those nasty things. He's an absolute marvel. He can even sweat."

She jerked her head to look at Coltrane. He was lounging against the armrest of the sofa, not saying a word. "I imagine he can. I'm supposed to be impressed?" Jilly said.

"Sweat pipes, dear. It's a rare talent."

"It's my blue-collar roots showing through," Coltrane murmured. "Not all of us are California bluebloods."

"California bluebloods?" Dean echoed. "What a concept. I wonder if there really is such a thing. We're definitely children of privilege, I won't deny that. Not that having Jackson as a father has been that much of a treat. I might honestly have preferred living in the Valley with an insurance salesman for a father and Donna Reed for a mother."

"It wouldn't have done any good, Dean," Rachel-Ann said. "You still wouldn't have ended up as Beaver Cleaver."

"True. What was it Sophie Tucker said? 'I've been rich and I've been poor and rich is better'? Too bad the money seems to have run out." Dean leaned forward and poured himself another glass of wine. There was no sign of food on the elegantly set table, and Jilly realized that on top of being tired, irritable and uneasy, she was absolutely famished. She hadn't felt like eating this morning when she took off, and she'd fed most of her fast-food lunch to a grateful Roofus. Not that this current get-together was giving her much of an appetite, but she needed to eat or she was going to pass out.

"As for me, I spent the day on the computer."

"So what else is new?" Jilly muttered.

"Ah, but it's been an especially informative few days. I know you think I spend all my time on the internet cruising gay chat rooms, but you'd be quite surprised at the things that can turn up if you know where to look," he said with innocence.

The sudden tension from the far end of the couch was palpable. "What sort of things?" Coltrane asked, his voice deceptively easy.

Dean waggled his finger at him. "All in good time, Coltrane. All will be revealed. Have patience, counselor."

"When are we going to eat?" Jilly demanded. "I'm finding your little games extremely tiresome."

Dean pouted at her. "Don't be harsh, darling. I so seldom get to enjoy myself. So do we have everyone accounted for? I spent the day on the computer, making great discoveries, Jilly wandered on the beach, probably brooding over some lost love. You do have lost loves, don't you, darling? Coltrane occupied himself with the plumbing, and Rachel-Ann... What did you do, my pet? Lie in bed and watch The Weather Channel?''

"I spent the afternoon down at the pool house."

Jilly shuddered. "In heaven's name why?"

An endearingly wicked little smile curved Rachel-Ann's lips. She looked younger than she had in years, clear-eyed and resilient. "The pool house isn't the same thing as the pool, Jilly. I used to have a lot of fun in that pool house."

"Meeting your blue-collar lovers," Dean said maliciously. "Coltrane here has proclaimed his blue-collar roots—why don't you take him down there and demonstrate how you spent your adolescence? If you tire of him maybe he could figure out what's wrong with that skanky swimming pool. Can you imagine a house in Southern California without a working swimming pool?''

"Would you use it if it worked?" Rachel-Ann responded, unmoved by his spite.

"It's entirely possible. Every now and then I'm interested in being healthy. And a nice tan is always an asset." He turned to Coltrane, who'd been listening with an unreadable expression on his face. "What do you think, Coltrane. Want my sister?" His eyes were glittering with amusement. "For that matter, which one would you like? You can't have both. Alan Dunbar tried that and it backfired. Not that Daddy hasn't been paying him off nicely ever since, and Jilly and Rachel-Ann are still close, but I wouldn't recommend it if I were you. Pick one and stick to her."

"You're drunk, Dean," Coltrane said.

"Not drunk, dear boy. Just celebrating. I'm getting ready to declare my independence, and it's a heady feeling. I haven't had much of a sense of power in my life, and it does tend to go to my head."

"I've had enough of this," Jilly said, rising. "If you're not going to serve dinner then I'll go out and get something. I'm not in the mood for this—"

"Sit down!" Dean thundered.

"Fuck you," Jilly snapped, as Roofus lumbered to his feet with a yip of annoyance.

"Make her stay, Coltrane," Dean begged in a petulant voice. "I've got it all planned."

"I can't make your sister do anything," Coltrane murmured. "You'll have to ask her."

Jilly was already halfway to the door when Dean's voice reached her. "Jilly, please."

Never in her entire life had she been able to say no to him when he used that sweetly plaintive voice, and he knew it. It didn't help that she knew she was being manipulated.

She tried to hold her ground. "Why, Dean? What's going on? What kind of game are you playing?"

"We're waiting for our final guest," Dean said.

"And who's that?" It couldn't be any worse than Coltrane, watching her out of those mysterious green eyes. It was a crime that such a dangerous man could be quite so tempting. But then, maybe that was exactly why he was dangerous.

"Who do you think it is, Jilly?" came a voice from behind her. "Your loving father."

As Jilly turned to look into Jackson Dean Meyer's brown eyes, she realized with a sinking feeling that things could get a great deal worse, after all.

Brenda de Lorillard pulled herself free from Ted's easy embrace, the song fading from her lips. She'd been singing "Night and Day" in her husky alto while they danced on the balcony. She'd always contended that was the most erotic song ever written, and Ted, bless his heart, agreed with her.

But right then eroticism was the farthest thing from her mind. She looked up at Ted with panic in her eyes.

"What's wrong, honeybunch?" he asked gently.

"He's here," she whispered.

"Who is?"

"The Bad Man. He's back. And he's going to hurt the girls."

17

For a moment Jilly was frozen. She could hear Roofus growling, low in his throat, and even Coltrane's restraining hand wasn't having a calming effect. "I thought you were in Mexico," she said, looking her father in the eye. She was taller than he was, a fact that made him acutely uncomfortable. One of the many reasons he'd never liked her, she supposed, though his lack of interest stemmed from when she was very little.

"What gave you that idea?"

"Coltrane."

"Coltrane lies for me at times."

"Fancy that," she said lightly.

He tilted his head to look at her, and she looked back, surveying him as offhandedly as she could manage. His tan, his hair, his suit were all perfect. If anything he looked younger than when she'd last seen him, in his late forties rather than the midsixties she knew him to be. "How long has it been, Jillian?" he said jovially, a perfect impersonation of an indulgent father. "A year?"

"Two and a half," she said, wishing to God it had been twice as long. It wasn't right to hate your own father, even if he'd never evinced the slightest interest in you. But she hated him, quite intensely. Not so much for what he hadn't given her, but for what he'd done to Rachel-Ann and Dean and their mother.

She couldn't remember if she'd ever loved him, ever trusted him, even when she was a young child. Her mother had loved her three children with unstinting love, but Jackson had only loved Rachel-Ann, and his two birth children had been of absolutely no importance. Neither had his wife, and as far as Jilly could remember he'd barely noticed when Edith had left him. Until she'd tried to take his children.

He'd even offered her a deal, Edith had said. She could have Dean and Jilly and he'd take Rachel-Ann. She'd said no, of course. They were all her children. But she'd failed to take into account how ruthless and determined Jackson could be. He'd taken her children and her only hope of happiness. And before she could get the courts to intervene a car accident had taken her life, leaving the three of them in Grandmère's hands.

Jackson Dean Meyer hadn't even bothered to accompany his children to Edith's funeral. That was when the hatred had begun, Jilly thought. And the last eighteen years had only solidified it.

"Still the revolting hippie look I see," Jackson said benevolently, reaching for her braid. "When are you going to cut your hair? And those clothes!" He sighed. "I would have thought you'd have inherited some clothes sense from your mother and me. If I can say one good thing about your mother, she knew how to dress. You seem to have missed out on that ability entirely."

"Daddy..." Rachel-Ann's troubled voice reached them, but he waved a silencing hand without looking at her. He hadn't finished his carefully orchestrated attempt at demoralizing Jilly. He used to be able to do it so well. He must have forgotten that she'd grown impervious, once she found she no longer cared.

"Why are you here?" she asked in an even voice. "It's not Christmas or anyone's birthday, though you usually don't pay attention to those, anyway. What blessed convergence of the stars do we have to thank for your appearance here tonight?"

"Your brother invited me." He smiled his affable smile at Dean, who raised his wineglass in salute. Jackson Meyer's smile had always been one of his most effective weapons. It reached his eyes, lit his whole face and convinced the recipient that this charming, wonderful man was totally enchanted with them. Until he slipped the knife between their ribs.

"I'm sure it's not the first time he's invited you. Dean hasn't given up on you yet," Jilly said.

"Ah, but you have, is that right, Jillian? Fortunately I have two other children to fall back on, since you in your infinite wisdom have decided my sins are unforgivable. It must be nice to be so sure of yourself, that you can sit in judgment on others."

"You're losing your touch, Jackson," Jilly said, unruffled. "You tried that tack two Christmases ago. It didn't work then and it won't work now."

Only the faint tightening in his handsome jawline betrayed his reaction. He smiled benevolently in her direction, but the smile faded slightly from his eyes. "Well, then, I'm sure we can excuse you for the rest of the evening, since you find my presence unacceptable. Dean and Rachel-Ann are glad to see me, and I know I can count on Coltrane."

"I know you can," she said sweetly.

"And take that hellhound with you," he added, another trace of his affability vanishing. "He sheds."

"Oh, I wouldn't think of going anywhere," Jilly said smoothly. "If you've finally decided to set foot in La Casa for the first time in my memory then the least I can do, as one of the owners, is to make you welcome. Are you here for dinner or are you just the appetizer?''

Jackson looked at her sorrowfully. "I must have hurt you very badly, dear girl. I'm so sorry."

Zing! She didn't betray the sting of fury. "I forgive you," she said sweetly, sweeping around him and heading back to the table. Roofus was still eyeing Jackson and growling low in his throat, but Coltrane's long fingers soothed him, and he settled back on the floor with a reluctant sigh as Jilly sat back down on the sofa.

Jackson took his time finding a comfortable chair and dragging it over to the table. He paused to give Rachel-Ann a kiss on her proffered cheek, then nodded at the two men in a manly, convivial gesture. He put the chair at the head, of course. He sat down, then beamed at the four of them with patriarchal majesty. "Isn't this nice?" he murmured.

"Lovely," Jilly muttered. Waiting.

"You can leave any time now." A note of annoyance was creeping into Jackson's voice, and Jilly made a mental hash mark. He wasn't the only one who could score points.

"I wouldn't think of it," she said in a sultry voice. "You're up to something, and nothing on this earth would make me miss it."

"I wouldn't count on the ghosts interfering, either, though they may qualify as on this earth," Dean said prosaically. "Anyway, I want you here. Our esteemed father has an offer to make, and it should be heard by all three of us."

"Then what's Coltrane doing here?" She'd glanced at him, just once, before tearing her eyes away from him. He sat in the shadows, watching, almost a ghost himself.

"As my chief legal counsel I felt he should be here," Jackson said smoothly. "Besides, the man's living here. It would hardly be polite not to include him. Where's your hospitality, Jillian? I would have thought your grandmother would have taught you better than that."

Jilly curled her feet up on the sofa, a small enough barrier between her and Coltrane. "I think this house has had too many guests and not enough family."

"Shut up, Jilly," Dean said. "I get tired of the two of you baiting each other. Father's here for a reason, and we owe it to him to listen."

Normally Jilly would have argued. Dean was always trying to win Jackson's approval, and he never would. At first she thought he was ready to crawl once more, until she recognized the odd glitter in his eyes. If it had been Rachel-Ann Jilly would have said she was on drugs. Dean didn't do any drugs but vodka, and the look in his eye was slyly triumphant. She found that even more troubling.

"Thank you, son," Jackson said. It was probably only the second or third time Jackson had ever called him son, and Jilly could see Dean's reaction, even as he fought it. Jackson leaned back, pulling a silver-chased cigar tube out of his pocket, making them all wait while he went through the ritual of lighting it. Coltrane shifted, letting his hand rest on the sofa. Between them. Near her feet.

After a long, faintly theatrical puff, Jackson leaned back in his chair, putting on his most paternal expression as he rested his hands across his flat belly. "You know I have a great interest in La Casa. I always have had."

"I know you've never set foot in it in more than twenty years, and that Grandmère left it to us rather than to you," Jilly said sharply.

"In trust. And it was for tax purposes," Jackson returned. "I know you don't like to think about the practical aspects of life. You're so busy with your lost causes, running around town trying to save buildings that are past their prime. And you consistently fail, don't you, Jillian? Because no one but you gives a damn."

"True," she said calmly.

"It's common practice to skip generations when

it comes to inheritance. Coltrane will be happy to fill you in on the legal ramifications at another time if you're fascinated, which I doubt. It seems unlikely you'll have any kind of estate to leave any children or grandchildren you might eventually produce if you continue devoting your life to lost causes.''

"I'll pass. I really don't care. And Grandmère didn't want you to have La Casa. She knew you'd have it bulldozed and turned into high-rises.''

"Then why did she leave it in trust? As long as you want to live here it's yours. But as soon as you leave, or it's inhabitable, it reverts to me.''

"That was explained to us when we inherited the place,'' Jilly said. "Tell us something we don't know.''

"This place is unsafe. It's a firetrap, and the next earthquake we get will probably have it collapse around you. I don't want to lose my children in a tragic accident,'' he said in such a concerned voice that any fool would have believed him. But Jilly had stopped being a fool long ago, at least where her father was concerned.

"We'll be fine,'' she said briskly. "Thank you for your concern, but we're staying put.''

"It was left to the three of you, Jillian. Aren't you interested in what your siblings have to say? I'm offering a substantial amount of money for each of you. Enough for you to buy all sorts of historic garbage heaps and restore them, enough for Dean to get the kind of place he wants.''

''And what about Rachel-Ann?'' Dean questioned in a silky voice.

Jackson leaned over and put his perfectly manicured hand on Rachel-Ann's slender knee, squeezing it. ''I was rather hoping she'd move in with me.''

The silence in the room was palpable. Jilly's recoil was instinctive, but she wondered if she was overreacting to a perfectly normal suggestion.

Not if she were to go by the expressions on everyone else's faces. It was as though Jackson had dropped a bomb in the middle of the room and everyone was politely pretending it hadn't happened, even as it was about to detonate.

Coltrane's face was frightening in its stillness, his eyes were like ice, and his hand had tightened into a fist. He said nothing, though, and the others couldn't see his terrifyingly quiet reaction. Only Jilly could, and she wondered what caused it. What she was missing.

There was no mistaking Rachel-Ann's blank expression. She didn't move, and Jackson's hand remained on her knee, softly kneading.

Dean was the first to speak, clearing his voice with a sound that was shocking after the deep silence. "Wouldn't Melba have something to say about that, Father?" he asked softly.

"Melba and I have agreed to an amicable separation. We signed a prenuptial agreement, of course, so it should all be relatively straightforward, and she had no grounds or interest in contesting it. I haven't given her any."

Jilly couldn't pull her eyes away from his hand, squeezing her sister's knee, a slow, hypnotic caress. "And...?" Dean prompted, his voice faintly hollow, the triumphant glitter still in his eyes.

"I've bought a place in the Hills. I'll need a hostess, and Rachel-Ann needs something to do. I'm sure she won't mind looking after her old man. Will you, baby?" Knead, squeeze, knead, squeeze. His fingers caressed her knee.

"Yes, Daddy," she said in a soft, little girl voice. "I mean, no, Daddy. I won't mind."

She was trembling. It took Jilly a moment to realize that her sister was practically vibrating in distress. She called him Daddy. Odd, none of the others ever had. Dean called him Father, or Jackson, and Jilly tried to call him nothing at all.

"Oh, I don't think so," Coltrane said, his voice cool, emotionless. "I think—" Before he could finish his sentence the candelabrum went flying, sailing across the room like it had been thrown by an unseen hand. The other candelabrum toppled from the piano, the coffee table shook, knocking the glasses to the floor as the rest of the lights went off and the house was plunged into darkness.

Rachel-Ann screamed in utter terror, and Jilly leapt forward, trying to reach her, only to collide with Coltrane in the dark. Tripped by Roofus's sudden leap, the two of them went down, directly into the middle of the glass coffee table in a tangle of limbs. A second later it broke beneath them. Coltrane was on top of her, heavy, overpowering, and they tumbled to the floor so that she lay underneath him, shattered glass beneath her back, digging into her skin. She could hear Roofus barking, Dean and Jackson were shouting, and she closed her eyes in the smothering darkness, feeling faint....

And then Rachel-Ann's voice came to her, clear and oddly close, as if she were whispering in her ear. "Yes," she said. "I will."

"Where are the goddamned lights?" Jackson shouted in fury. She could hear him crash into the furniture, all the while Roofus was barking wildly, unsure whether to protect her or to attack. There was no sound from Dean, who must have gone to find out what was wrong with the electricity, and Rachel-Ann had vanished. Escaped while she still could, Jilly was sure of it, even though there was no way she could have known for certain.

Jilly felt detached, almost floating, as she lay still in the darkness. She could feel the rubble beneath her—smashed glass and broken coffee table, digging into her back. And Coltrane on top of her. In the dark he seemed huge, almost smotheringly powerful, and she knew she should be fighting to get him off her. But for a moment she didn't move, absorbing the feel of him, the astonishingly safe weight of him in the darkness.

The lights came on in the hallway, and Jackson greeted it with a burst of profanity. "Where are the goddamn lights in this room?"

"Aren't any." Dean's voice came from over by the doorway, and the beam of flashlight washed over the room, stopping on Coltrane and Jilly. "My, my, don't you two look cozy? Should we leave you alone to enjoy yourselves?"

"Don't move," Coltrane breathed in her ear, ignoring Dean. Jilly said nothing, still in that strangely altered state.

"Where the fuck is Rachel-Ann?" Jackson demanded.

"Didn't see her," Dean replied, seemingly undisturbed. "Though I thought I heard a car drive away when I was looking for the fuse box."

"Fuse box? I told you this place was a firetrap. And Rachel-Ann couldn't have left—I boxed her in." Even from her strange sense of distance Jilly could hear the smug satisfaction in her father's voice.

"That doesn't mean she couldn't have taken another car," Dean said reasonably. "Looks like she got away, after all."

"Shit! You've got to help me find her. Bring that flashlight!" There was no missing the rage in Jackson's voice.

"But what about Jilly?"

"Coltrane will see to her."

"Assholes," Coltrane muttered beneath his breath when they were alone. "Are you okay?"

Still that odd, floating feeling. "I don't know," she said.

"There's broken glass all around us. I don't want to make things worse by moving too quickly. Are you bleeding?"

"I don't know," she said again, almost dreamily.

"Shit. Don't pass out on me!" He sounded oddly panicked. She couldn't imagine why. The darkness was soft, warm, and those annoying noises had gone. She wasn't particularly comfortable, but if she concentrated on the weight of his body on top of hers rather than what lay beneath her, she was happy enough.

He moved, his weight lifting off her as he put his hands down on either side of her, and a moment later he'd pushed himself back, a muttered curse escaping as he straightened up.

"Stay put," he said. "I'm going to find some lights."

"I wasn't planning on moving," she said in a wry, dreamy voice. It wasn't as nice without him covering her, though she was having an easier time breathing. And she definitely didn't like it when he left her alone in the room, in the darkness.

Reality was beginning to rear its ugly head. Her back was stinging, and she thought she could feel the warm wetness of blood beneath her. Rachel-Ann had disappeared, all hell had broken loose, and she was lying on a bed of glass....

She started to shift, but Coltrane was already back. "I told you not to move." He sounded harsh. A moment later a small pool of light illuminated the scene. The same damned bare-bulbed lamp that had lit the previous night's little scene. Embarrassing as that had been in retrospect, she still preferred it to tonight's absurd disaster.

"I'm going to pull you straight up," he said, looming over her like a huge, dark shadow. "Don't wiggle, don't squirm, just let me pull you."

"And if I've hurt my back?" She managed to find some of her usual tartness.

"Then you'll be paralyzed for life and you'll

stop annoying me,'' he said. He leaned down and reached for her hands. "One, two, three."

She was up, soaring, his unexpected force propelling her against him with such strength that the two of them fell back against the sofa, her on top this time.

"We've got to stop meeting like this," Coltrane muttered.

This time she didn't hesitate, putting her hands on his chest and pushing herself upward, away from him, only to shriek with surprise at the pain in her back.

"Shit," Coltrane said again. "Look at your back."

"An anatomical impossibility, slightly different from the one I was going to suggest to you."

There was a moment of stunned silence. And then he laughed, a great, whooshing sound of relief and something else. "You are amazing, Jilly Meyer," he said finally. "I'm taking you to the emergency room to get that back looked at. We can discuss anatomical impossibilities on the way over. You'd be quite surprised at what I can manage."

"I'm fine. I don't need to go anywhere with you."

"Don't argue with me," he growled, taking her hand. "I'm not in the mood for it." As they moved into the hall she could see he had something wrapped around his left hand, stained with blood. Blood on his khakis, as well. ''You're hurt,'' she said, pulling to a stop, trying to ignore the pain in her back.

''We're both hurt, sugar. And Dean and your father are out chasing ghosts, Rachel-Ann's disappeared, and it's up to us to get our butts to the emergency room. So stop arguing and come on. And try not to pass out. I could carry you, but I'm not in the mood if it's not going to lead to something more entertaining than a hospital.''

''No, you couldn't.''

''Couldn't what?''

''Carry me. I'm five eleven in my bare feet…oh shit.'' She looked down. Sure enough, she was leaving bloody footprints on the floor.

He sighed. ''Where are your goddamned shoes?''

''I don't remember. Where's my goddamned dog?'' She suddenly wanted to cry.

''I put him out in the back. I figured you didn't need him licking your face while you were lying there in pain.''

''I like having him lick my face.''

''You'll have to make do with me. Can you walk?''

''Of course I can,'' she said, pulling her dignity

around her. And she could even, with great effort, do it without a limp.

"Son of a bitch," he muttered, obviously not convinced. A moment later he'd swooped her over his shoulder in a fireman's carry, and they were out in the evening air.

18

Discovering his car missing didn't improve Coltrane's thoroughly foul mood. It was only a slight relief when he realized that Meyer's Mercedes G-Wagen blocked Rachel-Ann's BMW. She must have taken his car in a desperate bid to escape. He'd have to assume she'd be all right—at the moment he had more pressing matters, like the woman he was carrying and the fact that his left hand was bleeding like crazy.

"We're going to have to take your car," he said to Jilly, still slung over his shoulder. She was right, she was no lightweight, and apart from Rachel-Ann's escape, this night was going from bad to worse.

"My feet are cut," she said from halfway down his back. "I can't drive."

He strode into the garage, opened the passenger door of her Corvette and dumped her in. "You're not going to."

He ignored her protests, moving around to the driver's side. His left hand was hurting like hell, but it looked as if the bleeding had slowed. He'd managed to slice the hell out of it when he'd pushed off her, and he'd never been particularly fond of blood. He didn't have the choice of getting light-headed, not with Jilly's lacerated back and bleeding feet.

"I told you, you aren't driving my car," she said weakly as he got in beside her. "What's wrong with your car?"

"Your sister stole it, and a good thing she did. Let's just hope your father can't catch up with her. Stop arguing and tell me where the keys are."

"What if I told you they were back in the house?"

"I'd say you were a liar wasting important time." He flipped down the visor and the keys dropped into his lap. "Put on your seat belt."

He was having a hard time managing his with the dish towel wrapped around his hand, but it was too dark for her to see how bad it was. The engine of the Corvette purred to life, and he backed it out of the garage with total disregard for whoever might be wandering around in the dark. He would have just as soon run Jackson Meyer over—he was past the point of subtlety when it came to revenge. He wanted him dead.

Dean was pretty high on his shit list, as well. What the hell was he trying to pull tonight, with his obscure hints? What had he found on his god-damn computer that he thought could put the fear of God into Jackson Dean Meyer? For that matter, what had he found that could put a backbone in Dean himself?

He raced down the driveway, the lights spearing the darkness. Jilly was silent beside him, and he wondered whether she'd passed out. As far as he could tell his hand was bleeding more than the lacerations on her back and feet. Maybe he crushed her when they fell. Maybe she was in shock.

"If I didn't know better I'd say you engineered this entire thing in order to drive my Corvette," she said, and he laughed. Then again, maybe she was just fine.

"I'm not that manipulative," he said, running a red light rather than shifting gears. He needed to keep his right hand on the steering wheel, giving his left a break. It was bleeding again, soaking through the dish towel, and Jilly wasn't going to like having her precious vintage leather-covered steering wheel stained with his blood.

Though she was ruthless enough that she might enjoy it. "How are you feeling?" He glanced over at her. She was leaning back against the seat, safety belt fastened around her waist, her head back, eyes closed. She looked pale in the intermittent street-lights, and he pressed harder on the accelerator,

torn between appreciation for the car's responsive-
ness and worry about Jilly.

"Don't push it," she muttered without opening
her eyes. "I'm fine. You don't have to drive like
a bat out of hell."

"Are you ever going to let me drive this car
again?"

"Over my dead body."

"So I might as well enjoy it while I can." He
zipped around a corner, the tires taking it perfectly.
He'd thought he'd get her in bed long before he
got behind the wheel of this beauty. He'd been
wrong, unless you counted that frustrating erotic
partial they'd had last night.

And for some reason, being wrong about the car
wasn't particularly pleasing. He'd rather be inside
her than her vintage Corvette, no matter how sleek
it was or how beautifully the engine purred. He
wanted to hear her purr again. The hell with the
car.

He would have carried her into the emergency
room, abandoning the car, but they were ready for
them. Someone had called ahead, and it certainly
wouldn't have been Jackson. Dean must have been
more alert than Coltrane realized. He left the engine running while he helped her out, and she
reached for his hand when he started to turn away.

"Come with me." It killed her to say it. He

wanted to laugh, but somewhere his sense of humor had vanished.

"You want me to abandon your precious car here? It's illegally parked. Chances are it'll get towed or stolen. What's more important, the car or having me with you?"

It was a no-brainer, but she didn't let go of his hand. Thank God she hadn't grabbed hold of his cut one—he was busy keeping it out of sight. "Screw the car," she said.

They'd put her in a wheelchair and were busy wheeling her into the emergency room, and he had no choice but to go along with her since she wasn't about to let go of his hand. Moments later she was in an examining room, up on the stretcher, still clinging to him.

He heard Jilly's voice coming from a long ways away. She was talking to the nurse, explaining what happened, while they began to pick tiny shards of glass out of her bare feet. She was crushing his hand, or maybe it was his other hand that felt hot, heavy, crushed. He wasn't quite sure. He lifted it to look at it. The red kitchen towel swam before his eyes, then he remembered the towel had been white when he'd wrapped it around his hand.

He was the one who'd passed out cold, even before he hit the floor.

* * *

There was only one benefit to having made such an utter fool of himself, he thought three hours later when they were finally released from the emergency room. It had managed to put Jilly Meyer into an uncharacteristically cheerful mood. Maybe she liked to see men humbled. Or the ridiculousness of it tickled her. He didn't know and he didn't care.

"You'll need to stay off your feet for a day or two, as much as possible, Ms. Meyer," the nurse said, giving final instructions. "The cuts aren't deep but they'll heal better if you give them a rest. They're actually worse than the scrapes on your back, despite the amount of blood. The doctor sent along something for the pain, and it might make you feel a bit woozy, but that's understandable."

Coltrane didn't even blink. Blood, he thought. He really didn't like blood.

"As for you, Mr. Coltrane, once you drive home you should stay put. You've got seven stitches in your hand and quite a bump on your head from when you fainted in the emergency room. There's no sign of a concussion, but you should have someone check on you periodically to make sure you aren't developing any. It wasn't much of a blow, but we can't be too careful."

He thought he heard Jilly snort faintly. "I'm fine," he grumbled.

"Just keep an eye on each other. And next time, keep the sex play away from glass top tables."

"We didn't—!" Jilly gasped, but Coltrane simply took the wheelchair from the nurse and whisked her out the door. The car was still there, adorned with a parking ticket, but waiting for them. He breathed a sigh of relief and put the brake on the wheelchair.

"You stay here while I bring the car around."

"What did you tell the nurse?"

"Hey, it's L.A. I had to give her a believable excuse. Did you want me to tell her the ghosts scared your dog?"

"Is that what happened?" Her voice was hushed.

He paused, looking down at her in the wheelchair. She wasn't in nearly as bad shape as he'd thought. No stitches, and while her feet hurt, it had been more a question of cleaning the dirt and glass out of the tiny cuts and protecting them from infection. "I don't know," he said. "All I know is I want to get you home and up to bed."

"Don't count on it," she drawled.

"Still arguing? I'm talking therapeutic rest, not sex, sugar," he said. As usual, he was lying to her. He had every intention of carrying her up to the swan-shaped bed, stripping off her clothes and doing everything he'd been fantasizing about doing for the last three days. She was better off not knowing. It would give her less time to come up with objections.

She didn't want him to pick her up and put her in the front seat of the Corvette, but she had no choice. She held herself stiffly, making it even more difficult, but he didn't bother arguing with her. There'd be time enough for that when they got back to the house.

He had no idea what he'd find there. Jackson and Dean still storming around? Maybe the so-called ghosts had driven their sorry asses out of the place, which would be a relief. Unfortunately he didn't believe in ghosts any more than Jilly did.

Rachel-Ann did. They'd scared her away, which in fact was a good thing. Coltrane had been about to crash across the table and grab Jackson Meyer by the throat. Rachel-Ann had sat there, frozen, as her father stroked her knee, and Coltrane had been equally frozen in disbelief.

It had to have been an earthquake. Just one of those random tremors he was getting used to after more than a year in California. Or maybe Roofus had been stuck under the table.

Or maybe La Casa de Sombras really was haunted. If so, it wasn't by his mother, he knew that much.

Los Angeles streets were never empty, but at

two o'clock in the morning things were relatively quiet. He drove at a leisurely pace, enjoying the feel of the Corvette, when Jilly's quiet voice broke the silence.

"There's nothing wrong...that is..." She stopped.

"Nothing wrong with what?" He knew what she was going to say. He just didn't know how he was going to answer it.

"If people aren't related by blood," she said finally. "There's nothing wrong with them having sex, is there?"

He was half tempted to make a joke, come on to her again, but for some reason he wasn't in the mood. Oh, he was in the mood to take her upstairs to her bed at La Casa and fuck her senseless. He just wasn't in the mood to joke.

"You mean your father and Rachel-Ann," he said, not mincing words.

"It was that obvious?" she said in a lost little voice. "I'd never had any inkling. I mean, I knew he doted on her, but we all do. She needs looking after—she's always been so fragile emotionally. But I assumed he just gave her all his paternal affection. I didn't mind—I know it's unnatural but I really hate him. Not so much for what he's done to me but what he's done to the others. And for what kind of man he is. But since Rachel-Ann isn't related to him, it isn't really incest, is it? Even if it feels…peculiar. And maybe I was just imagining it. Maybe I was jealous. Maybe I—''

"Hush, Jilly," he said softly. He wanted to reach out and take her hand, hold it for some kind of comfort, but he didn't trust his left hand with the wheel. "You didn't imagine it. And whether or not it's incest, it's wrong. He's the only father she's ever known. Rachel-Ann knows it's sick. I think Jackson knows it, too, and he doesn't give a shit."

"Oh, God," she said in a quiet voice.

"He's not going to get her, Jilly. He's not going to put his hands on her again."

He had no idea what she made of his steely voice. It didn't matter. He'd wrap his hands around Jackson Meyer's carefully tanned throat and squeeze the life out of him if he ever put his hands on his sister again.

Jilly was silent. "I trust you," she said finally.

"Don't. I'm not someone you should ever trust. Just because I won't let your father touch Rachel-Ann doesn't mean I'm not dangerous on my own. Don't ever forget that." He had no idea why he was warning her. Particularly when he had every intention to taking her to bed within the next hour.

"Big bad man," she murmured sleepily.

"Don't say I didn't warn you."

"I consider myself warned. You're not nearly as evil as you'd like to think you are. I'm on to you. I should have realized when Roofus liked you so much. He has excellent instincts when it comes to people."

"You're out of your mind."

"It's been a long night—cut me some slack," she said sleepily. "Don't worry, I'll hate you tomorrow. In the meantime I like the novel sensation of someone taking care of me. Are you really going to carry me upstairs when we get home?"

"It's either that or you crawl up on your hands and knees."

"I think I prefer the Scarlett O'Hara scenario," she said dreamily.

"Just don't punch me when I'm carrying you."

"I'll try to resist the temptation," she said.

It wouldn't do her any good, but he didn't bother to tell her that. She'd already had a hard time resisting him, and tonight she was far more vulnerable. He wasn't going to leave her until he'd taken everything he wanted from her, wasn't going to leave her until she was so bone weary she'd sleep for weeks.

And he'd just have to hope that Rachel-Ann was safe somewhere. Far away from her father.

When Rachel-Ann ran from the house she didn't stop to think, to hesitate, to question. She ran blindly, down the path circling the terrace to the garage, only to find her car trapped by her father's G-Wagen. On instinct she grabbed her useless keys, then turned to look for another avenue of escape. Coltrane's Range Rover was parked beside it, and in a panic she tried the door. He hadn't locked it, and the beeping noise signaled that he'd left the keys in the ignition. She didn't bother to question her sheer good luck, she simply jumped in, started the car and took off down the long, winding driveway. She was shaking so badly she could barely keep the car on the road, and it slid into a side street, just barely missing an oncoming car.

She pulled over to the side, fastening the seat belt with shaking hands. "You'll be fine, Rachel-Ann," she whispered. "Just drive carefully and you'll be fine." She pulled into the street once more, after carefully checking the traffic, and began to drive, putting all her concentration into the simple act of keeping the Range Rover moving in a straight, steady line. She didn't want to think about them. About the voices, the hands that touched her.

"Run away," the ghostly apparition had said. "Your brother will stop him. Get out of here, quickly!"

And Rachel-Ann, numb with terror, had said, "Yes, I will."

She had no idea where she was driving, she simply drove, concentrating on the traffic, the lights, the simple mechanics of the car.

She should go to a hotel, book a room and hide there. No one could find her there, not ghosts, not her father. She'd be safe, alone.

She didn't want to be alone. And she'd run out without her purse, even her wallet. If the police stopped her she'd be ticketed for driving without a license. Maybe worse, since she hadn't stopped to ask Coltrane if she could borrow his car.

She picked up the keys she'd dropped on the seat. She had a change purse attached to the key ring—she usually kept a few dollars in there for parking. No credit cards, though, and not enough for even a fleabag motel.

She pulled up to a red light and unzipped the change purse. One lousy dollar bill—which would get her exactly nowhere. She was about to dump the key ring back on the leather seat beside her when she noticed the key.

It hadn't been there yesterday. She knew those keys very well—the key to her car, a key to La Casa, one for the gates that no one had closed in years. But there was a new key, next to the old, familiar ones.

The light changed to green, and she turned left. There was no guarantee, but she had a pretty good idea who had put that key on her key chain. It was worth the risk.

She'd never been particularly good at finding her way through the city streets, and yet she found herself back in Rico's neighborhood almost instinctively. It was Saturday night, and the street was jammed with people, lights and noise. She drove very slowly, past the rows of apartment buildings, looking for his. Looking in vain for a parking spot.

She found his building, but the cars were so thick she could barely drive, much less find a place to park. She was inching along, scarcely moving, when someone knocked loudly on her window.

It startled a little shriek out of her, but she pushed the button and lowered the window. It was the gang member from that morning, looking not the slightest bit safer by the garish streetlight.

"Hey, lady, you came back. Doc's at work, but he'll be back soon. You need a parking spot?"

"I don't—" But he was ignoring her, letting out a piercing whistle.

"Hey, *compadre,* move that rust bucket so the doc's lady can park her car!" he ordered in a loud voice. A spate of angry Spanish answered him, but one of the ancient cars pulled into the street in front of her, leaving her with just enough room to park the Range Rover.

"There you are. Nice car, lady. I like it better than the BMW. Is it new?"

"I stole it."

The boy grinned. "Way to go, lady! We'll make sure no one touches it. Just go on up and the doc'll be home soon. If you want I can let you into his apartment. I know how to jimmy his locks."

"That's okay. I think I have a key."

The boy grinned. "You go on up, lady. Don't you worry about the car. We take care of our own, and if you're Doc's that makes you one of us."

And for the first time in hours Rachel-Ann's panic began to fade.

19

It came as no surprise when the strange key fit Rico's door. She had no idea when he'd put it on the key ring, she only thanked God he had.

The apartment was still relatively neat, though there were dishes in the sink. She washed them. She wasn't quite sure why—it just seemed like the thing to do. She wandered into the living room, over to the wall of bookshelves.

She turned on the TV, but he only got three channels and they were grainy. No Weather Channel. She flicked it off again, then her eyes narrowed as she looked at the photographs on the shelf. There was Consuelo and Jaime, older than when she'd last seen them, looking happy and secure. One of Rico and a pretty young woman holding on to his arm. And one of Rachel-Ann, no more than sixteen years old, young and innocent and still hopeful.

She wasn't sure which picture bothered her more—the unknown woman clinging so happily to Rico, or the image of a youthful Rachel-Ann.

She took the afghan off the sofa and set it carefully on the desk, just as he had the night before. She opened up the sofa, stripped off all her clothes and crawled beneath the covers, waiting for him in the darkness.

Half an hour later, she got up, put her underwear back on, and got back in bed.

An hour later she got up and pulled the skimpy dress back on. Her panty hose were shredded, and she tossed them in the trash. It was cool in the apartment, or maybe she was just nervous. She found a T-shirt hanging on the back of the bathroom door—it smelled of soap and shampoo and Rico. She pulled it over her dress and it came halfway down to her knees.

Back in the main room, she put the sofa bed back together again. And then she took Consuelo's afghan, wrapped it around her, and curled up on the cushions, closing her eyes against the bright streetlights beyond the window.

When she awoke the night was still and silent, and she wasn't alone. Only the streetlights lit the apartment, but Rico lay stretched out on the floor, his head against the sofa, near hers.

He looked exhausted. For the first time she had a chance to look at him, really look. She was astonished she hadn't recognized him before. He still had the beautiful cheekbones, the sensuous mouth, the strong jaw. But he'd lost some of that youthful arrogance. Consuelo and Jaime's young son had been beautiful, proud, sleek and sexual, in love with her and in love with life. Nothing was beyond him back then.

Now he looked like someone who'd lived. There were lines around his eyes, around his beautiful mouth. There was even a trace of gray in his dark hair. And he was more beautiful than anything she'd ever seen.

She didn't want to wake him—he looked bone weary. Besides, she was content just to lie there and watch him while he slept. Staring at the smooth planes of his face gave her a sense of safety she hadn't felt in years. Maybe never. She didn't want to think about what had sent her running out of La Casa hours ago. Didn't want to think about Jackson, about the voices, about anything. She simply wanted to lie here and watch Rico sleep.

Almost on cue his eyes fluttered open, and he turned his head to look at her. Without a word she put her hand on his face, she put her lips on his mouth, and a moment later she lay on the floor beneath him.

He made love to her in silence, with such tenderness it made her want to weep. On the floor he took her like a virgin bride, with gentle hands and mouth, with strength and heat and fierce desire always in control, and when he slid inside her she came, for the first time in years, a sweet, tight orgasm that made her cry. He kissed her when he climaxed, kissed her tear-streaked face and her mouth, with his body and his soul. And then he held her as she wept, curled up on the floor with his body wrapped tight around her.

Sometime during the night they opened up the sofa and got into bed, under the covers. They made love again, and this time she felt freer, more open, ready to take him again and again, hungry for him. When she woke in the morning he was wrapped around her, his thumb stroking the scars on her wrist.

"So much pain, *chica*," he whispered.

"Yes," she said. Because it was only the truth.

"Are you all right? You can see why I didn't kiss you the other night. I knew this would happen, and I didn't know if it would only hurt you more."

She rolled over on her back, looking up at him. "You never hurt me, Rico," she said.

His smile was wry. "Now that's not true. I was an arrogant asshole, sure of myself and the world. Teenage boys are oblivious to the trouble they cause."

She smiled at him. "Well, then, let's say you hurt me less than most."

"What brought you back here to me, Rachel-Ann?"

"You put your key on my key chain."

"Yes, but I didn't expect you so soon."

"Should I leave?" She started to roll away from him, teasing, and he uttered a mock growl.

"I want you to tell me what made you run. What happened?"

She turned her face away from him. "Nothing. Nothing different. My father came for dinner last night. You never met him, so you wouldn't know how frightening he can be."

"Yes, I did. The day we left La Casa."

She opened her eyes. "He sent you away?"

"Who else? Your grandmother had a fit, of course. It's hard to replace good help like Jaime and Consuelo on a moment's notice, but she agreed that you needed to be protected from my mongrel influence. He didn't like the idea of a Hispanic son-in-law."

She was silent for a moment. "We never talked about marriage," she said finally.

"No. But I dreamed about it. I was in love, *chica,* desperately, passionately in love as only a teenage boy can feel it. I wanted to slay dragons for you, to fight anyone who dared to hurt you. In particular your father. Unfortunately I was badly outmatched back then."

"And now? Can you save me from him now?" she asked in a hushed voice.

"Yes," he said. "But I think you need to save yourself."

"And what if I'm not strong enough to? What if he wins? What makes you think I'm not more helpless than I was fifteen years ago?"

"You were never helpless, Rachel-Ann. He just made you believe that. It wasn't your weakness that got you into trouble, but your strength."

"I don't believe that."

He kissed her nose. "I know you don't, *mi alma*. And I can't convince you. You'll have to find it out for yourself."

She just looked at him, trying to find defenses against what she was feeling. The soft, melting need that was unlike anything she'd felt before. She knew what needs sent her to men, and it was a far cry from what she needed from Rico.

"Can I come here again?"

"Of course. I gave you the key, remember?" he said gently.

"Can I live here, with you?"

"Yes." He didn't blink, didn't hesitate.

"Will you make me go to AA meetings?"

He shook his head. "I won't make you do anything you don't choose to do, Rachel-Ann. If you like, I won't even mention the word *meetings* to you again. It's up to you to ask.''

"It's not the answer for me," she said, needing to convince him. "I know you can't accept that, but it doesn't work for everyone."

"I can accept anything you want to tell me," he said calmly. "But I can't give you the answers—you're going to have to figure them out for yourself."

"Maybe that's what I'm so frightened of."

"Maybe it is, *mi amor*. Maybe it is."

La Casa de Sombras lived up to its name when Coltrane drove up the winding driveway. Shadows everywhere in the moonlit night, and not a sign of life.

The massive Mercedes G-Wagen was gone, and so was Dean's Lexus. Rachel-Ann's sedan was still there, abandoned along with the ancient vehicle in the far bay. No sign of his Range Rover, which he accepted with equanimity. He was more interested in the Corvette, anyway.

He could only hope Rachel-Ann had found somewhere safe to run to. She'd sat at the table tonight like a meek fawn caught in the headlights of an oncoming tank, frozen, unable to move, with no idea of the disaster bearing down on her. She didn't know the extent of just how wrong Meyer's obsession with her was, even though she clearly had some inkling.

He'd wanted to kill him. It had been that simple, that direct, shockingly so. Coltrane always thought of himself as a man who used brains and trickery to get what he wanted. He'd never wanted the catharsis of physical violence before, not as much as he'd wanted it tonight.

And the damnable thing was, it had started earlier. Started when Meyer had first walked into the room and done his best to demoralize Jilly. It hadn't worked. Obdurate, that's what she was. Unflinching in the face of her father's bullying, unmoved by his malice. Clearly she'd let go of him a long time ago, and he no longer had the power to hurt her.

But Rachel-Ann hadn't let go. She sat on the sofa, shrinking into herself as Meyer clutched her knee like a ham-handed pervert, and she hadn't made a sound. And Coltrane had wanted to kill him.

He'd never had the slightest suspicion that Meyer's obsession went so deep with Rachel-Ann. He wasn't sure what he would have done about it if he had known—his reaction would have been violent no matter what the circumstances.

He pulled into one of the empty bays, parked the car and turned to look at Jilly. She'd fallen asleep—the pain pills they'd given her must have taken effect. He stared at her for a moment, taking a good long look at her.

She wasn't particularly beautiful, he supposed. Not stunning like some of the women he'd bedded. She wasn't particularly charming—she'd given him nothing but shit since the moment they met. Maybe that was part of her charm.

Because he was charmed by her. Effortlessly, completely. He'd been planning on getting her into bed ever since he'd realized who Rachel-Ann was. No, that was a lie. He'd been planning on getting Jilly into bed since he first set eyes on her in the waiting room at Meyer Enterprises. She'd been asleep then, as she was now. He'd never realized how sexy a sleeping woman could be.

He'd come up with a dozen excuses, wicked reasons, evil intentions to sleep with her. In the end, none of them mattered. Looking down at her while she slept, he knew why he wanted to take her to bed. For the sheer, simple joy of it.

And he knew he wasn't going to do it, after all.

She was primed, she was ready, she was half out of it on pain pills. He'd gotten her so turned on the night before she'd temporarily lost all sense of inhibition, and sexual need positively radiated from her. And he knew it was for him and no one else.

She'd been celibate, almost hermitlike, since her

divorce three years ago. Meyer kept private investigators on retainer, and there was nothing in his children's lives he wasn't privy to. And Coltrane, with unlimited access to Meyer's records, knew it all, too.

She hadn't wanted anyone in three years, and she wanted him. He'd gotten beneath her impressive defenses, and tonight should have been the night for the big payoff. He could do what he'd been planning all along. Take her to bed, screw her senseless, and then wait for Meyer to show up.

And Meyer would, eventually. His house of cards was tumbling down, and he had no idea why. The carefully balanced scams and schemes, the incredibly intricate orchestration of money and deals that danced on the head of a pin were about to come crashing down, leaving Jackson Dean Meyer penniless, disgraced and under indictment for a textbook of illegal financial practices. Coltrane had been leaking information to the Justice Department for weeks, anonymously. Today he'd sent the final file, and by Monday they'd be ready to pounce. Maybe they wouldn't wait for the weekend.

They'd take everything they could. Including, most likely, the house. That was what would hurt Jilly the most. Dean would be shattered by the loss of money and prestige, Rachel-Ann by the loss of her father.

But Jilly would still be there to take care of them as she always had. Somehow she'd survive, even without her beloved mausoleum.

But who would take care of her?

None of his concern. He wasn't in the business of taking care of people, and Jilly wouldn't thank him if he tried. She wouldn't admit weakness, wouldn't take help from anyone, even when it was perfectly all right to occasionally take a helping hand. She had to take care of the world on her own, and he'd gladly leave her to it.

The one thing he could do for her was not sleep with her tonight. Better to leave her with that much dignity. Better to leave him with an itch that couldn't be scratched, an annoyance underneath his skin that he'd get over eventually. She was half-drugged and half in love, the fool. It was just too damned easy.

She muttered something when he picked her up, but she was too zonked out to do much more than put her arms around his neck and curl up in his arms. He carried her through the empty house, up the winding stairs to her room, laying her down in the absurd, swan-shaped bed.

She didn't wake up. She simply snuggled into the bed with a deep, peaceful sigh.

He pulled a sheet over her. And then, on impulse, he leaned down and kissed her, softly, on her mouth. For a moment her lips clung to his, and her hand lifted to touch him, then fell back to her side as she slept on.

He stepped back, staring down at her for a long, thoughtful moment. And then he turned and left her, closing the door behind him.

"Isn't that the sweetest thing you've ever seen?" Brenda said from her perch on Jilly's dresser.

"Adorable," Ted grumbled. "The man's a fool."

"Oh, don't be so...so manly about it. That's the most romantic thing I've ever seen. He'd rather deny himself and walk away than hurt her."

"Don't start believing in your own movies, Brenda. You used to laugh at them yourself. He's a dope. She's crazy about him, he's in love with her, and yet he's being all noble and leaving her. He's a fathead."

Brenda didn't bother to deny it. "You think he's in love with her? I wasn't quite sure about that. Oh, I know she loves him. Typical, when there have been any number of more respectable men available, that she'd fall for a con man, but I can't say I blame her. He is gorgeous."

"Harrumph."

"Don't be jealous, sweetie. I wouldn't want him

even if I could have him. I'm just enjoying the movie. Here we've got the gorgeous, tormented hero, determined to do the right thing, and then we have the feisty, wounded heroine, who'd much rather he do the wrong thing and stay with her. I think it's more a romantic comedy than a weeper.''

"Most of those weepers were pretty funny," Ted said wryly.

"Pig," she said cheerfully. "So what are we going to do about these two? Let them screw up their lives? Walk away when they clearly belong together?"

"You're such a romantic, honeybunch. What makes you think people belong together? Maybe if these two don't hook up they'll find someone else in a month or so who'll be just as compatible."

Brenda was silent for a long moment. "Don't you believe in soul mates?" she asked.

"For the rare, lucky ones, I do. For you and me. I'm not convinced these people are worthy of the kind of eternal love you and I have."

"Eternal love," she said in a hollow voice. "Are you sure you believe it for us?"

He lifted her down off the dresser. She was a small woman, and he was a big man, and he lifted her as lightly as if she weighed nothing. Which she supposed was, in fact, true.

"I wouldn't change a thing about us, darling," he said. "We were meant to be."

She wanted to believe him, oh, so desperately. But he didn't know everything, and that knowledge ate away at her. She wasn't ready to deal with it. "What about them?" she said. "What if they were meant to be?"

"Then they'd better get busy doing something about it. Come on, darling. It's almost dawn. We need to settle down for our Sunday siesta. Let these poor fools work out their own future. We've interfered enough for one day."

Brenda took one last look at the woman sleeping alone in her huge bed. She'd never shared that bed with anyone but Roofus, and Brenda knew better than anyone the pleasure that could be had in that bed.

Jilly deserved to share it with someone she loved. But Brenda knew all too well, you don't always get what you deserve in this life.

Or the next.

20

"What the hell are you doing here?" Jackson demanded, his voice tight with fury.

"I work here, remember," Coltrane said with deceptive ease.

"Not at four-thirty in the morning you don't." Jackson had his laptop open on his desk, and when Coltrane had strolled in he'd been so caught up in whatever he was doing that he hadn't even heard him.

"Looks like the place has been burglarized," Coltrane said, glancing at the chaos around him. Files were strewn all over the room, a credenza had been toppled, and Meyer was still furiously tapping away at the keyboard of his computer.

"Get the hell out of here, Coltrane. I've got enough on my plate without putting up with your bullshit. You were supposed to protect me. You were supposed to make sure no one could get to me. I've spent thirty-five years doing business with no one interfering, and your job was to see that continued. Now the Justice Department has me under investigation, my wife's lawyers are getting ready to pounce, and someone's been tampering with my private files. What the fuck is going on here?''

"Maybe your luck has run out, boss," Coltrane said, taking one of the leather chairs opposite him and sitting down without waiting to be asked. He had a hell of a headache, his hand was throbbing, and yet he felt almost unnaturally calm. It was all falling into place, just as he'd planned. So why wasn't he feeling more satisfied?

Meyer looked up from the computer screen. "What the hell happened to your head?" he said, frowning.

"I hit it when I passed out in the emergency room. The sight of blood tends to do that to me. Unmanly, I know, but we all have our weaknesses."

Meyer's eyes narrowed. "Whose blood?"

"Your daughter's." He said it deliberately, just to get a reaction. He got one.

Meyer turned pale. "Rachel-Ann?" he said hoarsely.

"No. No one's seen her since she took off. Jilly got cut by the glass from the broken coffee table."

Meyer shrugged, turning his attention back to the computer. Deleting files, no doubt.

"Is she really your daughter?"

Meyer's reaction was even better this time. "What the hell are you talking about?"

"You don't seem to give a damn about Jilly. I just wondered if maybe her mother played around on you or something. Most parents have at least a trace of paternal feeling."

Jackson's chuckle was humorless. "Hell, yes, she's mine. Looks a lot like my grandmother when she was young. Edith didn't have the nerve to play around on me. It still surprises me that she thought she could leave and take my children."

"And you care so much about your children?" Coltrane asked.

"Not particularly. Rachel-Ann was all I needed, but Edith wanted more. It didn't matter one way or the other to me, and it kept her off my back and occupied. I'm not a man to let sentiment get in my way. I thought you knew me better than that, Coltrane. Why would you think I'd give a damn about someone I happened to father? I wasn't around when they were growing up, they aren't the slightest bit like me."

"Then why do you care about Rachel-Ann?" He wasn't sure if he wanted to hear the answer. Whether Meyer was fooling himself as he tried to fool everyone else.

Meyer shrugged. "Just goes to show that blood

ties are bullshit. She's my perfect soul mate and always has been.''

"Soul mate?" Coltrane repeated in disbelief. "Have you been reading cheesy romance novels? I'm not even sure if you have a soul, much less a soul mate.''

"Watch it, Coltrane. Don't get in my way,'' he growled. "I'll crush you. I've crushed stronger men than you in the past, and I don't have any qualms about doing it to you. I'll bury you.''

"How many people have you buried, Meyer?''

Meyer didn't even blink. "Don't call my bluff, Coltrane. You have no idea what I'm capable of.''

"I wouldn't be so sure of that. I've never underestimated you, boss.''

Meyer stared at him for a long, thoughtful moment. "That's why I chose you, Coltrane,'' he said finally. "Deep down, you're just like me. Ruthless, cold, practical. You can get the job done, no matter what the price, and you don't let the petty laws of little men get in the way. Am I right?''

Was he? Was he just like Meyer, deep inside? Just as cold and ruthless, ready to sacrifice anyone for his quest? Anyone like Jilly Meyer or even his own sister? It was uncomfortably close to the truth.

"Right, boss,'' he said easily, giving no hint at the disgust Meyer's words had engendered.

"And you can do one more thing for me, can't

you? I'll make it worth your while, you know I will. At this point you're the only one I can trust. My son's a weakling, but at least he didn't use to be troubled with ridiculous scruples. God knows who he thinks he is to pass judgment on me, the little bastard. He seems to have developed a conscience of late, but I'm sure I can acquit you of providing a moral influence.''

''I think we can safely agree on that.''

''So I'm getting out. Not just out of my marriage. Out of the business, out of the country. This has been in the works for quite a while—a wise man always keeps an escape hatch ready. I've done all I can do here, accomplished what I wanted to. Now's the time to retire, while I'm still a young man.''

You're sixty-three, Meyer, Coltrane thought. *I wouldn't call that particularly young.* But he didn't say a word.

''I don't trust many people,'' Meyer continued. ''But I trust you, Coltrane. Can I count on you?''

Meyer didn't trust anybody, including him, but he was adept at convincing people they mattered. If they had something to offer, that is. Coltrane wondered why he never bothered with Jilly, who had more to offer than all of them put together.

He had to stop thinking about her. After today he wasn't going to see her again. He just needed to put a few thousand miles between them, and he'd forget all about her.

"You can count on me, Jackson," Coltrane said. "What do you want me to do?"

"You can bring me Rachel-Ann."

It was dawn when he returned to La Casa. The sun was coming up over the lawn, fingers of pale lavender reaching out to touch the facade of the house. Neither Dean nor Rachel-Ann had returned home, and Jilly must still be completely zonked out, thank God.

He started up the steps to the terrace, then at the last minute changed his mind and turned around. He'd be gone from this place soon enough—he wanted to wander around one last time and see if anything jogged his memory. He had no idea how young he'd been when he first lived here—probably only two or three. He didn't remember his mother being pregnant, and Rachel-Ann was only a few years younger than he was. Maybe he just hadn't noticed his mother's rounded belly.

He walked down the gravel path, past the towering palm trees and tangled undergrowth. It really was odd to see vegetation grow wild like this in Los Angeles, where yard workers were plentiful and affordable. But then, Jilly paid the bills, and as far as he could tell she never ventured off the patio. There was something she didn't like about the grounds.

Then he remembered her reaction to his mention of the pool. Something about the pool bothered her, enough so that she let the landscaping grow up around it and practically obscure it, enough so that in the land where the climate cried out for a swimming pool, she kept it unusable. He wondered why.

It was simple enough to find. Even with the overgrown pathways the smell of rotting algae was easy to trace. He could see the roof of the pool house, half caved in, before he came to the actual pool itself.

It was surprisingly small, only about half full of dank, black water and some kind of plant life, and it looked as if it had been abandoned decades ago. The tile around the edges was cracked and discolored, and weeds grew up in the cracks. The diving board was long gone, the steps leading down into the pool were rusted, with a rung missing. It looked derelict and depressing. It was no wonder Jilly kept her distance. That the entire family kept their distance.

He walked forward, staring down into the murky depths. Even though there was only about three feet of water in the pool he couldn't see the bottom, which was probably a good thing. From the smell of the place there might very well be some decomposing wildlife in there, as well.

A shiver ran across his backbone. Maybe as a going-away present he'd pay for a bulldozer to come in and demolish this cesspit. It was the least he could do for Jilly—after destroying her family he could give her that much.

The wind had picked up, swirling dust into the air, and Coltrane grimaced. He'd be glad to be out of this town. There was usually nothing he liked more than a good storm, but the wind in L.A. made his hackles rise.

There were a few lights still on in the shadowy interior of La Casa, and he switched them off as he went, plunging the place into a predawn gloom. It suited his mood. He climbed the stairs slowly, silently. Jilly wouldn't be likely to wake up, but he didn't want to risk it. He'd walked away from her once. There was a limit to how goddamn noble he could be.

He didn't even glance at her door as he walked past, determined to put temptation out of his head. Now that he'd made up his mind not to touch her again, not to hurt her, he wanted her more than ever. Must be human nature. The more off-limits something was, the more you wanted it.

Which brought him back to Meyer, and his stomach knotted in disgust. Meyer wanted Rachel-

Ann, his own daughter, and it wasn't to act as hostess for him while he lived the life of a wealthy fugitive.

And Coltrane, far too much like his nemesis, wanted Jilly, when to touch her would destroy her.

Meyer was right—they were too damned much alike. Ruthless, amoral, out for their own agenda. It didn't matter that Coltrane wanted truth and justice and Meyer wanted money and power. They still shared the same merciless approach to getting what they wanted. And an hour ago Coltrane had looked into Meyer's eyes and seen himself reflected.

He was getting the hell out of La Casa, out of Los Angeles, before he lost whatever trace of decency he had left in him. He had no idea where he was heading, only that he had to get out of there.

But he had to finish off Meyer before he went. Or Rachel-Ann would never be safe.

It was no longer justice, it was no longer revenge. It was much simpler than that. His arrival in L.A. had set too many things in motion. He needed to salvage what he could.

He packed, throwing his clothes in his suitcase with a total lack of respect for their price tags or labels. The sun was just coming up over the edge of the trees when he heard the noise. A soft, slightly shuffling sound, and his blood froze.

The ghosts, he thought, knowing that he didn't believe in them. Knowing they were coming, anyway. Moving slowly, almost silently, only the faint, whispery sound announcing their approach.

He was too damned tired to think straight. He could hear a clicking sound—*click click, click click*—and he moved toward the French doors instinctively. Rachel-Ann wasn't even there—she was safe from them. And Jilly couldn't even see them—they'd wish her no harm.

But he deserved any kind of punishment he could get, in this world or the next, and he waited as the door slowly opened into the room, ready to face the walking dead.

Roofus leapt toward him in canine delight, his paws clicking on the marble floor. Behind him came Jilly, moving gingerly on her bandaged feet. Coltrane looked at the two of them and almost wished they'd been ghosts.

Jilly halted just inside the room. The pain pills must have been weaker than he thought, because she looked wide-awake. She'd changed out of her bloodstained clothes into what she probably thought wasn't provocative. On most people a baggy T-shirt and jeans wouldn't have been arousing. Right now all Jilly had to do was breathe and he was aroused.

Her hair was hanging loose, down around her

hips in a dark curtain, and her face was pale in the murky light of dawn. She looked at the suitcase on the bed, then glanced up at him. "You're leaving?" she said in an even voice.

"I told you I was."

"Why? Don't you want to cause more trouble?"

"What I love most about you, Jillian Meyer, is your sweet nature," he said wryly. "I'm getting out before I make things worse. I've got a couple of things to take care of and then you never have to see me again. Count your blessings."

"I don't want you to go," she said flatly. "I need your help."

He looked at her, not bothering to hide his shock. "You need my help?" he echoed in disbelief. "Strong, powerful Jillian, ruler of the universe, protector of the weak, defender of the family, needs the help of a snake like me? I thought you could do everything."

She limped across the room, over to the bed and sat down beside his suitcase. There wasn't any other place to sit in the derelict room, and her feet had to be hurting. But seeing her sitting on his bed unnerved him.

"I can't do everything," she said in a quiet voice. "I can't fix things, I can't save things, no matter how hard I try. I can't make my father love Dean more, I can't make him love Rachel-Ann less. Hell, I can't make him love me at all.'' Her faint grin was self-mocking. ''Not that I care, mind you. Jackson's very good at being charming when he wants something, but I learned years ago just how little that counts for. And that's why he hates me. I'm the one person who sees him for what he is, and nothing he does can fool me.''

''I wouldn't say you're the one person,'' Coltrane said. ''I'm not particularly deluded about him.''

''And you still work for him? Then you're worse than I thought,'' she said.

''Impossible. You think I'm pond scum. Not unlike the stuff that's growing over your abandoned swimming pool.'' He said it on purpose, just to test her reaction.

She shuddered visibly. ''I don't…like the swimming pool,'' she said in a tight voice. ''I don't like looking at it, I don't like talking about it. Something horrible happened there, long ago, and it infects the place.''

''Something horrible happened to you?''

''No. Not really. It's something else, something that happened a long time ago, something ugly and cruel. I don't know what it was, and I don't want to know. I just don't like it.''

''Okay,'' he said evenly. ''So I'm not pond scum. But I know what your father's capable of and I still work for him. What does that make me?"

"A snake," she said without hesitation. "But not without redemption. I can't let him win. I can't let him hurt Rachel-Ann any more. I don't know what he's done to her over the years, but it sickens me, the way he looks at her, the way he touches her."

"Do you think he's had sex with her? Do you think he abused her as a child?" It was astonishing how casual, almost clinical he sounded.

"I don't know. Maybe not. But even if he didn't commit physical incest he's committed emotional incest over the years. And she has to break free of him."

"Isn't that her problem? You spend your life trying to fix everything, trying to save everyone. You even think I'm salvageable which, trust me, I'm not. What about you?"

"Me?" She laughed, entirely without humor. "I don't think I'm perfect. I know what a fucked-up, codependent mess I am. I'm stubborn, judgmental, interfering, afraid of everything under the sun, un-responsive, bad-tempered—"

"What a litany of crimes!" he said softly.

"Don't tell me you disagree. You've said half of those things yourself."

"I never said you were unresponsive."

He shouldn't have said that. Not with her sitting on his bed, alone in the huge old house. Not when he was going to leave.

She hesitated, and he wondered if she'd ignore it. "No," she said finally. "That was my husband. And that's another story. We're trying to save Rachel-Ann."

"You're trying to save Rachel-Ann, Jilly. I'm trying to get the hell out of here."

"And you'd just turn her over to him? Just let it happen?" she said in disbelief.

She'd managed to startle him with her insight. "What makes you think I'd turn her over to him?"

"Isn't that what you're doing, by leaving? She needs our help, Coltrane! I thought you cared about her."

"He's not going to get her. And stop being so melodramatic—it's not your style. What makes you think I care about her?"

"I don't know. Instinct, I guess. Are you in love with her?"

"Jesus Christ, Jillian!" he exploded softly. "What kind of dream world are you living in? Do I look like the kind of man who walks around suffering from unrequited love? Do I look like the kind of man to harbor a secret passion?"

Her grin was wry. "No, I suppose not. Clearly

you don't give a shit about anyone in this household."

"And you care too much."

"Maybe I do," she said calmly.

"And maybe you should start putting a little bit of that prodigious energy toward yourself. Have you ever done anything in your entire life that was just for you and not for your damned family or this ruined old house?"

"Of course I have."

"Name one thing. Even better, prove it. Tell me one thing you want, something that's selfish, greedy and absolutely bad for you. Something everyone will scold you for and shake their heads and say 'She's just as bad as the rest of her family.' I dare you to. Something weak and indulgent, like an ice-cream sundae. Want do *you* want, Jilly?"

She looked at him across the dawn-swept room, her brown eyes calm and clear. "You," she said.

21

Coltrane was looking at her as if she'd suddenly grown two heads. Jilly couldn't blame him. If there'd been a mirror nearby she would have checked herself. Surely that word hadn't come from her mouth?

After a moment he recovered himself. "They must have given you more pain medication than I thought," he drawled.

"They didn't give me any painkillers, you idiot. They sent some home with me in case I needed them but I didn't take any."

"Then why did you zonk out in the car like that?"

The man was dense, and she was tired of being subtle. "Because I was exhausted. I haven't slept in days, mostly thanks to you, and I was too damned tired to stay awake. Besides, I was expecting you to put me to bed and then take advantage of me. You've been trying to since you met me, and there I was, completely vulnerable. And what do you do? Give me a chaste kiss and leave."

She let her thorough disgust come through in her voice.

"You really do think I'm a shit, don't you?"

"Yes. No. I'm not sure," she said honestly.

"If you feel that way about me why in God's name do you want to go to bed with me?" He'd moved closer to the bed, watching her with an obvious mixture of irritation and interest.

"Because you're wicked and selfish and bad to the bone, and I'm tired of being good and noble. You've been sniffing around me like I'm a bitch in heat—I'm offering myself to you." She tried to sound infinitely practical. Considering that he was looming over her in the shadowed room, and she had the unfortunate habit of reacting to him like an adolescent in the throes of first passion, she was doing a good job. He made her heart pound, her stomach knot, her breasts ache and her skin prickle, all without touching her. And she really, really wanted him to touch her.

"Charmingly put. And what if my motives are entirely evil? What if I've been trying to get you into bed for nefarious purposes that have nothing to do with you?"

She blinked. "I assumed that was the case. I don't tend to drive men wild with passion—you must have some ulterior motive."

"And you want to sleep with me, anyway?"

He'd come up to the edge of the bed, and she looked at him, keeping her gaze calm and steady. The only problem was that her lips were trembling when she tried to smile, and she certainly didn't want to frown at him.

He'd changed since he'd brought her back. He was wearing an old pair of jeans and a T-shirt, not his usual style. He looked a lot less civilized without his linen and cotton and Armani. A lot more dangerous.

And a lot more gorgeous.

"Ice-cream sundaes aren't good for you, either. They make you fat, they raise your cholesterol and clog your arteries. That doesn't mean people don't have them." She heard their prosaic conversation almost from a distance. As if she were one of the ghosts, listening, watching, removed from it all.

"So you want me to sleep with you. Knowing I'm leaving, you want a nice, old-fashioned one-night stand? Not your style, Jilly. Why?"

"I'm trying to change my style." She had a sudden, horrifying thought. What if he didn't really want her? What if all his looks, his talk, his kisses and touches were part of a game, part of whatever mysterious agenda he had? What if now that he'd decided to leave he had no interest in her? The possibility made her both cold and hot with shame, made her want to run. "Maybe this was a bad idea," she mumbled, moving toward the end of the bed. "Just forget it."

He moved quickly, kneeling on the bed and catching her wrist, pulling her back. "Oh, no, I think it's an excellent idea," he said. "And I don't think you get to change your mind." He shoved the suitcase off the bed, and it hit the marble floor with a bang, startling Roofus, who'd found a comfortable spot to snooze in a far corner. He lifted his massive head, woofed softly, then went back to sleep.

It suddenly felt a lot more real, his hand on her arm, holding her there. He was very strong—he had to be, to carry a woman of her stature up the winding stairs—and she knew a brief moment of fear. "And if I want to leave?" Her voice shook; there was no way she could disguise it.

"You won't," he said. And he kissed her, cupping her face with one hand, kissing her with a deep and long and wet kiss, so that she was shaking, drowning.

He slid down on the bed, taking her with him, and she sprawled beside him on the too soft mattress. He was so hot, so strong, so solid beneath her, and it was both frightening and arousing. He stripped off her T-shirt, over her head before she realized what he was doing, and then he reached for the waistband of her jeans. She put her hands on his, to stop him, but he calmly ignored her, stripping the jeans off her, pulling them over her bandaged feet with surprising tenderness.

"Nice underwear," he said calmly. "Was that for me?"

She was wearing teal silk, the sexiest, most feminine underwear she owned, a skimpy bra and a thong bikini. "Yes," she said.

"Good. Let's leave them on for a while." He pulled off his own T-shirt and sent it sailing across the floor, then reached for his zipper. "I better warn you—I'm not wearing any underwear."

"Why am I not surprised?" she said faintly. The room was getting steadily lighter with the approach of daylight, and she would have much preferred it to get darker. She turned her head, and heard the sound of him shucking off his jeans, his quiet laugh.

"Are you prudish, Jilly?" he murmured, and the mattress sank beneath his weight as he moved closer to her. "Or just shy?"

She turned back to look at him, keeping her eyes focused on his face. Except that his chest was distractingly gorgeous. She'd never been that impressed with a man's chest before, or muscles, but Coltrane was an exception. He was strong, muscled and gorgeous.

"No one on this earth would call me shy," she

said, wanting to touch his chest. Keeping her hand beside her, still and unmoving.

"I would," he said. He took her hand and placed it against his heart.

His skin was hot, and his heart was thumping, loud, steady against her hand. "Your heart is pounding," she said.

"That's because I'm aroused. Which you'd know if you could bring yourself to look past my shoulders."

Of course she did, instinctively. He was most definitely, thoroughly aroused. "Can I leave now?" she asked in a small voice.

"No."

"All right."

"No arguments?"

"I don't really want to leave," she said.

"I know. That's why you can't." He took her hand and moved it down his chest to his flat stomach, over the rough covering of golden hair, and when he took his hand away she left it there, absorbing the heat and tension in him. "You have some catching up to do. How's your back? Can you lie on it?"

"Yes," she said. "Why?"

"I have work to do." He pushed her onto her back on the new mattress, carefully, and she barely noticed the scratches. He loomed over her in the shadows, and she closed her eyes, waiting.

Nothing happened. She opened them again, to see him watching her. "That's much better," he murmured. "Now let's see if I can get you even half as hot as you've got me."

He put his mouth between her breasts, kissing her above the lacy bra, and she felt her heart leap in heated response. Tentatively she reached up and touched the side of his face, his shaggy blond hair, and he made a murmuring sound of approval against her skin as he moved his mouth across the swell of her breast. He covered her other breast with his hand, his long fingers squeezing gently, arousing, so that she felt her nipples harden in the warm room, felt the heat and tightness between her legs.

The skimpy bra had a front clasp, and he undid it, pushing the scant silk aside, and when he put his mouth on her breast she let out a soft cry, wanting him to stop. Her breasts were too sensitive, and the wet pull of his mouth stirred deep, scary feelings inside her. She opened her mouth to protest, but he put his hand over her lips to stop her from saying the words, and some dark, primitive instinct made her take his fingers into her mouth, sucking on them.

The sound he made was so utterly, completely

sexual that her arousal deepened still further, and she suddenly felt greedy. She slid down on the bed, ignoring the pain in her back, and caught his face in her hands, kissing him full on the mouth. She wanted him, there was no question of it, and she tried to pull him over her.

"I'm ready," she whispered.

"No, you're not," he replied. "But you will be." He kissed her on the mouth, a slow, drugging kiss, and the feel of his tongue in her mouth was another hot jet of desire spilling through her.

And then he moved, down her body, kissing, tasting, sucking, as he cupped her between her legs, his fingers dancing against the damp silk of her panties.

Sheer instinct made her arch against his hand, and as he slid his fingers inside the silk covering to touch her she bit her lip, afraid to cry out.

He must have known. He moved up, covering her mouth with his, and pushed his fingers inside her.

She jerked, startled, but he paid no attention to her instinctive panic, holding her captive with his hand and his mouth, touching, stroking, with his tongue, his fingers, and she was shivering in the darkness.

He lifted his head, staring down at her as he

touched her. "Don't!" she gasped in a choked voice.

"Don't what?" he said, sounding wickedly amused, as his fingers slid against her.

"Don't...stop," she whispered, as the first little shock of pleasure hit her.

"Not an option," he said, and the second wave hit her, harder.

Her body was spiraling out of control, and it frightened her. When the third orgasm hit her she fought it, freezing.

"Oh, no. You're not getting away with that," Coltrane said, pulling away from her. The flimsy panties ripped as he yanked them off her, and he pushed her legs apart, moving between them. "Stop trying to control everything. Sometimes you can just let someone else take charge for a little while."

He was angry with her, and it should have bothered her, but it didn't. In the last few minutes they'd gone far past that point.

"What if I'm afraid to give up control?" she whispered.

"I'm not giving you that choice. You're going to be so out of control you won't know where your body ends and mine begins. I'm going to make you come so hard you'll be blind and screaming. You only have one choice."

She was shivering, but it wasn't with fear. It was hot, naked anticipation. He was going to give her everything and it was no longer her responsibility. It was his. "What's my choice?"

"Do I use my cock or my mouth?"

The words should have shocked her. Instead, another ripple of frustrated reaction swept over her body. She felt hot, cold, hungry, so damned hungry.

"Your cock," she said, sliding her fingers down around the hard, silky length of him. He was damp, ready, and she suddenly wanted to put her mouth on him, to taste him, take him.

"Wait…" she said. "I want—"

"Later." He took her hands and pinned them back against the mattress, looming over her, and she could feel him against her, hard, solid. "There'll be time for everything later. Right now this is what I need to do." He pushed forward with his hips, just entering her.

She clutched at him, suddenly desperate. "More!" she cried.

"How much more? This?" He pushed in, a bit more, holding himself still inside her, and she wanted to scream.

"Please!" she cried. "I need…"

Another slow, inexorable inch. "What do you need, Jilly?"

"You."

He was almost in, and the feel of him inside her, hard and smooth, was a torment, a pleasure so sharp it was almost pain, a need so fierce she couldn't breathe.

"Me? Or my cock?"

She didn't know the right answer to end the torment. She only knew the truth. "You," she said.

He thrust deep, so deep she could almost taste him, and she tried to catch her breath but she couldn't.

He took her, slow and deep and hard, and this time she couldn't fight. She clawed at him, trying to hold on to something, but his shoulders were slick with sweat, and she knew there was no safety left.

It went on, endless, deep, forever, and she didn't want it to stop. She clung for a long moment, and then she let go, completely, her body exploding into a darkness beyond comprehension. Her skin burned, her entire body convulsed around him, and she could hear her voice, sobbing.

And even through the rich darkness of completion, she could feel him give over to it, his body pulsing into her, filling her, giving himself to her, and like a fool she began to cry.

She wasn't sure what she expected. She didn't even know whether she expected anything at all,

but certainly not what he did. He simply cradled
her in his arms, against his still-racing heart, his
sweat-damp chest, and held her while she cried,
stroking her hair, her tear-streaked face, saying not
a word. And when her weeping had finally begun
to shudder to a halt he kissed her, with such utter
sweetness that she began sobbing again.

She thought she heard a soft chuckle from him,
but she couldn't be sure, since he was holding her
so securely in his arms. She supposed she ought to
move away, but at the moment she couldn't. If it
were up to her the world could have ended there
and then, with her wrapped tightly against his
body.

"You see," he whispered a long time later.
"Sometimes I'm right. You don't always have to
be responsible for everything."

"Yes," she said, hiding her face against his
warm, smooth skin.

"That doesn't make you weak, or vulnerable.
Sometimes it's just nice," he said, stroking her
long, thick hair.

"Yes," she said.

"But you aren't going to make the mistake of
falling in love with me, are you?"

She moved her head to look up at him, her eyes
still swimming with the remnants of her tears.
"Yes," she said. "I am."

She would have thought that would drive him away. She didn't care—her defenses were long gone and right then there was no gaining them back. She heard his sigh, his muttered curse. And then he began to make love to her all over again, slowly, with infinite gentleness, this time without a word, just kisses, soft, sweet kisses everywhere.

It would have been one thing during the cover of a long dark night. During the brightness of the dawning day it was positively, deliciously decadent. Afterward he carried her into the shower, setting her down on the built-in tiled seat from La Casa's glory days, and proceeded to wash her with sweet, rose-scented soap. And then he knelt at her feet and used his mouth on her, bracing her legs on his shoulders as the water poured down around them.

They ended up in the swan bed in the bright daylight, and Jilly was past wondering if Dean or Rachel-Ann were going to come wandering in. All she could think about was Coltrane and the wicked, delicious things he was doing to her body. The wicked, delicious things she was doing in return.

He took her in ways she hadn't even thought of, and she lost count of how many times, or when one session blended into another. It was a blur of heat and passion, sex and love, and when she took control, taking him in her mouth, she climaxed from the sheer pleasure she was giving him.

And they slept. Sweaty, sticky, exhausted, they slept the day away, tucked up safely in the swan bed, while the ghosts kept watch over them.

There was nothing to be afraid of, Rachel-Ann told herself when she pulled into the driveway at La Casa de Sombras. Jackson's monolithic G-Wagen was nowhere in sight, neither was her brother's Lexus. Her own car was still there, as well as Jilly's Corvette, and she parked Coltrane's Range Rover in the stall beside it.

She slid out, looking around her nervously, half afraid something might jump out at her. Oddly enough, it wasn't the ghosts who frightened her this time. She wasn't sure if they'd ever frighten her again. They were the ones who told her to run last night, who tried to save her. She had a great deal more to fear from the living.

The house was quiet, still, deserted. The living room was just as she'd last seen it, before she'd run. The glass coffee table was smashed on the floor, broken dishes and glasses all around. No one had cleaned anything up.

And she wasn't going to, either. She was going upstairs, pack as much as she could carry and run, before anyone tried to stop her.

Jilly would lecture her. She'd be sure Rachel-Ann was getting involved in another disastrous relationship, the first step on the inevitable downward spiral into drugs and alcohol, and Rachel-Ann wasn't in the mood to argue or explain. She didn't quite understand herself the difference with Rico.

But it was very different, and both too new and too old to be dissected. Some things you just take on faith. Her future with Rico was one of those things. The details would sort themselves out eventually. Right now, for the first time since she could remember, she felt alive. Hopeful. Strong.

Coltrane might be around there, as well, unless Dean had given him a ride someplace. She didn't want to see him, either. She didn't like the way he looked at her, the worry and disapproval almost a match to Jilly's. She'd been fully prepared to sleep with him when she'd first heard about him, and then he turned around and acted like a stern older brother....

Older brother. The words echoed in her head. Or maybe they were the voices of the ghosts, she could never be sure. Older brother. He's your brother. He knows who you are.

She sat down, hard, on the sofa that Dean had abandoned last night, staring at the rubble on the floor. Her brother. That's who the ghosts meant, when they'd warned her. Dean wasn't looking out for her—not Dean with his one-track mind. Dean loved her, but he was unlikely to do anything about it, much less stand up to Jackson.

It was Coltrane who was looking out for her. Coltrane, her long-lost brother, who must have known all along.

She heard the voices then, drifting down the stairs, and for a moment she froze, listening for the ghosts. But in a moment she recognized Jilly's voice, unexpectedly husky with laughter. And Coltrane's response.

She didn't hesitate, didn't stop to think. She jumped up, raced out of the living room and up the stairs, storming into Jilly's room without knocking.

Coltrane stood silhouetted against the window, wearing a pair of jeans and nothing else. Jilly was sitting on the bed, wrapped in a sheet, looking like...

Looking like exactly what she was. A woman who'd just had the best sex of her life. A woman in love.

Her sister, and her brother. One by blood, one by heart. Coltrane was looking across the room at Rachel-Ann, an enigmatic expression on his face. In his green eyes, just like her own green eyes, she saw that she'd been a fool not to see it before.

"You're my brother, aren't you?" she said abruptly. Almost from a distance she could hear Jilly's indrawn gasp of breath.

"Don't be ridiculous, Rachel-Ann. He's no relation to us."

"No, thank God, or you'd obviously have a lot to answer for," Rachel-Ann said in a controlled voice. "He's only related to me. Aren't you?"

She half expected him to deny it. He glanced at Jilly, who was sitting in the middle of the bed, the sheet wrapped tight around her, that blissed-out expression vanished in the cold light of day.

"Yes," he said. "I'm your brother."

22

Jilly sat in the huge, swan-shaped bed, frozen, watching them. How had she missed the obvious? They were so much alike, and she'd never even guessed.

"What are you doing here, Rachel-Ann?" Coltrane demanded. "I thought you'd have enough sense to keep miles away from this place."

"I've never been known for my good sense," Rachel-Ann retorted. "Why was I supposed to stay away? So I wouldn't figure it out and tell Jilly? Well, guess what? I figured it out, and Jilly knows. Forget about me—what are *you* doing here? Did you come here to find me?"

Coltrane moved away from the window. He didn't even glance at Jilly, huddled beneath the sheets in a knot of pain and betrayal. "I didn't know you existed until I saw you," he said slowly. "I came to L.A. to find out what happened to my mother. Our mother. She died out here, over thirty years ago. My father told me she was murdered."

''Your father?'' Rachel-Ann echoed. ''We don't have the same father?''

''No.''

A spasm of fear crossed Rachel-Ann's pale face, and Jilly wanted to move, to comfort her, to protect her. But she was trapped inside her own sense of betrayal.

''Does Jackson know who you are? Why you're here?'' Rachel-Ann demanded hoarsely.

''No.''

''Why not?''

''He's the reason I'm here,'' Coltrane said in a cool, emotionless voice. ''My mother lived here with him and a bunch of others in the late sixties, and he killed her. He murdered my mother. Your mother. I came here to find the truth. And to make him pay.''

''You bastard,'' Rachel-Ann said softly. ''It's a lie! He couldn't—''

''Don't!'' He stopped her. Still refusing to look at Jilly. ''I don't give a damn what you think, but you have to get out of here. He'll be coming here. He thinks I'm bringing you here, keeping you for him. He's going away, leaving the country. He's about to be indicted for fraud, he's broken almost every law you could ever think of, and all he cares about is getting to a nice safe country where there's no extradition and enjoying all the money he squir-

reled away. And he expects you to help him spend
it.''

"And why shouldn't I? Why shouldn't I go
away with him? He loves me."

"Yes, he does," Coltrane said grimly. "Just a
little too much. He's your real father."

"Oh, God," Jilly said, breaking her shocked silence as it all finally made sense.

For a moment Rachel-Ann didn't move. And
then she crossed the room very slowly, ignoring
them, walking into the bathroom. A moment later
they heard the sound of her retching.

Finally Coltrane turned to look at Jilly, unflinching, unrepentant. "You have to get her out of here.
I thought she'd stay away and I wouldn't have to
worry about her."

"You just had to keep me occupied?" she said.

"It was your idea, Jilly. Not mine."

Of all the things he could have said, that was
the cruelest. She had no doubt that he knew it, that
he'd said it deliberately. "What will he do to her?"

"Force her to go with him. Your father doesn't
give a shit about laws or morality, he just doesn't
want to get caught. And he's not willing to give
up anything he wants, including Rachel-Ann.
You've spent your life protecting her, Jilly. Get her
out of here before he comes back."

"And what will you do?"

"I don't know," he said flatly. "I'll figure it out as it happens."

"Murder's against the law."

"Tell your father. And it wouldn't be murder. It would be justice, long overdue."

"You made a mistake with me, you know," Jilly said slowly. "You can't get to him through me or through Dean. He doesn't care about us. It was a waste of time trying to play your games with me. Sure, I fell for it. I'm only human. But it didn't get you anywhere you wanted to be."

He looked at her, letting those green eyes sweep down over her body, slowly, pausing between her legs. "Oh, yes it did," he said softly.

There was an art deco lamp on the bedside table. Without hesitation she picked it up and flung it at him, yanking the cord from the wall.

He didn't bother to duck. He didn't need to— the lamp didn't even come close, simply smashed on the marble floor. "Get her away from here, Jilly," he said again. "Take her and get as far away as you can. And with any luck you'll never have to see your father or me again."

Without another word he walked out of the room, not bothering to close the door behind him. Roofus rose with a huge doggy sigh and followed him with mindless canine devotion.

Jilly was still sitting there, motionless, when

Rachel-Ann emerged from the bathroom, pale, shaken. "What am I going to do, Jilly?"

It took her a moment to respond. She looked up at her sister with a kind of shock. "I'll get you out of here. Coltrane is right—Jackson's dangerous. He always was, but now that he's desperate I don't think anything will stop him. We need to have you out of here."

"You, too, Jilly. You need to come with me. If he can't have me—"

"He certainly doesn't want me," Jilly said. "He never has and he never will. Thank God." She tried to pull herself out of her momentary paralysis. Her sister needed her. "Rachel-Ann, did he ever…?" She couldn't bring herself to say the words. "When you were young, did he…?"

"No," she said in a shaky voice. "I wasn't sure, but it seemed as if he came close a few times, but something stopped him."

Jilly breathed a tiny sigh of relief. "Nothing's going to stop him now. You need to get your stuff together and we'll go. We'll drive up north, or maybe out to the desert where he can't find us."

"I have a place to go. Where I spent last night. He'll never find me there."

Jilly stared at her. "Who is he?" she asked calmly.

"Don't pass judgment on me, Jilly. He's not

some one-night stand. He's someone I cared about, a long time ago.''

There was a moment's weary silence. ''Actually I wasn't passing judgment,'' Jilly said. ''For once I was a little more preoccupied with the mess I've made of my own life, speaking of one-night stands.''

''Jilly…''

''Get packed and bring your stuff downstairs. I'll be down in a minute. Don't try to take everything—the sooner we get out of here the better.'' The sooner she got away from Coltrane, from the smell of sex that was turning her stomach and making her heart ache, the better.

They'd used up most of the hot water. It didn't matter—a cold shower was what she deserved. She dressed quickly, grabbing the first thing she could find. Jeans and a T-shirt, letting her hair hang free as she hurried down the stairs. The hall was deserted, and she headed straight for the kitchen, the heart of the house. The sun was already beginning to set, filling the rambling old mansion with shadows. She'd spent the entire day in bed with a cheat and a liar.

And the worst thing was, she still wanted him.

She was a survivor. They had their roles in the family. Rachel-Ann was the fragile one, Dean the scapegoat. And Jilly was the mother, comforter, the strong one who rescued and protected.

Right now she would have given anything to have someone rescue and protect her. But she'd already given that right to the man who'd betrayed her.

She was limping by the time she reached the living room. Twelve hours on her back hadn't quite effected a cure for her feet. All was still and silent, everything hidden in shadows, and she almost turned away when some small sound alerted her.

"Hello, Daddy," she said. "Looking for someone?"

Jackson Dean Meyer rose from the wing chair that had shielded him from sight. He looked smaller than she remembered, somehow diminished. And yet even more dangerous. Because what had been vague, instinctive warnings had now coalesced into fact. He was a murderer. A murderer fixated on his own daughter. One of them.

"You look like hippie trash, Jillian," he said calmly. "As usual."

"Takes one to know one, pops," she said flippantly. "Did Grandmère know you ran a commune in this place?"

"Why do you think she took it away from me? And I wouldn't knock it if I were you. This family was flat broke before I got started. Drug money went a long way toward making us solvent again. Toward supporting you and this house.''

But Jilly wasn't going to be distracted. ''You can't have her.''

Jackson's small eyes narrowed. ''Jealous?''

''You're disgusting.''

He didn't even react. ''Where's your sister? And where's Coltrane? He promised to have her here for me.''

''And you trusted him?'' There was no noise in the house. She could only hope and pray that Coltrane had realized Jackson was already there and had spirited Rachel-Ann down the back stairs, out of the house, away from danger.

''As much as I trust anyone. Why shouldn't I? He isn't troubled by morals.'' He cocked his head to one side, looking at her. ''Oh, I get it. You slept with him. I told him to try to distract you if he could—I didn't need you barging into my office, asking questions, demanding answers while I was dealing with the federal government breathing down my neck. But I never thought he'd do it. Or that you'd fall for it. I guess you're not the big, strong Jilly, after all. You're just as much of a weak-minded fool as your mother was.''

She didn't even blink. ''Rachel-Ann is gone, Jackson, and so is Coltrane. If you want to get out of the country ahead of the law then you'd better leave now.''

"How very interesting. Who told you I was leaving the country? As far as I know only Coltrane was aware of my plans.''

"Maybe you trusted Coltrane a little too much.''

"And maybe I didn't.'' Jackson was looking past her, into the darkened hallway. "What took you so long?''

It was Coltrane, of course. Dressed, looking like a stranger. Not like the man who'd spent hours in bed with her. And standing beside him was Rachel-Ann, looking stunningly serene, with Coltrane's hand on her thin upper arm.

Jackson smiled at Rachel-Ann, that fond, benevolent smile that had always made Jilly's blood run cold. Long before she knew she had a reason for her discomfort.

"We're going away, Rachel-Ann. You're coming with your old man and we'll roam the world having adventures. You'd like that, wouldn't you? I'll take care of everything, just as I always have, and you won't need to worry about a thing. It'll be just you and me, like always.''

Rachel-Ann was still, silent, watching him out of her betraying green eyes, so very like Coltrane's.

If Jackson was daunted by her lack of response

he didn't show it. "Where are your suitcases? Not that it matters—we can buy anything we need once we reach Rio. We're starting out in Brazil, darling, and then we'll see where we want to go from there. Thanks for everything, Coltrane. You've done a good job."

He reached out for Rachel-Ann, but Coltrane didn't release her. Jackson frowned. "What's the problem? Afraid I haven't taken care of you? Don't worry, I've left instructions with Afton—"

"I'm not going with you," Rachel-Ann said, her voice wobbling slightly.

Jackson's disbelief should have been comical. Instead it was even more chilling. "Don't be ridiculous. Coltrane brought you here to me—"

"I didn't bring her here," Coltrane said. "She insisted on coming. I was trying to get her out the back door."

Jackson's smile was benevolent. "Of course she insisted. I don't know what you've said to upset her, but all she has to do is look at me and know that I love her and always have. I'd never hurt her. Come with me, Rachel-Ann. You've always hated this house, hated this life. We'll start a new life, far away, where no one knows anything about us."

"I'm staying with my brother," she said calmly.

"Don't be ridiculous! Dean is useless, and who the hell even knows where he is—"

"No," Rachel-Ann said. "My real brother."

The silence in the room was chilling, deafening. Jackson's attempt at charm vanished, leaving him cold-eyed and dangerous. "You lying son of a bitch," he snarled in fury. "Don't believe him, Rachel-Ann. It's nothing but lies. I don't know what stories he's been telling you, but I don't know anything about him."

"He told me you murdered his mother. My mother. Why would you do that?"

"Baby, I wouldn't!" Jackson said, so charming, so believable that even Jilly knew a moment's doubt. "I don't know who he says he is, but it's lies. I don't even know who your mother was. You were an adoption case I was handling that fell through, and I decided to keep you for myself."

"If it was an adoption case you were handling wouldn't you have met my mother?" she countered.

"She died in childbirth," he said without hesitation. "Who are you going to believe, baby? A stranger, or your father who loves you? Walk away from him, now. Come with me. Just go upstairs and get a change of clothes and we'll get out of here. Go on, sweetheart." He must have sensed her hesitation, and he nodded encouragingly. "I'll be right down here waiting."

Like a sleepwalker she pulled herself out of Coltrane's grasp, moving away from them, up the stairs. Jilly watched her in numb despair until she disappeared into the shadows, and when she turned back Meyer was holding a small but undoubtedly effective gun on them.

"I'm going to have to kill you both," he said in a conversational tone of voice. "I really thought it was going to be easier than this, but you brought it on yourself. I never even guessed. You're good, Coltrane. Almost as good as I am. Who would have thought that snot-nosed little toddler would grow up to be you?"

"I'm nothing like you," Coltrane said.

"Of course you are. Much as you hate to admit it, we're the same, under the skin. Amoral, greedy, wanting what we want. Like your bitch of a mother. She was trying to blackmail me, you know. She'd left you and your father the year before and showed up here with the baby, demanding that I divorce Edith and marry her. Either that or she'd go to the police about the things that had gone on around here. It was a wild time—no one was to blame. Hell, I didn't even remember half the things I did."

"So you killed her."

"I'm afraid so," he said with unconvincing remorse. "I drowned her in the swimming pool. She put up a hell of a struggle, but she was no match for me. Things would have been a lot simpler if I'd just carried through and gotten rid of the baby, too. I've always been the kind of man who does what needs to be done. But I took one look at Rachel-Ann's eyes and I fell in love."

"Touching," Coltrane said.

"I thought so," Meyer said, unruffled. "She was only a newborn, but I knew she'd grow up to be just like her mother. I'd loved Ananda, you know. Before she turned on me. And even though she had to die, she brought me a second chance. Rachel-Ann."

"You are so sick," Jilly said in disgust.

Her father smiled at her with complete sweetness. "I do what I have to do. You're going to die. I can't leave the two of you behind. I made a mistake with Rachel-Ann, and I've never regretted it. But I won't make the same mistake with the two of you."

"I don't give a shit what you do with me, Meyer," said Coltrane, "but let Jilly go. You don't want to kill your own daughter."

"But Coltrane," Meyer said with the utmost reasonableness, "if I can plan to sleep with one daughter I can certainly kill the other one. Don't underestimate me. I have no morals whatsoever. No decent paternal feelings, no sense of right and wrong. I'm doing it."

"No."

Rachel-Ann had reappeared on the stairs, but she didn't have a suitcase in her hand. Instead she held the collar of a growling Roofus. And Dean was beside her, languid, unruffled, almost amused at the trauma in front of him.

Meyer had turned pale. "I can shoot him," he said. "I can shoot that damned dog before he gets anywhere near me."

"Give it up, Father," Dean said. "You're turning this into a bad soap opera. The jig is up. You've lost. Rachel-Ann knows. Jilly knows. We all know."

"It's lies...."

"And even better, I have proof," Dean said in a silken voice, coming down the stairs, leaving Rachel-Ann standing there, still gripping Roofus's collar like a lifeline. "I've had most of the pieces for months now, but I finally got the final bit of evidence today. The autopsy report on a young homeless woman named Ananda Coltrane. They found her body in the Pacific, battered almost beyond recognition by the rocks. But not so battered that they couldn't tell she had chlorinated pool water in her lungs, not seawater."

"I don't know what you're talking about."

"There's already proof that ties you to her, Father. And I think a simple paternity test, maybe combined with a DNA test, would prove all sorts of interesting things. I'm sure Coltrane will be glad to offer some of his DNA for testing."

"You're my son...." Meyer said hoarsely.

"And you don't give a damn," Dean said smoothly. "And neither do I. You have your chance. Go away. Disappear. Leave the country and enjoy what time you have left. I'm sure you've stashed away a comfortable amount in various foreign countries. As long as you go now then you can get away with it. I'll be more than happy to take over Meyer Enterprises, to pick up the pieces of the mess you made. You can get away with murder, Jackson."

Coltrane jerked, then stilled. Saying nothing, his face like ice.

Meyer turned to Rachel-Ann, holding out his hand. "Rachel-Ann?" he said, pleading.

"Go away while you can, Jackson," she said, her voice cool and dismissing. "Save your sorry ass and save us all embarrassment."

She couldn't have destroyed him any more effectively. He stared up at her with shock and hatred in his face. And then before anyone could realize what he was doing he raised the gun.

Jilly screamed and Coltrane hit Jackson at the same time, slamming him against the wall. The gun went off, the shot going wild overhead, and

Roofus leapt from the stairs with a furious growl, looking like a particularly shaggy hound of hell.

Meyer's scream was pure panic, high-pitched and girlish, and before anyone could stop him he ran out of the house, Roofus bounding after him, baying like a blood-crazed wolf.

"Roofus!" Jilly called, but the frenzied dog didn't hear her. Someone caught her arm, probably Coltrane, but she shook him off, running outside, after her dog.

Meyer was disappearing down the path toward the tangled rose garden, with Roofus close on his heels. She had no idea how dangerous Roofus could be, but she couldn't trust that he wouldn't rip Meyer's throat out if he got him down. Meyer deserved far worse, but she couldn't let Roofus get a taste for blood.

She ran after them, mindless of the branches that pulled at her long hair, scratched at her arms. The others were behind her, she could hear them, but she didn't care. They were heading toward the abandoned pool, and she didn't even hesitate, crashing after them.

She reached the clearing only a moment after they did. Meyer was teetering on the edge of the pool, his eyes wide and staring, and Roofus was stalking him, growling deep in his throat.

"Roofus!" she called him again, her voice urgent.

The dog turned, whipping his huge head around. And Meyer stumbled, backward, into the dank pool.

She heard the sound as his head smacked against the cement. The sickening splat of bone and blood, the splash as his body tumbled into the few feet of murky water. And then all was silent.

She hadn't moved when the others reached the clearing; she was simply standing there, holding Roofus's collar. Coltrane got to her first.

"Don't let them see him," she said with quiet urgency.

He glanced into the pool, then turned to look at her. Keeping his distance. "Still protecting them?" he asked in his cool voice, as if they'd never shared a bed, their mouths, their bodies.

"Yes."

"And who's going to protect you?"

"No one," she said. "No one at all."

23

Brenda buried her head against Ted's shoulder, shivering. He held her tightly, comforting, until they were left alone at the poolside. Alone with the body still floating facedown in the shallow waters.

"We couldn't stop him then, honeybunch," he murmured. "We can't help him now."

"Good," she said, her voice muffled. She didn't want to look. Too much death in this old house. Too much evil and hatred, when all she'd ever wanted was love.

"Look at me, Brenda," Ted said, putting a hand under her chin to lift her face to his. "At least it's over now."

"Is it? Who's to say he won't join us here. Forever? I don't think I could stand it, Ted, I just couldn't—"

"Hush, love. The woman he murdered didn't come back. I don't think he will, either. If he does, we'll get rid of him."

"How? We're stuck here, helpless...."

"Are we, love?"

The sound of his voice, tender and understanding, broke the last remnants of her formidable will. "No," she said finally. "You aren't. You could go."

"Go where?"

"Toward the light. If you wanted it would come to you. It wasn't your fault. You were just a victim, and you could move on if you wanted. To heaven, to paradise, whatever it is. You'd just have to go without me."

"Then I wouldn't want to go," he said simply.

Now that it was out in the open she couldn't stop. "But I lied to you, Ted. I never told you what really happened, and you didn't remember. You thought we had a suicide pact, and we were trapped on earth as punishment. But that wasn't what happened."

"I know."

"You see, I— You know?" She stared at him in astonishment.

"For all your efforts at trying to distract me, there have been enough people over the years talking about it for me to figure it out, honeybunch. You killed me, and then yourself. I don't know why you did it, but you must have had a good reason...."

"No," she said.

"You didn't have a good reason?" He smiled wryly. "It was a whim?"

"How can you joke about this?" she demanded tearfully. "We're talking about murder. Death."

"It was a long time ago, sweetness. But if confessing will make you feel better, go right ahead. I'll love you no matter what."

"I didn't kill you."

She'd managed to startle him. "You didn't? Who did?"

"You were sound asleep, and it was a hot night," she said, remembering that night so long ago. "I went for a swim. To this same, goddamn pool."

"You used to like midnight swims," he said gently. "Did you wear a bathing suit?"

She smacked him in the chest. "Of course not. But I had my robe. When I came back to the house my robe was trailing in something, and I thought I'd dipped it into the pool. But it wasn't water, it was blood. Your blood. On the terrace, on the stairs, in our bedroom."

He was no longer amused. "Poor angel," he murmured. "How awful for you."

"How awful for you! You were dead. I ran the rest of the way, and found you lying in bed. The back of your head…" Her voice broke at the memory.

"The back of my head is very nice right now, sweetheart. Don't distress yourself. What happened then?"

"I ran to the window. We'd given the servants the night off, and no one was there. I looked out and I saw her, covered in blood as she ran for the car."

"I can guess," he said. "Adele. My ex-wife."

"She didn't consider herself ex."

"She never would. And no one ever suspected her. They thought you did it? What happened, love? Did she see you and come back?"

"No. She drove away. She'd left the gun on the bed. I think she probably knew me better than I knew myself. I took the gun, crawled into the bed, and—"

"Oh, love!" he said tenderly.

"So, you see, you can go. You didn't do anything. But I did. I've had fifty years with you, love, and it's more than I deserve. You need a chance—"

"I don't need anything but you," he said calmly. "But what makes you think we can't go together?"

"Because I killed myself."

"Your God is a lot more unforgiving than mine," he said gently. "Are you ready to leave this place?"

She stared up at him in disbelief. "I can't."

"You can. Give me your hand, honeybunch."

He held his out, and without thinking she placed her small, perfectly manicured hand in his big, strong one. His fingers closed around hers, and a moment later they were enveloped in a blinding white light.

"Ted," she whispered, afraid.

He pulled her into his arms, and the light filled them, buoying them up. "Eternity, honeybunch," he whispered. "It will be fine."

And it was.

Rachel-Ann drove blindly through the busy streets. They'd tried to stop her, make her stay, but she pulled away, eerily calm, and in the end they'd let her go before the police got there to fish out the body.

She had no idea where she was going until she ended up there. The Unitarian church was brightly lit, and several smokers congregated on the sidewalk outside the entrance. People she recognized.

She gave them a tentative smile as she walked past them, into the meeting room. It was crowded, and instead of taking her usual seat in a far corner, away from prying eyes, she sat in the front, still, silent, waiting as the seats filled up behind and around her.

"Does anyone here have something they need to talk about tonight?" the leader asked after the opening rituals had been conducted.

It was Rachel-Ann's cue to avert her gaze, to pull inside herself so that she almost disappeared. But not tonight. She raised her hand, and the leader nodded.

"Hi," she said. "My name is Rachel-Ann, and I'm—" Her voice cracked, and the room was silent. "And I'm an alcoholic," she finished in a raw voice.

"Hi, Rachel-Ann," the voices came back at her, welcoming.

"Hi, Rachel-Ann," came Rico's soft voice, directly behind her. She reached out, blindly, and he caught her hand, holding it tightly.

"My father died tonight...." she began.

"Where's Coltrane?" Dean asked. Jilly was sitting at the table in the kitchen, staring silently into a cup of cold coffee. It was after midnight, the police had left, along with the coroner and the ambulance, and they were alone in the house.

She roused herself to look at her brother. "He's gone," she said simply. "I don't think he wanted to answer questions for the police."

"No, I imagine not. Our friend Coltrane had a lot of secrets."

"Don't most people?" she asked wearily.

"I think he had more than his share. You didn't make the mistake of falling in love with him, did you?"

She jerked her head up. "You think I'm that stupid?"

"Yes. Or let's say, I think you're that vulnerable. You aren't always the strong one, Jilly."

"I don't really have any choice right now, do I?" She stirred the coffee.

"Is he coming back?"

"Coltrane? I doubt it. He got what he wanted. Jackson's dead."

"Are you sure that's all he wanted?"

"Positive," she said. "What else?"

"You, big sister?"

She shook her head. "In that case he'd still be here. He wouldn't have taken off without a word. Now would he?"

"Maybe. Maybe not."

"Besides, it's Rachel-Ann I'm worried about. Where do you think she is?"

"Stop it, Jilly! Stop fussing about everyone else and start thinking about yourself. Rachel-Ann will be fine. She's a lot tougher than we give her credit for."

"And what about you?"

"You just can't stop it, can you? I'm fine, too.

I haven't had any illusions about Jackson for years. You're the one who thought I still needed his approval. I just wanted the old bastard to get the hell out of here and leave me the company. Which he's done. A little more violently than I expected, but it's for the best.''

"Dean!" She stared at him, horrified, but he seemed completely unruffled.

"Rachel-Ann and I can take care of ourselves. It's past time for you to start concentrating on Jilly. You need a life, sweets. Beyond this old house, beyond your foolish siblings. You need a new project to renovate, a new soul to save. I was hoping it was going to be Coltrane, but if it's not, so be it. Time for all of us to stand on our own two feet, sis.''

"Yes," she said, not wanting to hear it.

"And time to get rid of this old place. You know it as well as I do.''

She looked up at the cavernous ceiling, the stained sink, the cracked dishes behind the tall, glass-fronted cupboards.

"Yes," she said. And she started to cry.

24

Eight months later

Jilly Meyer balanced a bag of groceries on her hip as she fiddled with the key to her apartment. It was a tricky lock—the building with its Spanish court-yard dated back to the 1930s, and as far as Jilly could tell the locks had never been changed. She didn't mind the extra trouble, especially when she looked at the ornate key hanging next to the key to her Saturn. She'd sold the Corvette—it was too powerful, and she'd somehow lost her impervious-ness to traffic tickets. After piling up three in a row she decided she needed a more sedate car.

She'd sold La Casa de Sombras. Well, the three of them had, to an independent film studio who planned to restore it to its former glory and use it as offices. She'd warned them about the ghosts, but for some reason no one ever saw them, not even Rachel-Ann.

She'd had a hard time finding an apartment that would let her bring a dog as big as Roofus, but

Dean had grown into his role as corporate shark, and he'd found this place for her in a matter of hours, once the sale of La Casa was agreed upon. And the apartment had been perfect, in dire need of having the wallpaper and woodwork stripped, the leaded windows reglazed, the walls replastered. Unfortunately it was finished now, perfect, and there was nothing to occupy her. Rico and Rachel-Ann flatly refused to let her do anything to their new bungalow, so she had to make do with buying baby clothes before her sister was even four months along. Even though Consuelo insisted in shocked tones that it was bad luck. Rico and Rachel-Ann were unconcerned with bad luck.

She had no one left to take care of. Rachel-Ann was happier than she'd ever been in her life, surrounded by her huge, extended family of in-laws. If Rachel-Ann missed the brother she only knew she had for a few hours, then Consuelo and the cousins made up for it. As did the child growing within her.

And Dean had blossomed. Smooth, sure of himself, though still attached at the hip to his beloved computer, he didn't need her at all. The only creature who seemed to need her was Roofus, and even he was getting tired of the small apartment.

She braced herself as she opened the door, waiting for Roofus to bound out in an excess of canine enthusiasm, but instead she heard a soft, plaintive woof from within the dark confines of the apartment.

She dropped the bag of groceries, stumbling into the living room in sudden panic, calling his name. Only to find him sitting peacefully, his tail wagging, his huge head on Coltrane's lap.

Eight months. Eight months without a word, and there he sat, in the middle of her new apartment.

"How did you get in here?" she demanded. She didn't make the mistake of calling Roofus to her side. He looked so pleased there was a good chance he wouldn't come.

"I actually know how to pick locks. An old skill, acquired under circumstances you're better off not hearing about," he said. His voice. She hadn't realized how much she missed the sound of it.

"Then why don't you pick your way out?" she said sweetly. He looked different. His hair was no longer bleached by the sun—it was more a sandy color, and it was shorter than she remembered. His clothes were different. No more California Armani.

"I want to talk to you."

"I'm sure you do. How did you find me?"

"I've always known where you were."

"That's more than I can say about you."

"I went back to New Orleans."

"And you think I care?" She was quite proud

of herself—the brittle anger, the cool disdain. She was a better actress than she'd realized.

"Yes," he said. "You know what my name is?"

"Probably not. You lied about everything else."

"It's Coltrane. I mean my full name. Zachariah Redemption Coltrane. I thought it was time to start living up to it."

"So you've redeemed yourself. I'm overjoyed to hear it. Now go away."

"What do I have to do, Jilly? Crawl through fire?"

"What do you want from me? If it's Rachel-Ann's phone number I imagine Dean will give it to you."

"I've seen her a number of times since last fall. I like her husband."

Her eyes narrowed. "You were in L.A.? Because I know for sure that Rachel-Ann hasn't left."

"Yes."

Her icy composure was cracking fast, and she needed him out of there. It had taken her months to stop crying at the drop of a hat, months longer to finally feel like she'd have a life again. All he had to do was break into her apartment like a sneak thief for her to know she'd been fooling herself.

"What do you want from me?" she asked again.

"I've got a date tonight, and I don't have time for chitchat."

"You're still not very good at lying. You don't have a date."

"You think no one would want me?"

"No. I think you don't want anyone but me. Don't throw that lamp at me," he added hastily, as she glanced around her.

"It's my lamp. I can throw what I want. I'm asking you one more time. What do you want from me?"

"I have a house in the French Quarter. It's a disaster, even though it's a historic site. They used to hold Quadroon balls there. Lots of historic preservation going on. People actually care about the past in New Orleans."

"And?"

"I've got a lousy job for shit wages. I'm a public defender, defending every kind of loser."

"Why?"

"Because someone has to do it. Someone has to watch out for people who can't watch out for themselves."

"Codependent," she said.

"Takes one to know one," he replied. "There's a huge yard at the house. Lots of room for Roofus."

"I see," Jilly said calmly. "You came back

after all this time without a word, picked my lock because you want to take my dog away from me?"

For a moment he thought she was serious. "Jilly!" he exploded, and then stopped. "You're not going to make this easy for me, are you?"

"Crawling through fire is a nice image," she said.

"I went away to see if there was any way I could still be a decent human being. You don't deserve less."

"And now I deserve you? Lucky me," she said lightly.

His slow, lazy smile was absolutely devastating. "Well, I doubt you'll ever be bad enough to really deserve me. But you were showing a real talent for being wicked and selfish, and I thought it was my duty to encourage that side of you."

"Did you?"

"Hell, if you won't come for yourself, come for me. I need taking care of. Rescuing from my inner demons, and you're so good at that, Jilly. You've had so much experience taking care of everyone else."

"Asshole," she muttered.

"Or you could come for the best sex either of us have ever had or ever will have in our entire lives."

"Not good enough."

"Then come with me because I love you."

And in the end it was that simple. "I love you, too."

"I know," he said.

Roofus barked as she threw the lamp at Coltrane's head. The boy had a lot of redemption left to seek, but she was going to make sure he found it.

With her, in a ruined old house in New Orleans. And maybe there'd be a little redemption left for her, as well. Even the strong one sometimes needed help.

"Are you going to marry me?"

His slow, sexy grin made her dizzy. "If you'll stop throwing things at me."

"I want babies."

"If you stop throwing things at me."

"I want you."

"Well, that, Jilly, you may have. Any time you want."

And she did.